THE PLEDGE

THE PLEDGE

LAIRDS OF THE CREST

KIM SAKWA

Taggart
Press

ISBN: 978-1-7371142–4-6

Library of Congress Control Number: 2022918853

Published in Clarkston, Michigan

PROLOGUE

SCOTLAND, 1400

The wind whipped something fierce, loosening the tartan wrapped around Ella MacPherson's shoulders. With dusk fast approaching, she quickened her pace and continued her climb up the craggy hillside. Worried about losing her footing and hurting the babe growing inside of her more than any harm the chill might cause, she let the train of fabric fall with the next gust and kept going.

When she neared the crest, she began to smell the faint, familiar scent of burning wood from the fire, and breathed a sigh of relief when a short time later the welcome sight of the small, one room cabin came into view.

Ella loved this cabin, a small hunting lodge her grandda had built some years ago. She had fond memories of visiting throughout her childhood, though the times she'd spent here recently were even more special.

Her breath caught when the door opened and she saw

Lachlan standing in the frame, his mighty size filling it entirely. At the sight of him, her heart quickened, then nearly burst as he started forward and ran to meet her as she crossed the meadow. Suddenly, he was lifting her in his arms, holding her tight.

"Ella, I was coming to meet you shortly," he chided, his voice muffled as he spoke into her hair. "You must be careful."

At the sound of his voice, and the warmth and concern in his tone, she burst into tears.

"Och, Ella. What's this, love?" he asked, pulling away to look at her. When her attempts to speak failed, he picked her up again and cradled her in his arms. She felt his warm lips and hot breath on her brow as he calmed her with sweet endearments, and she sunk into his embrace, knowing it was most likely the last chance she'd have the opportunity to do so.

Once inside, Lachlan set her by the fire and wrapped her in a blanket. Then he knelt in front of her, his large hands cupping her face.

"Whatever has you so distraught, I swear I will fix it," he promised, looking deeply into her eyes. Her savior, her knight, her everything. She knew he would do just that, if only her problem could be fixed.

Years ago, Ella had met Lachlan at the spring festival, and they'd both been smitten at once. But Ella was a MacPherson and duty-bound by a lifetime of honor to marry Ethan MacKenna. She and Ethan had been promised to each other before birth. The MacKennas, once a large clan, had dwindled down to just a handful, and all hope for their lineage seemed to rest on this union. So, after a few days of flashing smiles, long and lingering looks, whisper-soft touches, and even a stolen kiss or two, Ella and Lachlan had parted ways, knowing they'd had all of each other they ever could.

For five years Ella had devoted herself to her new husband, a good man, a nice man, handsome even, but deep inside, her heart had still belonged to Lachlan. And in all that time, Ethan's hope—and the weight of his family's hope—of expanding the MacKenna clan seemed doomed, for their efforts to conceive were fruitless.

Called away one blustery winter night, Ethan and his horse set out, never to return. The following week, word came that while crossing a river Ethan had been caught by a wretched current and never resurfaced. His death, said the messenger, was all but guaranteed. Ella had mourned his loss, she truly had, but when Lachlan came to pay his respects, they couldn't deny their feelings. Their love rekindled, they'd begun meeting discreetly, thinking they could give the MacKennas a bit of time before making their union official.

The cabin was the easiest and most accessible place to meet, at least for her, as it was halfway between the MacKenna property and her family's. Soon after they began meeting, Ella realized she wasn't barren after all. There'd been a few telltale signs, and she'd known she was in the early days, but hope had filled her so.

Now, just a scant month later, they sat at the small table where Lachlan had had a hot supper waiting, rabbit and crusty bread thick with butter. He'd even collected some wildflowers that grew by the water and placed them in a pottery vessel. The meal was temporarily forgotten, however, as Lachlan waited patiently for her to gather her thoughts.

It was hard to look into his eyes when she gave him the news, and although she'd never doubted his love for her before, she knew now they were bound, as well as cursed, heart for heart, together, forever.

"You're sure, Ella?" Lachlan asked, once she'd told him the news, holding their hands between them.

"Aye," she said softly. "Horace said he received word a week ago and rather than buoy false hopes by saying anything, went to see for himself if it was truly Ethan. He says it is, that Ethan was wounded and for a time thought to be on his deathbed but is more improved by the day. According to Horace, he'll be well enough to travel by week's end."

For a split second, Lachlan's eyes showed his grief, and Ella would swear he'd aged right before her at the news. Then, using every bit of the strength and honor she knew he possessed, his will like none other, Lachlan said, "You must go home, Ella. I will not knowingly bring dishonor upon any of our families."

"But the babe!" Ella cried.

"If there *is* a babe," he whispered, his voice so hoarse on the word, he had to look away to compose himself.

When his eyes were on her again, they were swimming with tears as his large hand reached out to cover her belly, which could at this very moment, be home to a living testament of their love. She threw herself at him. God help her, but she was distraught at the thought of having to leave him again. She was truly beside herself. Lachlan held her close as she sobbed, and when she finally pulled back and looked at him, she saw that his lashes were spiked from his own tears, his cheeks damp. "I will love you forever, Ella," he told her, but said no more about their babe.

What followed was an emotional, bittersweet evening, during which Lachlan ensured she ate before holding her close on the bed as she cried herself to sleep.

The next morning Ella awoke alone. She discovered a hearty breakfast awaiting her upon the table with freshly picked wildflowers next to her plate, and next to that, Lachlan's perfectly folded tartan. Ella noticed something nestled within, and gingerly fingered the object strung with a leather thong. When she took it out and held it in her hand, she recognized the item's significance, and tears filled her eyes as she rubbed the wooden medallion etched with a griffin.

'Twas something Lachlan had oft told her stories about—the mythical creature that was half eagle and half lion. Extolling the virtues of the king of all beasts: noble, fierce, and protective. It was his favorite, and she knew he'd given it to her for their babe.

Ella would name her son—she just knew it was a boy—after the man who would be her rock, if only in thought, and she knew their boy would indeed extoll the virtues of the mighty griffin his father had bequeathed to him.

CHAPTER 1

Celeste Lowell checked her bags one last time, leaning over the bed to skim the neatly stacked piles. Satisfied with her handiwork, she zipped her suitcase, duffle, and tote, then made a few trips downstairs to place them by the side door.

On her last pass, the setting sun caught her eye, and she used her hand to block the rays. An unfortunate move as her shift in vision drew her attention to the étagère set against the wall in the hallway—or, more specifically, the photographs lining its shelves. At first, the photos had brought her comfort, but as time went on, she'd started doing her best to avoid looking at them.

It seemed like every time Celeste tried to plan something that would distract her or help her move on, fate stepped in and said, "Nope, I don't think so." By now, Celeste had thought that after all the tragedy she'd experienced, she'd surely be left to find a bit of peace.

As ever, Madame Fate said differently.

With a sigh, Celeste relented and focused on the pictures, moving closer to gingerly finger their frames. The first, a family portrait taken when she and Derek were still quite young, Derek flashing his mischievous smile as he put up bunny ears behind Celeste's head.

Another, shortly before her parents' car accident, when Derek was a freshman in high school and she had just begun middle school. In this one, Derek had an arm wrapped around her neck from behind, affectionately pulling her close. He'd taken the role of older brother and protector quite seriously.

There were others, too, a couple of just Derek and Maggie, a few of Celeste with Derek at various times throughout college and law school, and another of the three of them together.

Celeste picked up one of her brother from when he'd been about twenty—his eyes were gleaming, his mischievous smile bright—and kissed the glass. "I miss you every day," she whispered. She tried to avoid looking at any of the photos with Maggie in them, but when she ultimately failed, Celeste immediately shut out her feelings and thoughts on the subject with a forceful, "Don't." Speaking aloud to herself was something she did when faced with ill feelings and bad thoughts. Some famous astrologer swore by the technique. Sometimes it worked better than others. Right now, not so much.

Really, how did one deal with the unexplainable? The utter uncertainty of what had truly happened to her best friend. At least with her parents and Derek, she had closure. Not to say their deaths still weren't horrible, but with Maggie, well... She shook her head and tried again. "Shhh."

To distract herself, Celeste walked through the kitchen and out to the back porch (the second technique she used when the first wasn't enough), and looked longingly over the backyard.

Though she'd only be gone a few months, she'd miss this place. The gorgeous wood table and pergola that Derek had built. The bistro lights Maggie had strung just so. How many meals had they shared there, the three of them together? She could still see Derek, spatula in hand as he flipped steaks, Maggie sitting happily in a chair and watching him. Oh, how she'd kill for one more of those moments.

A few months after Maggie's disappearance, Celeste had given up her apartment and permanently moved back into the house. It wasn't the family home that they'd grown up in, but one that they'd all picked out together after Derek and Maggie finished law school. It was technically Derek and Maggie's house, but Celeste had always loved it here; during school, it was where she'd spent the holidays and summer breaks, and they'd always told her she had a spot there anytime she needed it.

After Derek died, it had become her home, at least part time, when she'd come back because neither she nor Maggie wanted to be alone. And then she'd stayed because she just couldn't leave.

In recent months, she'd finally started sprucing up the back porch, which was going to be Derek's next project. A nice rug, some potted plants and a very comfortable club chair. She loved having coffee in the morning while sitting in that chair, her new favorite spot. A few months ago, she'd ordered a porch swing, something she'd always wanted, but it was back-ordered and had arrived only yesterday. The box was now in the detached garage and would have to wait until her return at the end of the season.

Celeste considered it a small feat that she'd even managed to store the box in there, given that it had taken a year before she could even step into that place. The garage. Derek's tools, his sports car, the Harley. Maggie was never a fan of the motorcycle, but Celeste secretly loved it. While she'd been helping Maggie sort through Derek's things after...well, *after*, Maggie hadn't wanted to cover them up. Celeste had. It was just too much on top of everything else.

She was pulled from her musings by the sound of her neighbor opening his side door. A pretty wood fence separated their properties, but it was more for aesthetics than privacy. Celeste was happy to see him come and go, and enjoyed the small feeling of community.

"Hey, Nick," she said with a wave and a smile.

"Hi, Celeste. You taking off tomorrow?"

"Yeah, don't forget my cousin may come and stay for a bit— he's traveling around from Scotland, and may or may not be in the area—so don't be alarmed if you see some strange guy in the house." She thought better of what she'd said and corrected herself. "I mean, if something's *off*, be alarmed. Please."

"Don't worry." He winked. "I got it."

So, she supposed that was that. Celeste fired off a text to her cousin—her favorite on her mom's side—to let him know the code for the lock in case he wanted to use her house while she was away, then looked around, pleased with herself. She'd have one more cup of coffee in the morning and then head out.

Celeste had spent her summers in the Hamptons since college and was looking forward to another season on the beach. An old friend who owned a yoga studio always needed extra help during the season, and honestly, it was a nice distraction.

The summer before, one of his clients had asked her to sing at their club, which was surprising, but fun. She liked to sing, at least recreationally, and picked up gigs at local bars or clubs when she could fit them in. Celeste was hoping for the chance to do that again this year—another good distraction.

Now, she grabbed some leftovers from the freezer and threw them in the microwave before turning on the bistro lights to have dinner at the table outside under the pergola.

In the morning, she enjoyed that last cup of coffee in the club chair, taking the wolf figurine that she'd kept in her pocket since Derek's death—the one he'd carved for her back when she was in high school—and traipsed it across the side table.

She cleaned and dried her mug when she was done, looking around one last time to make sure she hadn't forgotten anything, then locked up and headed toward her car. Once situated in the driver's seat, she took a deep breath to steady herself.

Just two more stops before the Hamptons.

CHAPTER 2

SCOTLAND 1431

"Be gone." Darach MacKenna spat the words, then crumpled the parchment he'd been handed, looking the bearer dead in the eye. Without looking away, he threw it into the crackling fire, then turned, leaving the stunned calling party in the wake of his heavy footsteps.

"You cannae dismiss such an order," one of the men shouted to his retreating back.

Dar stopped in his tracks, his entire body stiffening as if he *were* the mighty oak for which he was named. Tall and broad, he knew his size caused intimidation and fear, and at times such as these, he used it to his advantage. When he turned, the four men retreated a pace as he stalked back to where they stood. Dar pointed, wielding the full force of his sinewy arm. "I just did," he declared firmly, his anger close to boiling over.

He doubted these men knew just how precarious their situation was, for at the moment he wished wholeheartedly for a bloody row to ease his strife. Knowing he shouldn't continue to entertain such thoughts, Dar purposely distracted himself by turning to the fire, where the order as it was had already turned to soot. Although its form still held ever so slightly atop the crackling tinder, 'twas no more than dust, and it was a stark reminder of how fickle life was, how it could all change in a blink.

"I won't see him," Dar avowed, calmer now as he turned back to the waiting men. "You tell Lachlan regardless of the rumors, he's not my sovereign." *Or my father*, Dar thought warily. "And I will not heed his summons."

While it was true that Lachlan hadn't made a public declaration, 'twas only a matter of time. Lachlan MacTavish was (or at least, had been in his mind's eye) a man of great honor and wisdom. Someone who until only a short time ago, Darach had deeply admired. Respected even. God help him, he'd emulated the man. A man well known for his good deeds and great honor; one who had risen to wield immense power and reverence. That both he and Lachlan wore the crest of the griffin had at one time drawn Dar to Lachlan, though he'd told himself it was only coincidence. Still, he'd treated it as if it was a message from the gods that they were brethren. *Brethren*, not father and son.

That had all shifted in a flash as Dar's mother lay dying last fall. When she had asked to see the man, Dar had been confused, but had nonetheless sent word. Then, God rest her tortured soul, she'd confessed her sins. The one of most importance *and* consequence, that during the short time his da had been thought dead, she'd lain with Lachlan MacTavish. She held

Dar's hand, and with a strength Dar had not thought she still possessed in her weakened state, admitted that she'd loved Lachlan, deeply.

A memory had jumped to his mind then, of a moment when years ago he'd asked MacTavish why he'd never taken a wife. The intensity that had flashed into MacTavish's eyes as he'd reached out and tapped the medallion Dar wore was something he would never forget. Not the force of it on his chest, nor Lachlan's stern words. "The griffin mates for life."

At the time, the answer was confusing, insufficient at best, but at his mother's deathbed, Dar finally understood the man's meaning—and who it was the great man had loved and lost. MacTavish had born the weight of his vow, never marrying.

Two days later, Lachlan MacTavish had walked into his home like the tall proud warrior he was, moving straight up to Dar's mother's chamber. Dar, who'd been in a chair next to her bed at the time, stood when the man entered the room. They nodded a brief acknowledgment, then Dar said goodbye to his mother, as he always did, but this time with the feeling this would be the last goodbye. That Lachlan's visit had been all she'd held on for.

An hour later, Dar watched from an alcove as MacTavish descended the stairs and made for the doors. The powerful man had stood for a moment in the center of the empty hall. Fingers to his eyes, he'd heaved a mournful sigh, and Dar would swear he'd heard his mother's name on the other man's lips. 'Twas the last time he'd seen him and Dar had felt ire, whether toward him, the situation, or both, he wasn't sure.

He recognized it now as the same ire his uncle, his da's

brother, felt toward *him*. Dar couldn't even blame him anymore. He wanted to, but his uncle was entitled to his feelings. And presently, those feelings declared that the once "golden" child had become a bastard.

Dar loved the man he'd thought was his father—who *was* his father, who had raised him—and if his da had ever known of his mother's transgression he'd never let it show.

"He *will* come to you, Dar," one of the men standing before him declared, breaking Dar from his revery. "Don't mistake his patience for acquiescence. And I promise you this, he won't wait much longer."

With spring almost upon them, Lachlan had thus far waited two seasons. Emboldened by that knowledge, Dar stood his ground, and with a sweep of his hand gestured to the door. A few grumbles later, Lachlan's calling party finally understood—official summons or not—he would not be joining them on their journey back. They let themselves out.

Grateful they were gone, and even more so to put the entirety of the situation out of his mind, at least for now, Dar took the stairs to his chambers. Once inside, he peeled off his tunic, shucked his boots and trousers and stepped into the steaming, hot bath that awaited. The servants had no malice toward him—bastard or not—and their loyalty showed. His muscles slowly relaxed as he pressed his neck to the rim, relieving some of the tension there. He turned it this way and that until it cracked, then heaved a sigh of relief.

Yet the relief he experienced was short-lived. In truth, he felt like a man without a home, when for his whole life his home, *this* home—Remshire—had brought him great pride.

Now, here he was, back to collect some personal belongings and be gone again on the morrow.

He spied the ledger atop his bedside table out of the corner of his eye. Leather bound and filled with parchment, 'twas scribed with meticulous notes, ones he'd taken over the past months to help him navigate his way in the future. Now, he reasoned, a *new* future.

Come all you want, Lachlan, you won't find me here.

CHAPTER 3

The drive took Celeste forty minutes out of her way, but it was a route she'd taken so many times that her car passed the city outskirts and turned off the interstate as if by rote. A short time later she drove through the iron gates of the Maplelawn cemetery. It hadn't been that long since her last visit, Mother's Day, just a couple weeks ago, but since she'd be out of town for a few months, Celeste wanted to stop by once more before leaving.

She parked halfway down the narrow street that divided the grounds and hopped out of the car. She'd made it just far enough to be annoying when she realized she'd forgotten the flowers she always brought.

Celeste groaned, turned back, and grabbed the bouquet from the passenger seat before beginning down the familiar path again. She always felt a bit distracted here. Like all the parts of herself fragmented until she became something of a jumble. She floated in the midst of all her identities: dutiful daughter and sister, still-grieving adult who despaired of visiting her family *here*, and the baby of the family, the lost little girl who just wanted them all back, wanted a secure place in the world again.

Winding through the rows of headstones, Celeste smiled at Jimmy when he waved at her. He'd been here as long as she could remember, taking care of the grounds. "Hi, Miss pigtails," he called out, his traditional greeting. She hadn't worn her hair like that in years, but Jimmy had been there that day they'd buried their parents, when Derek had held her up entirely, tight against his side as she sobbed. The horror of watching their caskets lowered into the ground and throwing a handful of dirt on top was still a painful memory.

Years later, it was she and Maggie who held on to each other when Derek was lowered. She remembered at the time how they'd sunk to their knees and stayed there long after the groundskeepers were done.

Those memories almost always accompanied her to their family plot. A pretty patch of grass her parents had picked out shortly after they married. It was a large swath of earth, big enough for several to be buried. Celeste had always assumed that at the time they'd bought the plot, her parents were picturing all of them and their spouses and children laid to rest there one day.

Years later, and no one new had been added to the family. The thought saddened Celeste, but she took a bit of solace in the fact that at least her parents weren't there to see how small their family had become. Or to bury their son. Or how this little piece of real estate had been put to use much too soon.

Celeste knelt between her mother's and Derek's headstones, placing the flowers in the little cup she'd nestled into the ground for that purpose. Then, she brushed off the letters of her mother's name—not that they were dirty, Jimmy looked after their plots with care—it was just something she always did. She played with the stems of the tulips until they stood just so, then breathed, "Hi, Mommy."

Saying the words never failed to bring a rush of tears to her eyes. A bittersweet smile crossed her lips as she added, "I brought you some tulips." Tulips had been her mom's favorite, and Celeste could remember vividly how their house would be filled with them every spring. From large vases in their foyer, kitchen, and dining room, to smaller arrangements in the living room, den, and powder room, she even went so far as to place a flower or two in a drinking glass on all of their nightstands.

Her mom had wanted them all to be surrounded by happiness and beauty. "Life can be tough, sweetie," she'd say, stroking Celeste's hair. "Sometimes even cruel. It's important to bask in a few small or simple pleasures whenever you can." Celeste never bought flowers for herself like her mom had, but after their parents died, Derek had always ensured there were tulips in the entryway each spring. Celeste knew it was his way of trying to carry on their parents' torch, and he'd done a darn good job of it.

Now, as the last of the torch bearers, each year when the tulips started to bloom, Celeste bought them for her mom. Even so many years later, the ache of missing her struck Celeste in all kinds of moments. What she wouldn't give for one of her hugs right now. Losing one's mother was tough at any age, but

Celeste had been in middle school, and so it was especially difficult.

Mom had always been the one who made everything okay, even when it wasn't—she always saw the glass as full even when it was empty. Celeste wanted her back—all of them back—so badly. She heaved a sob, surprising even herself. It wasn't often she cried over her parents anymore, but when she did, it was raw and heavy. She knew she might seem okay on the outside— Celeste worked hard to give off a cool, composed detachment— but inside, she felt truly alone.

When she'd gotten into the New Age theories, karma, tarot, and whatnot, she'd asked a local healer and spiritual leader, Why? Why *then*? And the answer had surprised her. "Maybe their fate was simply to experience the joy of having a wonderful family, to meet their purposes as being incredible parents, and once that was accomplished, their souls' mission here was done." Whether it was true or not, Celeste liked to believe in things like that. It made the unbearable a bit more tolerable.

Turning to her father's headstone now, Celeste whispered, "Hi, Daddy," and traced the lettering of his name. A vivid memory jumped to the fore of her mind, one of him cheering her on when she was up to bat at a softball game in middle school. She'd made a base hit that night, and he'd been so proud of her. Then, as always, they'd gone for ice cream after. Ice cream as the answer to everything was another tradition that Derek had carried on afterward. According to her brother, trips for ice cream were always necessary, but *especially* to celebrate.

Celeste had given up softball for theatre when she entered

high school and it turned out to be one of her best decisions ever. Though she was sad her parents never got to see her perform in any of the plays they produced, the yearlong program was a lifesaver.

She considered herself lucky to have been part of it each subsequent year, to be given the space to shed her own life and inhabit someone else's, even if just for an hour or so. It really was her saving grace. Not only did it give her something to do before and after school, but it also came with ready-made friends, and extra time with Derek too.

Since Derek had played football, they'd both woken up early and headed out the door at the crack of dawn to make practice or fit in extra studying time. When Derek wasn't playing or training, he came to her rehearsals, helped build sets, and, of course, sat front and center for the actual shows. In return, Celeste worked concessions at his games when she had downtime and cheered him on from the stands.

Although their aunt had stayed with them at first, Derek proved himself capable of being a parent to her, and had quickly been able to get custody. They'd always been a team, the two of them, and that only strengthened after their parents died. Then, their duo easily transitioned to a trio when Derek met Maggie. As it turned out, Maggie was Celeste's kindred spirit. She'd also lost her mom, but it was more than that. It was like they were two halves of a whole.

They had taken so quickly to each other, all of them, really, and they'd never looked back. Not once. They'd been so blissfully happy, ecstatic to have found each other, that when Derek was killed, it wasn't just the shock of something God-awful happening, it was that he was gone, taken from them, when they'd both felt like they'd all already been through enough.

When Maggie disappeared a few months later, the tiniest part of Celeste felt relief. Not that she wasn't devastated, not that she wouldn't give everything to have her back, but at the very least, she didn't have to worry about losing anyone else. There was no one else to lose.

"Hi, Dare," Celeste said, turning finally to her brother, fingering the stone. She wished she had an update on Maggie for him. *I still haven't found her, but I know in my heart I will.* Or, *You'll think it's crazy but she's supposedly happy now,* but though true, that seemed inadequate. Instead, she fished out the wolf figurine and tapped it across his headstone, which had become something of a ritual of hers.

"Mighty pretty flowers you brought your mama."

"Thanks, Jimmy." Celeste was happy for the interruption. Somehow, Jimmy always came over with something nice to say at just the right time. An occupational hazard, she supposed.

"I'll keep my eye out until you come back, don't worry none."

Squinting from the sun, Celeste pocketed the small wooden wolf and smiled, ready to wrap things up.

She looked at her watch, making sure she still had time to make her last stop. There was one more person Celeste had to say goodbye to before leaving.

CHAPTER 4

SCOTLAND, 1431

Dar made good on his word, at least to himself, and left Remshire for Dunhill proper after only one night. Between the scornful looks from his uncle—the man had yet to forgive him for not being his brother's natural born son—and that last underlying threat from MacTavish's men, Dar couldn't get out of there quickly enough. The thought of having to speak with, let alone *see* MacTavish (aye, he'd reverted to formalities), stuck in his craw.

And if that weren't enough, there was the discomfort he'd lately felt when in residence, as if he truly didn't belong in his own home. 'Twas a crisis he'd never imagined befalling him, and one that seemed to have no solution.

Before his mother's death, Dar had devoted himself to the upkeep of Remshire, and, as a result, had felt the gratitude of its inhabitants. One visit from MacTavish, and all of that had changed. For someone who always prided himself on seeking the answers to any matter, Dar was simply at a loss. Neither philosophy nor logic were of aid to him now, and the further away he felt from the truth, the angrier he became.

This anger fueled him as he put his full force into another backward swing, letting the axe in his hands fall and rip through the wood in front of him. He'd been at it awhile now and a fair pile lay beside him. While he'd been hoping for a bit of peace and solitude, much to his chagrin, a few moments later he heard the familiar voices of his brethren.

"Margret asked for an addition on the south-east corner," he overheard Callum say as he and Grey approached. "I told her you'd have it done by month's end."

Dar snorted at the sarcasm mid-swing but didn't stop. Though Callum's assessment wasn't far off. Dar *had* been a workhorse of late—an ideal distraction from his internal strife. Quite timely, too, considering he'd learned of his shocking parentage on the heels of coming to Dunhill. Aside from his brief trip home, he'd been in residence nigh on two seasons now, helping Callum on his and Maggie's quest to bring the keep to and beyond its former glory.

Continuing to ignore the twosome, Dar carried on with his task in silence, knowing it wouldn't be long until Grey chimed in.

A moment later, he did. "At this rate, I told Gwen you'd commence at Seagrave by the summer solstice," Grey said dryly, bending down to grab a piece of wood.

Funny, Dar thought wryly as he swung again, pleased that at least they'd decided to make themselves useful—Grey had begun tossing logs to Callum, who was placing them atop the block in front of Dar.

They remained silent all of two minutes before Grey started up again. "Do you want to talk about it?" he asked, all joking was gone from his tone. Still, Dar bristled.

Dar let the axe fall again, splintering the log thrice, then gave his brethren a narrow-eyed look, hoping it conveyed the magnitude of his displeasure. "If I wished to speak of it, you'd know," Dar spat. He didn't wish to speak of it. And especially not to Greylen or Callum, both of whom had exemplary parents. Something Dar had thought was true for himself until a few short months ago.

Now it seemed he had an axe to grind, so to speak.

His mother and father—the man who'd reared him, who he'd always think of as his father, no matter what had tran-spired—had been less than perfect in the end. All of his thoughts and feelings, the preconceived notions of who he was and from whence he came had become a jumble. Worse, a lie. His whole identity was shattered. How could he still stand tall on principal and integrity, honor even, when at the core, his very foundation was unsound?

"Lachlan's a good man, Dar," Callum said, as though he'd been able to hear Dar's thoughts, which raised Dar's ire even more.

"What of *If I wished to speak of it, you'd know*, didn't you understand?" Dar growled. *Lachlan*, he thought, *och*. 'Twas the last name he'd wanted mentioned. *Lachlan, Lachlan, Lachlan.*

Dar's erstwhile admiration of and obsession with the man was not a welcome reminder either. Was he acting childish? Aye, what of it.

Dar paused his wood-splitting for a moment and surveyed his brethren. He sighed. They had only wanted to offer support. And Callum and Grey were right, despite his history with Dar's mother—a history that existed only because both parties had assumed his father dead—Lachlan MacTavish was as honorable as they come. Only a righteous man would stand tall and claim parentage like that. God almighty, he'd made that public declaration after all.

Dar heard tell that MacTavish and his men had come upon a crowd rife with boisterous gossip and tossed a blade right in its center. No, Lachlan MacTavish was a man who did not go unnoticed. And not just for his height and breadth, which were, Dar had to admit, much like his own. He continued to be a man of high regard despite it all, well known as a warrior, a fighter, and with a considerable collection of coin to boot.

From his years idolizing the man, Dar knew that he always traveled with three others, their colors amber and purple, their fierce stance enough to cause doubt in even the surest of men.

Dar had heard that that day with the talebearers, MacTavish had knocked a few to the ground before proclaiming loudly enough for the dead to hear, "Darach MacKenna is no bastard. He is blood of my blood and if that displeases any soul, by God, he'd better take it up with me. No, I did not raise him—that boy was reared by Ethan MacKenna with love and pride—but it's the same love and pride I have for Darach."

Dar shuddered at the memory of it, loath to even reimagine

the scene again, but grateful he hadn't been a witness, at least. He wished to be gone from this place *now*; hell, permanently. His offer to help Maggie deliver a letter to her kin in the mysterious future now seemed a Godsend.

At first he'd thought it more of a distraction, a way to escape his current circumstance, but more recently, the idea had come to him that mayhap he'd use this errand as an opportunity to begin anew. Why not? Hadn't Gwen and Maggie done the same? 'Twas true they'd had no choice in the matter, but still, the rebirth had been just as fulfilling. If they'd found happiness *here*, in this time, what was to say he couldn't do the same, but there, in the future? What's to say that wasn't the ultimate intent, anyway?

Considering the acts of destiny that had already convened upon two of their five, with this imminent, oddly *celestial* errand, Dar couldn't help but wonder if Celeste might be the key to finding his own Maggie or Gwen. Then, feeling a tad foolish, he banished the thought. Mayhap 'twas merely the future itself—and the man he could become there—where his destiny lay.

As he was about to utter a word of apology to his brethren for his snappish behavior, he heard riders, four to be exact. He wasn't sure why, but he had a feeling it was MacTavish—the number of riders suited that assumption, at least. The three men he traveled with were as loyal to him as Darach and his brethren were to one another.

His suspicions were confirmed when Dar heard MacTavish ask one of the men in the courtyard, "Where is he?"

"Lachlan," Callum said in greeting, calling him over.

"Callum." He nodded toward him. "You've done well, here, son. Bouncing back from a loss is not easy. Fergus would be proud. But then, he always was."

"Grey," Lachlan acknowledged before peering past him, his eyes landing on Dar. As Dar turned to leave, he called out, "Don't you dare walk away."

"You did." Where that came from, Dar couldn't fathom. But the color drained from MacTavish's face before his eyes narrowed.

"Is that what this is about?"

Only a moment ago, Dar would have said nay. Now he wasn't so sure. "I don't know."

At that, MacTavish nodded in what Dar thought might be understanding. "You want to do this here?"

His men hadn't moved from where they flanked him, while Grey and Callum inched a bit closer to Dar, in a clear show of solidarity. Dar shrugged, not really sure *what* he wanted to do.

"I loved your mother. From the moment we laid eyes on each other at the spring fair all those years ago. But she was already promised and, if nothing else, *we*," Lachlan said, stressing the word, encompassing all in current company, "are honorable men. You were conceived out of love, Darach Grifud MacKenna, at a time we thought Ethan dead. Ella was never truly mine. But you, *you* will always be mine. Your birth and rise to manhood, I would trade for nothing."

Dar felt a tug in his chest, a pricking behind his eyes, but he ignored both, pushing them aside. It was too late. Too much had happened, had changed. While Lachlan's sentiments were

all well and good, Dar refused to have any of it. It was too difficult, too complicated. And besides, he wasn't long for this
world—in this era, at least. He turned to leave.

"That's it?" Lachlan asked, a hint of exasperation seeping
into his words.

"Aye," Dar said, keeping his voice even. "I made it this far on
my own and still managed to find myself amongst the finest of
men."

Dar had never been so happy to be one of the five of his
brethren as he had been lately. At times, especially these last
few years, it felt as if they'd all been chosen for reasons unbe-
knownst, even to them, but chosen they had been. Dar wasn't
sure if Lachlan understood the meaning behind the Lairds of
the Crest, but by the look on his face, it was clear he knew Dar
spoke of his brethren, and he seemed none too happy that Dar
had named it as an accomplishment.

"Do you know why you're a part of this fold? A member of
this brethren?" Lachlan asked, his words laced with incredulity.

That caused Dar to pause. 'Twas something he had often
wondered, though he was loathe to admit it. Grey and Callum
came from great wealth, Aidan and Ro not far behind. They
were naturally from the same circles, with parents who had
grown up with one another too. But Dar, Dar's family—the
MacKennas—had not reached that level of nobility. In the past,
Dar had brushed the question aside, assuming it was a good
deed his father had done that had brought the men together, or
something of the sort.

When Dar said nothing, but made no further move to leave,

Lachlan continued. "The Lairds of the Crest exists because—" he paused and took a deep breath, looking away as if considering whether he should keep going. When he turned back, he said, "Allister and Fergus made sure you were taken into their brood out of esteem for me."

He hadn't said them cruelly, but as Lachlan's words hung in the air, Dar felt his fists clench. So it hadn't been fate after all. 'Twas something much more deliberate, manipulated. Suddenly, everything he thought he'd known and believed about their brotherhood seemed a lie.

Unable to reply, Dar turned on his heels and left, feeling more uncomfortable in his skin than ever. Which was something, considering the revelations of these last six months. For the first time, he questioned his place among Greylen, Callum, Aidan, and Ronan. No matter that Callum and Grey were following fast behind him. Had they known? Dar had only just closed the doors to his quarters when a solid rap barely preceded his men's entry.

"It matters not, Dar," Grey said without preamble. Being the eldest held weight and Grey took the responsibility seriously.

Dar was shocked he could so easily brush this aside, though at least it made clear that his brethren had been as in the dark about the reasons for his being a part of their group as he had. This, however, on top of a mountain of seemingly ever-changing facts, helped not.

"Everything I believed," Dar said, shaking his head. "Everything I knew to be true. The very reason I at one time stood tall and implacable is now in question."

"You believe that deems you unworthy?" Grey had a

penchant for seeing through to the heart of a matter, and oft did so with the care he used now.

Feeling somewhere between anger and defeat, Dar asked quite truthfully, "Does it not?"

"We are brethren for a reason, Darach. You as much as Callum, Aidan, and Ro are blood to me. You are still blood, regardless of these divulgences."

"I feel unworthy."

"Let me tell you something about feeling unworthy and standing upon tenuous ground," Grey said, imploringly, "I've been there, Darach. I failed, if you do not recall. I failed my wife. Horribly. I had never felt so inadequate in all my life."

Dar averted his eyes, feeling suddenly ashamed he had forgotten about Gwen's abduction and abuse at Malcolm MacFale's hands. Forgotten that his brethren had suffered despite the advantages they'd had in life.

"'Tis nothing wrong with acknowledging the truth, and coming to terms with it," Grey continued, "but a time comes when a man finds his footing again, and makes it right. And he is all the better for it. Humble after realizing his humanity, and all the stronger too."

"I failed, too, Dar," Callum said, and Dar nodded slowly. Of course. Callum was deeply happy with Maggie, but before her there'd been Fiona and their babe. "It took a long time to move past that failure, too, if you remember. It was only with Margret's arrival that I found a real purpose and a reason to truly live again. I couldn't do it on my own. God's bones, you were a part of the restoration."

A few minutes later, Callum and Grey left Dar with a firm

smack on the shoulder each, and words suggesting that he needed to give things time to settle. Though mollified, Dar couldn't rid his mind of what Lachlan—*MacTavish*—had said. Dar's departure was growing nearer. He could feel it.

CHAPTER 5

SCOTLAND, 1431

Dar was still tense a few hours later when he joined his friends to dine that night, though it was difficult to be forlorn with Gwen around. Gwen merely wanted everyone to be happy. Her smile was infectious and her heart one of the warmest Dar had known.

She and Grey were in residence, partly to check on Maggie and the progress of the babe still growing inside her, but also because Dar knew Grey worried about his imminent plans. Dar was glad they had come when they did. If not for bearing witness to what had transpired with MacTavish, Dar wouldn't have had Grey's and Callum's words after, words he'd taken to heart.

Once the meal was served, Maggie closed the large doors to the intimate dining hall. It was her signal, a not too subtle one, that she wanted to speak again about his plans, especially with everyone in attendance. They were plans they'd been over hundreds of times by now.

Dar sighed but then smiled, at the ready to reassure her. "I know, Maggie. I'll travel using the sword," he placated.

She pulled in her lip, her telltale sign of worry. Callum covered her hand. "You needn't fret, Margret," he told her patiently.

Dar knew, and had observed, how nervous Maggie grew whenever the sword was discussed. Though it was now hung high upon the wall in the great room, and no one ever touched it but Callum—at least not since that day it had glowed for Dar —she still worried it might alight her back. While they continued to assure her she was in no danger of such, she'd come to treat it as an idol of sorts, giving a curtsey and sign of the cross when in its presence. It would have been funny, were her fear not so palpable.

Dar had also been awed by the sword's power when he'd first grasped the hilt. He remembered how its warmth had seeped through his entire body; its glow nearly blinding him. Momentarily entranced by its magic, he'd held tight before rationale took over and he dropped it quickly. Still, Dar always felt its energy when he neared it. And they all believed the moment he touched it, it would transport him. No one was sure how, or why, but they all agreed it was so.

In Maggie's case, it had taken her where she'd needed to be. The safety of the Abbey and the care of Callum's Aunt Cateline. And in the case of Gwen, while it wasn't the sword that had transported her, she did alight to exactly the place where Greylen would find and rescue her.

Then, there was the matter of the mystic. Dar always came back to her in his mind. Not only had she given Maggie words from the prophecy, the very prophecy that foretold Greylen and Gwen's fate, meaning they were connected, but she'd all but named Dar as the next person it would touch. *Prepare him well,* she'd said. Those words rang in Dar's ears often, along with her referencing the future, and Maggie's friend Celeste, the one to whom he was to deliver a message.

At first, the women had been filled with excitement at the prospect of him traveling to the future to find Maggie's kin. They'd spent hours, days, and months going over the particulars—preparing him, as instructed. Things like modern daily rituals, the crush of people constantly milling about, and the importance of following modern laws, which apparently included *not* walking around with the sword.

Often, it sounded like they were talking nonsense, and Dar found himself turning to Grey and Callum absolutely dumbfounded. His brethren seemed equally so. Though they had heard some tales of the future from their wives, hearing the details laid bare was shocking to them all. And honestly, at times impossible to comprehend.

While Dar prided himself on his keen mind and memory—something the women referred to as pho-to-graphic—even he conceded to the use of a ledger for certain details. City locals, street names, numerous number sequences, the workings of modern luxuries, and according to them, necessities.

They'd both shrugged and laughed at that once they'd said it, considering they'd lived without those "necessities" for some time now, and done quite well without them. Dar reasoned with only a small twinge of envy, it helped that Grey and Callum were both wealthy. Though Dar would never say it aloud, he suspected their shared experiences and upbringings were most likely why the two were the closest.

In hopes of pulling Maggie away from her worries now, Dar turned to Gwen to liven things up. "If you could have one thing from the future, what would it be?" he asked, thinking, too, that he may bring her a favor from his journey—that is, if he was ever able to return.

At his question, Gwen's smile filled the room, her eyes gleaming with delight. They all knew Gwen liked what she liked because she made sure you knew. She might be a bit mercenary about it, but only because she was so intent on sharing something she thought fantastic or superior and wanted you to have a taste or experience it firsthand.

"Oh my goodness, Dar. What a question." He could see the gears turn as she thought long and hard, a myriad of emotions crossing her face. She squeezed Maggie's hand, asking, "Could you imagine, Maggie?" But then she looked at her husband and shrugged, shaking her head as she replied, "Honestly, I have everything I've ever needed or wanted."

Grey's noncommittal grunt belied the warmth in his eyes at her words. They all knew Gwen took it upon herself to collect any culinary luxuries—spices and fruits and herbs and other exotic flavors—she missed from her time, things that hadn't yet found their way to their nook in Scotland. She left lists for Greylen, who indulged her every (possible) request and sent said lists to his ships' captains.

"Maggie? What of you?" Dar asked next.

Maggie took no time at all with her answer. "I just want you to be safe, Dar. And for Celeste to have some closure."

There was a moment of silence, and then Grey leveled him with a stare. "Dar. What if you *can't* come back?"

Dar nodded. 'Twas something that had crossed his mind, of course—after Maggie had traveled here using the sword, it had never "powered" for her again—but he'd given it thought and reconciled that mayhap his plight *was* to go forward in time. To stay. It would account for the complete detachment he'd been feeling of late to Remshire. After all, evidence was before them all that neither Maggie nor Gwen would choose to return to their time, even if they still missed aspects of it. Still, it was something that he hadn't discussed with the others.

One would think that would be devastating, to never return home, but Dar had seen firsthand how Maggie had reacted when she thought the sword was sending her back. She'd panicked because it was the last thing she wanted. Maggie had found peace here with Callum, and she wanted to stay.

And then there was Gwen. Gwen had first appeared in the midst of a storm, and though Dar had heard tell of her once walking back into said water during a particularly bleak time, there was never a true moment when she might have returned. Her husband was here, her children. She spoke often of her happiness and feeling of being settled.

Though he'd thought about it often, Dar realized that he'd always considered the possibility of not returning to his time as just that—a possibility. But that wasn't the case, was it? It seemed that once the sword had fated a person to a new time, it was permanent. And the destiny of each member of their brotherhood—along with a wee bit of magic—seemed to be tied into it.

"It's crossed my mind, Grey," Dar said softly. "And should that be the case, then I must believe I'm where I'm supposed to be. As the others who have traveled feel they are."

He looked at each pointedly. These were his brothers, men he'd known most of his life. And Gwen and Maggie meant just as much. He couldn't imagine never seeing them again. In truth, he didn't want to. "Let's stick with the plans we've made. I'll bring along a few jewels to barter for money so I can secure lodgings, then as soon as I can, I will find Celeste and gain access to Maggie's things."

There was a moment of silence as Dar's words sunk in, and he saw the others look around, catching one another's eyes. It seemed there was an unspoken agreement between them that Dar was correct, and when Maggie turned back toward him, her face held a new calm.

"The ledger? You have it?" she asked

Dar smiled. "Aye. Upstairs, filled with notes and addresses."

"And the letter, Dar."

"Aye, Maggie, the letter too."

"So you'll…" She waited for him to tell her.

"I'll travel safely and in one piece. Then I'll secure means and find Celeste. I'll deliver your letter to her and settle any affairs, if necessary. After which, I suppose I'll have to wait and see."

As one, Maggie, Callum, Grey, and Gwen said, "Add more jewels."

There was laughter at that, which diffused any remaining

tension, and dinner turned into a pleasant affair, more like what Dar was used to at Dunhill.

IT WAS MUCH LATER that Dar sat within his chamber, working by candlelight. He leaned over the wooden table, dragging the candlestick closer, adding a few more details to the sketch he'd created.

He'd stared so often at the pictures of Celeste that Maggie had shared, he'd memorized her image, and knew he'd be able to recognize her on sight. On the sketch, he smudged the fine lines of her long neck to soften the edges. Then he dipped the quill in ink, carefully dotting indigo to fill in her blue eyes, the act one of meditation more than anything else (though she was a beauty, that had to be said).

When he finally crawled into bed, head on the pillow, his last thought was of finding her, delivering Maggie's message, and settling into his future, whenever and wherever that might ultimately be.

When Dar awoke a short time later, he felt the sword's energy drawing him from upstairs and knew in his bones it was time. Lachlan's proclamation yesterday had only spurred the moment. He needed a change, he needed to prove himself as worthy unto himself, and that was something he didn't feel he could do here anymore. Despite Callum and Grey's kind—and truthful—words, Dar was still grappling with all that had been revealed to him, all that had happened in the last months.

Aye, he needed to *go*.

Dar reached for the ledger he'd left on the bedside table then collected his satchel, double-checking that it contained Maggie's letter; the gemstones, now ten instead of the original four; some other things Maggie and Gwen had insisted he take; and strange clothing they'd had Nessa and Anna fashion that they assured wouldn't make him stand out overly much.

He pulled out the odd tunic—something Maggie called a "tee-shirt"—and held it up, shaking his head at its flimsiness. His reaction was much the same when he stepped into the breeches—pants, they'd called them—before securing his dagger in a sheath under his pant leg.

He pressed his hand to the door as he passed Callum and Maggie's chamber and then again at Grey and Gwen's. "Until we meet again, my friends."

When he entered the Great Hall, the stone was already ablaze with life. The sapphire's glow was spectacular, and the blade buzzed with energy such that he heard its hum from across the room.

He strode to it, his sure footsteps quickening the nearer he got. In all his years, he'd never been so certain of anything as he reached above the hearth and clasped the sword's hilt.

The sensation he felt as the magic took over made him stumble, but he didn't fight it; instead, he eased into it, becoming one with the sword. Scant seconds later, the room began to blur, and his head felt thick, a sensation similar to being underwater. He didn't fear the sensations. Maggie told him what she'd felt, so if anything, he was buoyed by the feeling.

Confident in what was to come next, he held fast, said a prayer, and nodded to the stone within.

CHAPTER 6

On her way out of town, Celeste pulled up to the now-familiar odd-looking cottage with its cobblestone walk and funny mushroom-shaped roof. It had been three months since she'd last parked her car on this street, but she'd made sure to stop here last as it seemed this was the only place she felt a sense of ease or peace. A deep sense, actually. The only place where the truth about Maggie was known, where she could speak freely about her.

It wasn't like she was beside herself every day anymore. She wasn't. But still, what she wouldn't give to have done things differently.

What a stupid idea she'd had after Derek was killed. She'd heard about the old crone in some dumb Facebook group and told Maggie about her in the hopes that it would bring her some closure. She could kick herself for her own stupidity. But now, the messages—as cryptic and as vague as they had been the afternoon she'd brought Maggie here—were all she had. They brought her comfort; as did the old woman who delivered them.

As was usually the case, the front door opened as if on its own, but that no longer freaked Celeste out; she merely walked straight through the narrow entryway and past the sitting area before pushing aside the sheer curtains that separated it from the parlor. She sighed as she sat down at the cloth-covered table and stared out the window into an enchanting, magical-looking backyard, and waited.

It wasn't long before the mystic came out from the kitchen, carrying a tray laden with steaming cups and a plate of delicious refreshments. Celeste expected this from the other times she'd come—at first to question and demand answers, and later for company from the only other person who knew. There was a kind of camaraderie in that. Call it crazy, but Celeste really didn't care anymore. She shared a look with the wizened old woman as she stood to help her.

"Off for the summer, sweet?" the woman asked, her eyes filled with warmth and compassion.

Oh, how Celeste missed those things: warmth and compassion. Recognition. It wasn't that people didn't care, they did. It was just that for as long as she could remember, she'd been closest with Derek and Maggie. They'd been her people and she'd never really needed anyone else. And after losing them both, so quickly and so close together, she didn't really trust anyone. She didn't trust herself. And, if she were being honest with herself, the last thing she wanted to do, considering her track record where loved ones were concerned, was get close to someone new. Okay, yeah, she had issues, but who wouldn't?

Celeste answered the woman, "Yes. I just...just..." Celeste wasn't sure what she needed but she always felt better for coming here because it was the only place where she could just *be*. "I just want her back." She shrugged feebly. "I know that's all I ever want to talk about, but do you really think she's okay? That something awful hasn't happened to her?"

"I swear to you, Celeste," the crone said as she took Celeste's hand. "Margret is safe and whole. More than that, she is happy. You *will* see her again. I know it. I don't know if it will be permanent, but I promise you'll be reunited, even if only for a time."

On its face she knew it was irrational to trust the crone, but she did. When she'd first returned to the mystic after Maggie's disappearance, the woman had told her that Maggie was safe and whole and in the time she now belonged.

If Celeste ever told the detectives at the police department about this mystic on Crabapple Lane, she'd probably get a seventy-two-hour psych hold for her efforts. It was the only thing she'd left out when they'd called her for information about Maggie's disappearance.

She knew the detectives had questioned the woman, given that they'd tracked Maggie's recent cell phone locations to her cottage, but they hadn't given her much credence. On the other hand, Celeste was practically resting her very life on this woman's words.

Celeste would never forget the day Maggie disappeared. One minute they were speaking on the phone and in the next, all she heard was dead air. The call had ended. Celeste tried calling back, texting, emailing, all of it, but Maggie never responded. Not ever.

Celeste had rushed over to their house, using the keypad to open the side door. She'd called Maggie's name as she ran up the stairs to the bedroom, but aside from the mattress and box spring on the floor, and an odd swath of burlap and twine in front of the bed frame, it looked pristine. No Maggie, no sword, no jewel, no phone, no nothing.

When the detectives had come, they'd found nothing unusual either. The doorbell camera and those on the side and back doors revealed nothing. Like, literally *nothing*. No sign of Maggie leaving the house at all. And Nick, their next-door neighbor, swore that no one had come or gone except Maggie herself, who he'd seen come home.

So really all Celeste had to go on were the words of this woman, this ancient woman who sat in front of her patting her hand.

"You'll have your answers soon. I feel it," the woman said, pushing the hot delicious brew her way and tilting the plate piled with tea sandwiches. Celeste took a few of her favorite, cucumber with a creamy dill sauce on soft, crustless white bread. It wasn't something she'd normally eat, but here it was a treat, because somehow, it reminded her of home. Not her house-home, but nostalgia of her childhood and everything that was good about it.

She stayed for close to an hour, chatting about nothing and everything with the mystic— her summer rental that was close to the water and the porch swing that she couldn't wait to use.

It was so easy to speak with this woman, and Celeste never felt rushed or wanted to leave when she came here. When she finally did stand up to go, Celeste eyed the box in the corner, the one from which the crone had pulled out the jewel she'd given to Maggie; the one she'd said had aided her in her journey to the past.

"Are you sure there's nothing for me in that box?" she asked, as she did every time she visited the cottage.

The crone offered her a wrinkly smile. "The jewel is yours, too, sweet, but it is not in that box. It will come back to you, I swear, and then you'll know peace once again. True peace."

The woman stood and came around the table to embrace her. Celeste relished in the hug from this woman who was her only link to Maggie. And Derek.

And whatever might be.

CHAPTER 7

When Dar opened his eyes, he was standing in a strange room. Immediately he noticed a large bed piled high with lavender and white bedding that sat between two windows, which the sun shined through, catching and refracting the metal that framed extraordinarily life-like images on the night tables— they were like the images that Maggie had shown him on her "phone," but you could pick them up and hold them.

Pulling his eyes away from the images of Maggie, Celeste, and a man he assumed must be Derek, Dar scanned the entirety of the room, including the dresser and mirror above it on the opposite wall. Another large, framed mirror, taller than him, mayhap by a foot or two, sat on the floor, leaning against the wall. There were two doors on either side of it—one led into a wardrobe area, and the other, a modern bathing chamber.

Dar ran his hands along the stone countertops, the large porcelain tub, and what must be a glass-enclosed shower, an invention for bathing that the women had told him about. According to them, he would love it. He gave it a dubious look and decided he'd give it a try in a bit so he could draw his own conclusions. Another small room housed what he guessed was the water-filled latrine Maggie had described to him. Maggie and Gwen had told him much of the future, but actually being here was entirely different. Everything was so bright, so clean, so peculiarly lucent.

Before he made a ruckus as he explored, he decided to make sure he was in fact alone. He suspected he had landed in the home Maggie and Celeste had once shared, and if Celeste were away for the season as Maggie had presumed she would be, he would have these quarters to himself. Timely, as a period of adjustment would be necessary.

As he made his way through the upstairs, he peered inside the two other rooms. One, another bedroom, much smaller in size and, if he deduced correctly, mayhap an odd room of worship, replete with an altar of sorts that displayed crystals, candles, and, based on the scent, sage. A small bathing chamber lay between these two rooms, each connected by a door. He saw a white rectangular panel on the wall and touched it.

Suddenly, light blared from the ceiling, and he touched it again to put the room back into darkness. Ah, the light-*switch*. He'd have been terrified of evil sorcery if Maggie hadn't explained this to him. He touched it a few more times, a wee bit amused, then headed for the stairs. The wood floors and stairs were covered in various rugs—tastefully mismatched in a way Dar appreciated.

Two long side panels flanked the front door and a table

topped with many different items, including a crystal and some candles. A bench was next to the stairs, the wall opposite filled with a few framed pictures.

Dar stood there a moment looking at Maggie's likeness. She appeared very happy with her first husband, Derek, by her side. He had piercing eyes, a strong chin, and a gleam in his eyes that reminded him very much of Callum. Another photo was of Celeste and Derek, who Dar knew had been her brother. A few more from when they were wee youngins with grown people who were presumably their parents. Poor Celeste. She'd lost her entire family.

Suddenly, he could see the purpose behind the timing of things. Perhaps philosophy and reason were not lost causes after all. If not for his circumstance at home—his loss and the crack in his very foundation that had called his worthiness into question—he'd have not been so eager to embark on this journey. But now he had a noble quest. Something to build upon, to earn for himself. He'd layer a lifetime, beginning with the protection of this family. Aye, a noble quest indeed. One he could be proud of.

The mighty griffin rises.

At that, Dar felt an odd pang, a moment of shame for his diffidence. Truth be told, he thought of Lachlan, and the difficult circumstance Lachlan had found himself in so many years ago. The strength it must have taken for him to walk away back then, and do so nobly. Dar had been looking at it as an escape, as a skulking out the back door, but he saw now that hadn't been the case at all.

Lachlan had never said a word, and if not for Dar's mother

bringing their relationship to light, Dar was positive he wouldn't have. Aye, his father ('twas easier to acknowledge when he was in another century) was noble indeed. Mayhap that crack in his foundation was less substantial than he'd imagined.

A chime blared throughout the house then, followed by barking and someone pounding on the door. Dar had been schooled by Maggie, and felt prepared—at least he hoped—for interacting with the people of her time. Remembering the futuristic custom that one didn't always carry a weapon in plain view, Dar spied what he hoped was a closet and made haste to tuck the sword away for safekeeping. Reaching down, he made sure his dagger had made the trip, and tucked that away too.

All sound, he headed toward the door, hoping he didn't look too out of place in his short tunic, black trousers, and leather boots. It would have to do for now.

"Hey! Open up already!" came a voice, along with more barking from the yonder side of the door.

Dar opened it with a whoosh, using a hand signal on the animal that quieted him immediately. He'd spent many years training the dogs at Remshire, and was known locally as an animal whisperer. "May I help you?" Dar asked as if he owned the dwelling.

"Who are you?" the man asked skeptically, glancing down quizzically at his now obedient dog.

Using Maggie's directive, he replied, "I am a distant cousin of Celeste's from Scotland." Too late, Dar realized that he might have been a bit too forceful with his words, if the man's expression was any indication. Maggie *had* told him that interactions in her time were more—what was the word?—*civil.* "Who are you?"

"A friend and neighbor of Celeste's." The man peered around him before adding, "She did tell me a cousin might be staying here."

Dar couldn't believe his luck. "Yes. 'Twas a spur of the moment trip."

"She's gone for the summer, you know," the man said.

Dar kept his expression bland this time. "I know." He held out his hand, and looked the man solidly in the eye, aware he needed to forge an alliance. "Darach MacKenna."

The man still seemed a bit wary, but looked down again at his hound, who was staring at Dar with adoration. "Nick Anderson."

"Where's your car?" the man called Nick asked.

Quickly, Dar mentally flipped through the pages of his ledger. Maggie had told him what to say if someone asked him about "driving" or a "car" or a "ride." Trying to sound casual as he spoke the strange word, Dar uttered, "Uber."

Nick nodded and Dar breathed a sigh of relief at having passed this first test, then gave the dog a solid pat.

"Well, if you need anything, my number's in the kitchen next to the fridge. Better yet, give me your phone." He reached his out toward Dar, and though the gesture seemed friendly, not threatening, Dar faltered.

All had been going well, until this moment. Dar remembered that Maggie had impressed upon him the importance of procuring such a device, but God almighty, he'd only just arrived.

"'Tis lost," Dar said. An easy enough explanation when necessary, the women had assured, but based on Nick's ghastly look, you'd think that he'd spoken of losing an appendage.

"Did they send a replacement?" he asked, darting a glance down around the doorway as if it would magically appear.

"Nay, I can't say that they have," Dar answered, as if he knew who *they* were.

"Well, I can take you to get another, just let me know when you want to go." Nick's eyes suddenly widened before he smacked his forehead. "Dude, I have a burner you can have."

From the way Nick looked at him, Dar assumed *he* was Dude. He wasn't so sure what precisely it meant, though could concede that Celeste's neighbor was beginning to grow on him with his warm smile and friendly nature. Besides, the man had a hound with a pleasant disposition, which boded well for Nick's character.

"Why don't you come over after you've settled in, and I'll grill us some steaks. It's the least I can do for Celeste's family. I'll set up the phone for you too."

It seemed a worthy alliance. With a smile, Dar extended his hand in a custom Maggie and Gwen had practiced with him. Nick's grip was firm, another good mark. "Many thanks."

With that, Nick and his hound alighted yonder, and Dar got back to the business of familiarizing himself with Celeste's home.

A few hours later, Nick was back, pounding on the door.

"Dar! Dude! You okay?"

If it were not for the infernal blasting of some beacon affixed to the ceiling he would have been. But presently, smoke was aloft in the small kitchen, and if that weren't enough, he had welts on his back from scalding water, and his toe was most likely broken. Some Griffin he was.

Dar consoled himself with the thought that his brethren, and even the griffin himself, would have fared the same in this strange new world. Though Dar fervently hoped this period of trial and mostly error would pass quickly, his confidence needed to be shored, not shirred. No wonder women from the future were daft, it was a jumble of chaos here.

Dar opened the door, letting Nick rush past him toward the kitchen. By the time he followed, Nick had pulled a chair over and taken the infernal blaster off the ceiling.

"All you have to do is take out the battery, see?" he explained after twisting the device apart and showing Dar a rectangular shiny whatnot. "Don't they have smoke detectors in Scotland?"

Aye, he supposed they just might, but not in his time. Dar made a noncommittal grunt and went back to the sink where the paper he'd set afire was now a mess.

"*Dude.* What the heck happened to your back?" Nick asked with a gasp.

Ah, his back. That would be the shower. The very thing Maggie and Gwen swore he would like so much. Having figured out how to turn on the water, and stepping inside, Dar couldn't imagine why on earth they thought being blasted with cold water would be enjoyable. Cursing with displeasure, he'd made haste to turn it off and end the torture. As he'd fumbled with the lever, he'd found the release for hot, and it was suddenly as if someone had set him to boil. He'd made for escape only to be caught by a stone lip under the glass door; hence, his already blackened toe.

"I turned the wrong dial," he said truthfully, though as he said it, it dawned on him that perhaps the trick was to turn a bit of each dial to find an adequate temperature.

Nick made a face. "Is your water on the wrong side, too?"

Dar, unsure what that meant, grunted again, which seemed to appease Nick. When his stomach growled not a moment later, Nick laughed and said that he'd come by to let Dar know that dinner would be ready soon. Little more than an hour later, Dar found himself sitting with Nick and the hound, behind his dwelling, a cold bottle of ale in hand, sharing a meal comprised of delicious prime cuts of meat and some vegetables cooked on what Nick had referred to as a grill.

When Dar had showed up in the same clothes he'd had on when they met earlier, Nick had asked if he'd lost his luggage too. A pile of modern clothes later, Nick had come to the rescue yet again. It seemed he had two brothers; one a "bear," according to Nick, who was obviously referencing his large size, which was presumably similar to Dar's. Nick added a trip to the "mall" to the ever-growing list of things Dar needed.

Celeste's neighbor was turning out to be a Godsend, Dar mused. Mayhap with Nick's help and a bit of time, he'd have what he needed to understand the cadence of his odd new world—and to find Celeste and embark on his quest.

CHAPTER 8

With three weeks in the Hamptons under her belt, Celeste finally felt like she'd settled in. It always took a little while, but each summer, she found a new way to make this place feel like home. The newly renovated one-bedroom rental by the water was perfect. Even more so now, considering she'd taken her time cleaning, unpacking, and organizing everything to her liking, which included rearranging the furniture.

She also had a set schedule at the yoga studio five days a week with a class early every morning and another later in the afternoon. And, for the second year in a row, the moment Becky Adelman saw that Celeste was back in town and teaching yoga, she made a beeline toward her, and asked Celeste point blank if she would come work for them too.

Becky and her husband, Stuart, owned one of the hottest attractions in the area, a bar and restaurant about twenty miles north that hosted live entertainment on the weekends, giving it a bit of a low-key club feel. They also had an outdoor patio where Celeste had spent most of her weekday nights singing last summer, under the pretty wood pergola, nestled between the bar and an assortment of intentionally mismatched tables. It was right up her alley: a guitar, bar stool, mic, and the casual weeknight setting. It was low stress and she really couldn't ask for more.

This year, Celeste was thrilled to be asked back for the same gig. It was nice to do something she loved so much without the added pressure of pursuing it full time. Kind of the best of both worlds. Her voice was good, she knew that. It wasn't special or unique, but she could entertain a room full of people and at the same time lose herself in the music for a bit, which added a therapeutic element to her work too.

The summer was off to the best start she could envision—if she could only drown out the heavy stuff, Celeste would almost be able to imagine things were quite perfect. A bright summer by the water, a pretty little house, yoga, and singing for an appreciative audience. Voila, perfection. Well, a girl could pretend, couldn't she?

After finishing her nine o'clock class that morning, Celeste called out, "See everyone tomorrow. Don't forget I'm off the weekend schedule for now."

She'd been offered those slots too, but needed the extra time to get ready and then drive over to the club where she'd be singing for her first weekend gig. Shortly after Celeste had reprised her weekday night singing spot from last year, Becky had asked her to fill in for their usual Saturday house bands' lead singer, who was out for the next few weeks. Although a bit nervous to face the weekend crowd for the first time, Celeste had said yes.

Eager to get a move on, she wiped herself down, necessary after a hot yoga class, poured some water from the pitcher in the fridge, then closed up shop. After a quick shower back at her place, she headed down Main Street for a proper sit-down lunch at one of the trendy restaurants on the block. They made her favorite salad *ever*, and Celeste hadn't had a chance to have it yet this summer.

An hour later she'd just sat down at the bar—her seat of preference when she was dining alone—and was staring mindlessly out the big picture windows when a group of ridiculously good-looking and well-dressed men walked into the restaurant. Her attention drawn, she began to wonder about them: Secret service? Private security, maybe? She gazed at them absent-mindedly for a moment, before her spine began to tingle at realizing she recognized one of them. Celeste pushed her menu aside, scooting the bar stool back to get a better view as the group sat at a large round table.

She could feel all eyes on her as she approached, but she was too busy focusing on Stanley Finch. He was a schoolmate of Derek and Maggie's, and she hadn't seen him since Derek's funeral. Last she knew, he worked for one of the top law enforcement agencies in the country. She'd actually tried to contact him a few months after Maggie had disappeared but hadn't had much luck.

When he focused in on her, Celeste noted a narrowing in Stan's eyes for a fraction of a second before they softened in recognition. She let a breath out; she didn't know how she'd have reacted if he hadn't remembered her. Stan stood as she got closer, and his arms opened a second before he pulled her in close. Unexpectedly, Celeste teared up. She felt a little silly about it, but aside from the crone, she couldn't remember the last time she'd received an affectionate hug like this. And coming from one of her brother's friends, it meant so much. It felt so darn good.

When Stan pulled back, she tried to wipe her tears quickly, but she knew he saw them anyway.

"Did you hear about Maggie?" she blurted out.

He gave her a quizzical look. "Hear what about Maggie?"

Celeste swallowed back tears again. "She disappeared."

"*What?* When?" He looked shocked by the news, but then something caught his attention behind her. "Give me a minute," he said, then headed toward the front doors before Celeste could respond, let alone react.

Curious about his interruption, Celeste turned as three more blasts from the past entered the room: Amanda Marceau, Samantha Gilchrist, and Jenny D'Angelo.

Celeste vaguely remembered thinking that Jenny and Stan were an item back when they were all in college together, but then Jenny had married a real douchebag, that guy John Monroe. Celeste shuddered at just the thought of John—she barely knew him, but still, she knew he was a creep. What Jenny had seen in him, she'd never understood. The guy had actually had the nerve to hit on her a few times—while he was seeing Jenny. She'd almost said something, but in the end, was too self-conscious. After all, as much as she knew the girls *liked* her, she'd never been able to shake the feeling of "just" being Derek's little sister.

Seconds later, Celeste was broken from her revelry when a commotion broke out as the women rushed toward her. Then Jenny was embracing her and giving her the same love and warmth she'd gotten from Stan moments ago and there was nothing Celeste could do to stem the waterworks this time. She leaned in and let go, overcome by the onslaught of affection. A few moments later, she pulled back, a bit embarrassed that she'd so thoroughly lost it.

"Are you okay?" Jenny asked, her eyes filled with concern as she stroked the side of Celeste's face.

"Did Stan tell you?" Celeste managed to ask.

At this, Jenny shook her head. "He was too busy correcting my bad behavior. Tell me what, sweetie?"

"Maggie…" Celeste's eyes welled with tears and her voice cracked. "She disappeared two and a half years ago."

"Oh my God, that's horrible." Jenny pulled her closer at the news, covering Celeste's head protectively. She could hear Jenny saying something to Stan, though Celeste didn't care about anything in that moment but the feeling of being welcomed, of being wanted, of being cared for.

"I don't know why I didn't think of contacting you sooner," Celeste said when she pulled away. "You and Maggie were always such good friends. It's so odd to have run into you today."

"I'm sorry, Celeste. Things have been crazy for me these past couple of years. But that's no excuse. I should have reached out to you."

Celeste shook her head, then gave Jenny another hug. "It's okay. I'm just so glad that I came in here now and saw Stan. And you. And Sam. And Amanda," she said as the hugs continued.

Visiting Derek and Maggie on weekends and holidays when they were in law school had often included seeing Jenny, Sam, and Stan—even Amanda the few times she'd been there. Seeing people now who had been so close to her brother and best friend brought a little bit of that time back for Celeste, and she was grateful for it.

They added a chair at their table for Celeste and after settling in and placing their orders, Celeste told them how she was in town for the summer helping a friend who owned a yoga studio. She decided to leave off the gig at the club considering her current company—award-winning singer Amanda Marceau—but barely finished the thought before Amanda chimed in with, "You didn't pursue your singing, Celeste?" She sounded almost disappointed. "Derek and Maggie always gushed about all the leads you snagged in theater. Do you know how many programs they proudly shoved in my face?" She laughed. "But seriously, it's a shame, because you have such a beautiful voice."

Celeste blushed at the praise, especially considering the source. "I wasn't going to say anything, but I *am* performing at a club about thirty minutes or so from here." She shrugged. "It kind of happened by accident. But I'm happy it worked out because music is my therapy."

The girls exchanged looks, and within seconds, they'd solidified plans to come to the club the following Saturday.

Celeste loved every moment of the next hour as she was caught up in the cadence of the group. It felt like being part of a big family, and she was sad when it ended even though she knew she'd see them the following Saturday. Luckily, they were in the Hamptons for most of the summer, which meant more time spent together.

Just before they left, Stan pulled her to the side. "Hey," he said, concern flashing in his eyes, "I'm going to reach out to the lead on Maggie's case and use my resources at Calder Defense, my security company, to see what I can find."

While part of her wanted Stan to do just that, the bigger part, the part that believed in the crone, didn't care. Who was to say Maggie *wasn't* happy in another time. Seriously, *who?* Maggie had all but disappeared into thin air and the crone was the only person Celeste had come across who could give *any* explanation for her whereabouts. Besides, people had been writing about time travel for years—books, movies, TV series— it wasn't so farfetched, was it?

But, Celeste reasoned, this wasn't the place to blurt it out and especially not to Stan, of all people; the man was as "by the book" as they came. Telling him that the mystic on Crabapple Lane had assured Celeste that Maggie was just where she was supposed to be, in a different century, happy and whole—yeah, *no*. Stan would probably take her to the psych ward. No, for now she'd keep this to herself and just be grateful she'd run into them.

CHAPTER 9

Dar slipped on a pair of jeans, probably the article of futuristic clothing he liked best, and headed to the kitchen. He poured a cup of coffee and took both it and his computer to the back porch, marveling yet again at the routine he'd comprised for himself in his new life. With the early morning sun and soft breeze, he found the porch to be the best spot, and drank deeply from his mug before putting up his feet and pulling the laptop over onto his legs. He chuckled, *lap-top*, brilliant.

Dar had been in the future for all of fourteen days, but with Nick next door, he had been given the accelerated version of entry into the twenty-first century. All the notes he'd taken from Maggie and Gwen, and the few they'd scribed in secret (much to his surprise) had paled in comparison to the experience of learning firsthand how this time worked, or, more importantly, how to *work* things in this time.

He'd been thrust into the fray, but his guide made it quite palatable, especially since Nick seemed to chalk all of Dar's ignorance up to being from a foreign land. In his words: "Your hometown must be pretty archaic, Dude." *Aye, my friend, to say the least.*

Dar's confidence now much restored, he'd begun to feel as though he might just accomplish what he'd inadvertently set out to do. Begin anew, and whilst in the process, look after the fair Celeste. Maggie or Gwen, mayhap both, had also seen fit to slip his medallion into his satchel, and he'd found it tucked away in a pocket beneath his personal items. It brought him comfort. A link to his brethren in spirit and in blood.

In his new world, he was especially pleased to see this attribute of the griffin noted on a website he'd looked up on his new computer: "King of all creatures—noble, fearsome, and above all else, protective."

When he'd begun to discover his new home, Dar had thought it best to skirt the rules, to pass by as undetected as possible, but once again, Nick, who seemed to have the answer for everything, had shown him the way.

ID, done. Instead of using the name and number Maggie had warily suggested to procure "fake" papers, Nick's friend who worked for a utilities company simply opened an account in Dar's name, thus providing "proof" of residence.

With Nick's guidance, once it arrived in the "mail," it wasn't difficult to take said paperwork to a storefront and request formal government identification. When pressed by the nice woman behind the counter to produce *more* such identification in order to get *this* ID, Nick had launched into a tirade about the difficulties of "getting proof without showing proof" and demanded that Dar, his dear friend, brother from another mother, have his due.

Flustered, the poor woman had issued the ID, even though Dar suspected that this was highly unorthodox—which was confirmed by Nick's "holy crap, Dude, I did *not* think that would work!" after they left. Though Dar offered many apologies to the woman for his friend's behavior, in the end, he had his ID and owed Nick much for his theatrical efforts. Still, he'd find a way to make it right with the woman, a gift of some sort. Aye, he'd see to it.

When it came to selling one of his gems so he'd have some tangible money, Nick had jumped in to help there, too ("Dude, I've got this. Bible," was Nick's oft ready reply. "Bible," Dar realized after the third or fourth time he'd heard it, meant "I swear to it.").

After a tense negotiation with a dealer of fine gems, Dar walked away with a cash deposit and note that guaranteed a small fortune three days hence. Even Nick was surprised by the sum, though Dar had to take his word for it that the sum was substantial.

Dar still had nine gems left, but they lay hidden in a safe he'd found in the basement, which had also contained all of the documents Maggie had said it would: IDs; numerous magical cards loaded with money, each marked with the sum written on it; and stacks of currency.

He'd found nothing of Celeste's in the safe, which he knew

meant she hadn't found it after Maggie disappeared. Another stroke of luck, though Maggie was fairly confident Celeste wouldn't have been able to sell their home without a death certificate. Macabre subject, but Maggie had insisted it bore repeating.

With his new identification, and a made-up nine-digit number that apparently everyone had, they'd opened several bank accounts—Nick insisted—and a set amount of the money he was due was deposited within each on the appropriate date. Then, they'd dropped off the gem.

When he realized that a conduit to everything lived but steps away, Dar had nearly stopped trying to figure things out on his own. But on a deeper level, he felt their connection becoming one of brethren status, and Dar knew Nick's ready help and good-spirited friendship were invaluable. Brother from another mother, indeed.

Over the following days, they'd shopped for clothes and toiletries, and secured a phone and computer too. When he'd seen Dar still wearing only the clothes Nick had lent him, he'd asked him whether the "airline" had lost his bags for good, whatever that meant, but he seemed to find it a reasonable enough explanation for why Dar had no clothes or possessions of his own, and so Dar had just agreed.

Maggie had filled him in on much, but her best advice in case she'd missed something was to use a search engine on a computer. He could type in anything that he needed instructions for, and a miniature moving person would alight on the screen and show him what he needed to know.

It had frightened Dar at first, but once he confirmed that

there was no way this person could reach him, he'd settled into the routine. With the help of the computer, he'd done laundry, perfected the coffee maker, and repaired a slow leak in one of the upstairs bathing rooms. There were a slew of tools in the garage, which must have belonged to Derek, that Dar used to fix a few loose door handles, hinges, and even the railing around the back porch.

Now, as he took another long pull from his coffee mug, he studied the map of various towns in the Hamptons that he'd printed with Nick's help, paying special attention to where Celeste was residing and working this summer. Not only did she teach some kind of exercise class, but the lass was a bit of a performer, Nick had explained, apparently a noble profession in these times, and oft found work at a "club" in a nearby town.

With a housing reservation in the same hamlet where Celeste worked, Dar was ready. He confirmed it once again over the phone, speaking slowly so as to be understood. Again, Maggie's wisdom. But also, Nick's, who had a penchant for raising a brow and waiting for Dar to repeat his words.

Dar waved as Nick headed off to work.

"Grill tonight?" Nick asked.

Dar smiled but shook his head. "I'm off to visit Celeste."

With a thumbs up, Nick replied, "Say hi for me. I'll keep an eye on the place."

"Thanks, man," Dar returned, using a term he'd learned from Nick.

After he finished his coffee, he took a long shower—pleasantly warm this time. As it turned out, the women were correct, it was indeed one of the many pleasures of the future. Once one knew how to use it properly, of course.

It wasn't much later that he packed up, locked the house, and settled into the car service that would drive him to Long Island.

Dar smiled. His first in a long time. Purpose did that to a body.

CHAPTER 10

In a rush to get to work, Celeste drove as quickly as she was allowed down Main Street, guitar in the seat beside her. She was still quite early for her actual set, but with Stan, Jenny, and the Montgomerys coming to have dinner at the restaurant first, she was a whirl of nervous excitement. Giddy, almost. She couldn't remember the last time she'd felt this way. For the first time since Maggie's disappearance, she had plans, real plans with real people she was looking forward to seeing. Her people. People she had a history with and who, it seemed, truly cared.

Celeste allowed herself a moment to marvel at the odd way it had come together, and stranger, how she felt okay with it, despite the fact that she hadn't had any interest in spending time with people since Maggie's disappearance. She reasoned that it must be *these* people in particular—their warmth and familiarity. Otherwise, she'd never have felt so comfortable letting them in. It reminded her of when Maggie first came around. Instant connection, instant camaraderie, instant friendship. It wasn't unheard of, Celeste just hadn't felt it in a long time.

Since running into them last week, Stan and the girls had all been in touch, calling and texting here and there to check in with her. Their interest and concern felt genuine. Suddenly, Celeste felt like she had a family again, and a big one at that.

Pulling into a spot behind the restaurant, Celeste grabbed her guitar and garment bag together in one hand and made her way to the front entrance. She exchanged greetings with a few employees who were taking a break in the side alley as she passed, then turned on Main, all but flying down the street; like she had a date with destiny.

She glanced down for just a second as she hurried, to make sure she had everything, and in that moment, *thwack*, ransmack dab into someone—someone really tall and really broad.

"Whoa, slow down, lass," drawled a deep voice with a heavy Scottish accent. "Ye'll hurt yourself that way."

The breath escaped her as Celeste craned her neck back until her eyes landed on the face of the man she'd slammed into. Her thoughts came at her in a rush. *Oh boy... big boy... bad boy... pretty boy all in one.*

Something about the man kept Celeste frozen, and after a moment, she realized she was staring. Flustered, she pulled back, noting sheepishly that her cheek had been squished into his shirt—literally smushed, like pressing into her eyelids smushed. But that accent had hit her out of left field.

She glanced at his button-down, thrilled her makeup hadn't left a mark—*thank you, waterproof liner and mascara*—and hoped her face wasn't a wreck because she was literally being held up by this hot, bad-boy fantasy of a man. Shoulder-length hair, chiseled cheekbones, strong chin, perfect nose, and deep dark eyes framed by thick spikey lashes. *Wow.*

He looked down at her, concern apparent in his eyes. "Are you alright?"

Speak Celeste. Speak. She flushed as she realized she was *still* staring, and stumbled back.

"Whoa there, lass," he cautioned, his words laced with that pleasing Scottish lilt as his large hands righted her before retrieving the garment bag that she hadn't even realized had fallen.

Finding her breath and her footing—but not yet her words—Celeste slowly craned her neck all the way back to get a better look at his face. *Oh mama.*

Finally, she registered everything that had just happened and things slipped into clarity all at once. "I'm okay—Are *you* okay—I'm so sorry," she said in a rush, completely flustered.

He chuckled and flashed a smile and Celeste felt herself blush. *Omg, stop doing that!* she silently reprimanded the hot Scottish stranger. A look she couldn't quite put her finger on crossed his features.

"No apologies necessary," he murmured, his voice a low rumble.

She was struck by his relaxed demeanor, how unruffled he seemed by the whole incident. More than that, it was how in control he seemed that impressed her most. Satisfied by what appeared to be his genuine reaction, Celeste glanced down at her watch and groaned.

"Listen, I really *am* sorry," she repeated, then reached out to brush her hand over the area she'd plastered herself against, a bolder move than she would normally pull, but something about this man made her feel bold.

Hot to the touch, his pec flexed in response, and damn if she didn't touch him again. His shirt was really nice, a silk blend for sure. Very expensive. *Rich*, bad-boy rocker, she thought, absent-mindedly rubbing the material between her fingers. It wasn't until his hand clamped over hers, holding it still, and their eyes locked that Celeste realized she'd been pretty much feeling him up—a perfect stranger—on the street.

Oh my God, what was wrong with her? She blushed, shrugging to cover her embarrassment before rushing on, and giving a half-hearted explanation. "I don't think I left a mark, but if I did, I'll cover the dry-cleaning bill."

Figuring she'd humiliated herself enough, Celeste turned and hurried away, but when she reached the entrance to the restaurant, she paused. She really couldn't help herself, something about him set off a spark in her, she wasn't sure what it was, she just knew that she wanted to talk to him again. It was another out-of-character move for her, but *why not?* She'd chalk it up to the full moon or something, then she'd dismiss it all to hell afterward. She turned around, and tried to suppress a grin when she saw the guy was still standing there, watching her.

"I'm here for the next few Saturdays," she called out, "I perform here—" She gestured with her head but forgot how close the door was and banged it instead. He flashed a smile, his eyes dancing with amusement as she rushed on, "I mean, I sing here—if you wanted to come by," she shrugged, "or um, if your shirt needs to be cleaned, I'll, uh, I can take it in myself, or you can bring the bill in, or whatever's easiest for you. Again, I'm so sorry, seriously!"

Celeste reddened and realized she was rambling. *Holy moly, shut up already.* So, before she could embarrass herself any further, she gave a small wave and darted into the restaurant. Thrilled to be inside and away from rocker-boy's force field, where she only seemed to be able to mortify herself, she sagged against the closed front door and took a deep breath, silently repeating her *dismiss, dismiss, dismiss* mantra, one she'd learned from the famous astrologer, before turning her attention to the bustle inside.

"Hey, Stu," she said, waving toward Becky's husband at the bar, then scooting out of the way as two hostesses rushed by in a close call. They were obviously knee-deep in prep for a big night. It was well known that Amanda Marceau was back in town, and the once-private songwriter and sometime performer had really come out of her shell now that she'd married the stunningly handsome British billionaire Alexander Montgomery. She'd sung in public twice now, and with their reservations on the books and word of it leaked on the street, tonight was gearing up to be epic.

Celeste blushed again thinking of that epic run-in she'd had with rocker-boy on the sidewalk, then quickly dismissed it from her mind so she could focus on her upcoming set as she got changed.

Although she was most comfortable performing alone with a guitar, she'd found she was really enjoying playing with the restaurant's band, who were all great, and so gracious about having her as a sub. The members were all locals to the area, super talented, and totally low-key. Kind of how she felt about singing. It brought her joy, and she enjoyed doing it, but beyond that, she wasn't chasing any dreams.

Amanda had called her twice during the week, wanting to be prepared for tonight. They'd decided that Celeste would stick to her normal set, and Amanda would join her in the middle.

When Celeste finally peeked out of her dressing room an hour later, she saw that the whole gang had arrived and were already seated. Grinning, she hurried over. "Hi, everyone," she greeted, her cheeks almost frozen from smiling so hard. They said they'd be there, and she'd believed them, but actually *seeing* them there was something else.

It reminded her of past events, when she'd had a built-in support system in her family. Even later, when she'd only had Derek and Maggie, *they* were always there, beaming and cheering her on.

As she got closer to the table, all the guys stood, and the girls hugged her hello, then gestured to an extra chair they'd requested for her. Grinning even larger than she'd thought possible, Celeste sat down to join them for appetizers.

Time flew by and before she knew it, she was on stage. It was hard to see past the lights and even though people always applauded, her friends—it felt good to say that—were extra loud and proud. When Amanda came up, they sang two of her hits and three covers they'd chosen earlier. Singing with Amanda Marceau. It was such a rush. Even better, after Celeste finished her set for the night, they waved her back to the table to join them.

When the DJ who was on after the band started playing old favorites, they all got up on the dance floor. Celeste was so happy, she teared up at one point. She felt silly about it, but she was just so overwhelmed by how well the night was going; though, of course, she also felt a little guilty for having so much fun. The girls noticed and pulled her in for a group hug.

When dessert and coffee came, they settled into easy conversation. Samantha had just started in on a story about their college days when, suddenly, all hell broke loose.

Celeste had no idea what was going on, but when Stan shouted, "DOWN!," she went down. The guys drew their weapons and the table they were at was literally flipped on its side as cover. Amanda gripped her hand and held it through a frenzied few minutes until, just as suddenly as it had started, it was over. The overhead lights came on and soon after most of the crowd was gone and all the festiveness had evaporated.

From what Celeste could work out, Jenny's ex had shown up, and though she didn't know the whole story, she remembered enough about John to intuit that just him showing his face was threat enough. Stan and some of the guys had run after him, but came back empty-handed, shaking their heads.

Celeste was just getting to her feet when Stan strode directly over to her.

"Where's your security?" he asked, his eyes flashing.

Confused, she asked, "What security? I'm flattered you think I warrant a security team but—"

"Your bodyguard?" Stan interrupted.

Celeste shook her head. "I don't have one," she said, still a bit shaken, wondering if she'd missed something.

Stan sighed and waved her off, and while Celeste still wondered what he was talking about, she was grateful to just sit down with the girls. It was at least another hour before they all left, one of the Calder trucks following her home, watching until she was safely inside.

After a night like tonight, Celeste mused, maybe a body-guard wasn't such a bad idea.

CHAPTER 11

By Dar's estimation, the past week had been monumental. And not necessarily in a good way. For one, his affection for Celeste lay on an entirely different plane than he'd first imagined.

And two, he was discovering that danger seemed to lurk everywhere in this new world. It was rocking his newfound footing and now here he was, teetering yet again. Fate's fickle hand, he supposed. Run from one troubled circumstance and land in the bubbling cauldron of another.

Dar knew better than most that to be truly evolved, one could never really run from a situation—the universe had a way of making one sort through their issues regardless. Well, that was the word of a spiritual guru on one of the podcasts Nick had downloaded for him anyway. It was one of many future inventions that Dar had taken to, and he'd even capitalized on the scholar's advice by browsing a local shop that sold crystals, much like the ones Celeste had in her home. He now carried an amethyst in his pocket, alongside his medallion. This griffin had best get his act together.

Before his encounter with Celeste last week, Dar had seen no point in rushing things, especially as he was still getting used to how things worked in this new era. Besides, it wasn't as if he could walk up to her and blurt out the truth of it. She'd probably have him taken off in cuffs, absurd as his story was.

As far as he was concerned, things had been going smoothly. He'd kept an eye on Celeste, but from a distance—observing her, trying to figure out his best means of approach. Of course, this was before their run-in.

Maggie had tasked him with making Celeste his responsibility, especially with her brother, her last protector, gone, and Maggie living in another realm. And up until their run-in, he'd been focused only on the duty he had to fulfill, at most entertaining that mayhap they would become friends, but that was secondary to his quest.

But now, a week after Celeste had collided with him—a week after he'd realized she was more than just a pretty face, and a week since he'd given chase to that brute of a man who'd clearly only had ill intent—Dar was a bit vexed. As he strolled down Main Street, keeping a safe distance from Celeste and her friends as they browsed the storefronts in town, he couldn't stop thinking about her and the way she'd looked at him that evening.

One minute he'd been innocently walking down the street, and the next, she'd literally *run into* him. His reaction to her had hit him full on, and after she'd dismissed herself, prettily and with an endearing self-conscious coyness, he'd gone back to the inn and headed to the beach for a run, a much-needed distraction.

Gwen was an avid runner and had introduced him to it a couple years ago when he'd visited Seagrave. Athletic shoes were high on the list of essentials Gwen had had for him, "Just wait, Dar, the support is amazing," she'd crowed. "Oooh, and make sure you get a hot stone massage, you'll love it." She was correct about the shoes, and although the hot stone massage sounded like something pleasant, he hadn't yet tried it.

When he'd returned to the eatery later that evening—at Celeste's invitation, he was thrilled to admit—he nodded to one of the bouncers he'd befriended on the previous occasions he'd been to the establishment, then spotted Celeste at a large table with the family she'd had lunch with the week before. With Nick's help, he'd later discovered that they were modern-day royalty of sorts. Alexander Montgomery was the owner of a vast security business and wed to a world-famous entertainer.

He'd watched her that night from the wall by the entrance, easily blending in amongst the crowd. When Celeste had taken the stage, he'd found himself transfixed. Though his preference was for when she sang by herself, sitting upon a stool with her instrument in hand, he could listen to her all night in any setting. She had a beautiful voice, mesmerizing eyes, and a charming presence.

Dar smiled just thinking of how she'd looked up there on stage, totally immersed in the music—so different from her self-conscious shyness offstage. Then, he realized he'd been daydreaming for at least a full five minutes and forced himself back to the present, to the task at hand.

He'd gotten good at blending in, and had always been a good tracker, so he was able to spot Celeste and her friend quite easily on the crowded sidewalk. When the women went inside one of the shops, he stopped to keep an eye on them from beneath an awning across the street. While he waited, his phone vibrated in his pocket, and after retrieving it, a picture of Nick's hound appeared on the screen, with the words *Miss you but your steak was great!* He chuckled, happy to see Brutus well, though admitted to himself that he missed them both.

Dar had been in the Hamptons for almost three weeks now, which had given him plenty of time to acclimate to the area and the cadence of the coast. As it turned out, this hamlet was a fine place indeed. The lodgings he'd secured with Nick's help—a two-room suite at a waterfront inn—were quite luxurious, and the purveyor of the establishment clearly had a penchant for getting to know her guests. Within days of his arrival, his favorite drinks, snacks, and hors d'oeuvres were always at the ready.

There was a coffeehouse nearby in town that opened early and provided a selection of hot and cold delights he knew Gwen would have loved. In fact, he'd swear that last time he'd visited Seagrave, Cook had prepared such a drink as the one he'd had that morning.

Dar had expected some trouble settling in or sticking out, but with so many people about, it wasn't all that hard to watch, learn, and emulate, especially now that he wasn't nearly as inept at how things operated in this new century. Besides, he had his ledger, Nick was a call away, and the internet to help. All of that, and keeping an ear attuned to passersby had served him well in learning modern English and even some slang.

Across the street, he saw Celeste and her friend (Jenny, he thought her name was) leave the shop, and, as Dar scanned their immediate surroundings, his chest tightened, all languidness evaporating from his body.

He already knew that he wasn't the only one watching them, the men from Calder Defense security had seemed to be keeping the women on a tight tether since Jenny's former husband had come into the club looking for trouble the other night. Dar had given chase to him but the brigand had gotten away.

Dar hated men who preyed on women, always had. Now, his eyes were drawn to a truck that looked similar to the ones that the Calder men drove, but his hackles rose as the girls made a run for it after it pulled up next to the shop.

Distance be damned, he ran, weaving in and around the crowds, and shouting at people to move out of the way.

The man who got out of the driver's side was wearing a cap, but Dar knew at once he was not Jenny's man, not a Calder man at all. But both women had their heads bent, avoiding the rain as they got into the truck, and Dar knew they weren't aware of the danger they were in. He was closest to the passenger side, and he almost ripped the door off its fastenings before he reached to pull Celeste out of the truck, grabbing at her with both arms, and scooping her up as her friend stared blankly at them, not moving.

Once he'd removed Celeste from danger and set her out of the truck's way, he dove across the seat to reach for Jenny. He could see in her eyes, she'd somehow been incapacitated, drugged, mayhap. He grabbed at her with both hands, intent on ripping her from the vehicle, too, but that bastard leaned over her and jabbed him in the neck. He reached up, but it was no ordinary weapon he'd been stabbed with. It was smaller, flimsier, but powerful in a way he'd never known.

Suddenly, Dar felt woozy, his senses swirled, and before he knew it, the truck was pulling away and he fell from the open door as he heard Celeste's muffled scream.

Her voice sounded far away, and though she tried to catch him, he knew his deadweight was too much. A few pedestrians helped lift him off her legs and she cradled his head while calling for help. Her hand brushed his forehead, and stroked his hair, as his mind fought for control.

By the time the Calder men arrived, the effects of what he'd been jabbed with—because surely the strange dagger had been covered in some kind of poison—had worn off. He was furious, and clutched at Celeste's wrist, her blue eyes widening as he sat up and then stood, taking her with him.

"You good?" one of the men asked him.

"Aye," he said, rubbing the back of his neck again, his eyes still on Celeste.

"Let's go then, get in."

Dar helped Celeste up, and followed quickly behind, barely closing the door before they were speeding down the street.

He leaned toward her, looking into her eyes as clarity began to return. "You're alright?" he asked, sure he'd grabbed her before harm came to her, but still, his heart clenched at the very thought of what might have happened. His fingers brushed her wrists and arms, then swept the nape of her neck as he checked for marks. Malleable, she moved with him, even pulling her hair back for his inspection.

"He didn't get me," she whispered, her soft voice washing over him like a balm. Her eyes misted as she held his gaze. Gratitude oozed from them.

He nodded a silent acknowledgment as they pulled into a parking lot, converging with three other vehicles.

"He was jabbed with something. Jenny, too," Celeste said to the other men, gesturing toward Dar.

"Check him out," one of the brothers directed.

As Dar's neck was examined, he listened to the exchange between the men. While the women worried for their friend and offered their wish that the bastard be dealt with, Dar didn't hold back.

"Slay him," he sneered. Dar, for all his distaste of warfare, could see no other option.

Aye, that got their attention, especially the brothers who'd introduced themselves as such. The older one caught his eye and gave him a curious look that Dar couldn't decipher.

"Get the girls home," the other said as they made for the trucks again. Then they were gone.

A delicate hand held his arm as the women were ushered to the remaining vehicle. When he looked down, Celeste's eyes were big blue saucers, her breathing still erratic. He declined the ride the men offered but before they left, he gave Celeste the reassurance she needed.

"They'll find her," he said, tamping down the anger flaring inside of him again for the man who had scared her so, and taken her friend. "These are good men. Honorable and capable."

Celeste looked at him and shook her head in what seemed like wonder. "I can't believe you saved me. I don't even know your name."

Despite the dire circumstances, Dar felt lighter inside than he had in days. Finally, a step in the right direction. "Darach," he said, unable to keep a smile off his face as he held out his hand to her, "Darach MacKenna."

"Thank you, Darach," she said, placing her hand in his and returning his smile. "I'm Celeste. Celeste Lowell."

Assured that she would be seen safely home, he watched as they pulled away. She turned to look out the back window as they drove down the block, her hand pressing the glass. That hand. Dar could still feel her touch. He stared back, knowing in his bones their connection was bigger and deeper than he'd ever considered.

CHAPTER 12

Celeste told the Montgomerys she would stay through dinner, but insisted on going home to sleep in her own bed later. As much as Amanda and Sam wanted her to stay, she needed to decompress by herself, in her own space.

It had been a highly charged, emotionally draining afternoon, much of it spent pacing while she and Sam and Amanda waited for news about Jenny. When word came that she'd been rescued, Celeste had cried with the rest of them, then mobbed her with major hugs when she reappeared, safe and whole.

After Jenny showered and changed, Stan, who hadn't left her out of his sight, escorted her over to the rest of the women. "We have some business to take care of," he said, making sure Jenny was okay before leaving her in their care and heading downstairs.

When they all met again on the terrace that evening, Celeste had sat back in awe. My, how she envied this group. The warmth, love, and care around that table were astounding, like a big happy family times ten. Amanda caught her watching and said, "We're short a couple tonight, but rain or shine, we eat together every chance we get."

Those words shifted Celeste's worldview. She decided right then and there that if she was ever lucky enough to become the matriarch of her...of *a* family, she would emulate the very essence of what she felt at this home.

At some point between salads and entrées, Stan turned to her and asked, "What do you know about Dar?"

This startled Celeste so much, she did a double take, not only at the question but at his sharp tone. "Dar?" she repeated, not sure who he was asking about.

"Darach MacKenna. The guy who pulled you from the truck today."

Oh. Him. Dar. Celeste had had so much on her mind throughout the day, she hadn't had time to process it, him, yet. This was the second time she'd been near him, and the second time they'd ended up sharing a sudden, intimate embrace of sorts. It was overwhelming to say the least.

Celeste had dated in the past, obviously, but she'd *never* felt anything like she felt with this veritable stranger, with *Dar*. Her actions had been as immediate and second-nature as they had been intimate. Cradling his head in her lap, rubbing his forehead, stroking his hair, those were all things she'd never done before with men she ostensibly knew much better.

"You don't know him?" Stan asked, jarring her from her thoughts. "He was at the club the other night, too—gave chase to John that night we were all there. I asked you about him then, remember? I thought he was your bodyguard, but you looked at me with such confusion I asked Stuart instead— apparently Dar started coming around the week before."

That was news to Celeste. But now that he'd brought it up, she remembered Stan asking her who her security was that night. She felt herself blush and hoped it didn't show, suppressing a smile because Stan didn't appear to be too keen on him. But the fact was clear: Darach had come into the restaurant that night after all her nervous babbling on the street. He had wanted to see her again.

Celeste found herself feeling defensive on Darach's behalf. He'd saved her from God only knew what today, and if Stan was correct, he'd chased after a truly bad man the night she'd performed with Amanda at the club. No way was he on the wrong side. He was one of the good guys, she knew it. She felt it in her bones.

"I ran into him last week," she said, meeting Stan's eyes. "Literally. And today was the only other time I've seen him." *So back off*, she thought.

"Just be careful. And cautious," Stan advised.

"I will," she promised, though mostly just to appease him because now her curiosity about Darach MacKenna was thoroughly piqued.

Looking around, Celeste noted that Amanda's husband was staring at them intently.

"Boss?" Stan asked, clearly also catching the odd look on his face.

"I know that name from somewhere, but it escapes me at the moment."

"We'll have the rest of the intel shortly," Stan assured.

"You're having him checked out?" Celeste interjected, louder than she'd meant to.

All eyes at the table turned to her, and she shrank back. They were just looking out for her. This was their business, it's what they did for those under their protective umbrella—and that included her now. Still, she couldn't shake feeling like the teenage daughter who'd brought the wrong boy home.

When the conversation around her steered toward the possibility of an upcoming family trip, Celeste sank into the relief of no longer being the center of attention. It also gave her an opportunity to process what Stan had told her, and to think about Darach.

After dinner, Celeste found herself breathing a sigh of relief as she got in the back seat of a Calder truck to go home. The whole day had been a bit too much for her, and she felt like she was on sensory overload.

A few blocks from her rental, she startled, thinking for a moment she'd glimpsed Darach walking along the side of the road. She told herself it couldn't be him—that he was just on her mind after the two intense run-ins, him literally saving her from being kidnapped, and after his being the topic of conversation at dinner. But damn if her heart didn't skip a beat at the possibility.

Celeste had never been in a relationship. Or, not a real one at any rate. One of the many tragedies she'd been through must have turned off that internal switch. Between the loss of her parents and the subsequent adjustments she and Derek had made with school and their living arrangements, Celeste had turned inward, focused on keeping what she had left secure.

For years, she'd been content third-wheeling her brother and Maggie, with her close relationships with each of them individually too. She'd never given boyfriends a second thought until college. She *had* thought about it then, had accepted a few dates here and there, but always shied away from real intimacy. And then she'd lost Derek. And Maggie.

So, looking for love? No. She'd been scarred by life and figured if and when she was ready, if she was ever ready, she would know. It wasn't so much that she didn't trust people, but that she didn't trust life.

Before her parents died, there had been a boy she'd liked. She used to get this rush when she saw him, in class, down a hallway, at a baseball game, wherever they happened to be in close proximity. It had been years since she'd felt that kind of thrumming attraction, but she recognized it now. The thrill of seeing the boy she might be crushing on. And maybe, too, the boy she was warned to stay away from.

After being escorted safely to her door, Celeste showered and changed into some loungewear. It was too early for bed, so she grabbed a cup of tea, turned on some music, and opened the windows in the living room to the beautiful night outside. A soft breeze rustled the curtains, and she waved when she saw the Calder truck parked across the street a few houses down, there to keep an eye on her overnight.

When she looked the other way, her heart skipped a beat again. There was a man down on the sidewalk who could only be Darach. It wasn't an illusion, was it? No, it had to be him. In jeans and a t-shirt, he walked down the block like he owned it.

How did he know where she was staying? Celeste wondered. Although she knew she should be at least a little uneasy about this virtual stranger showing up outside her house, something deep inside of her felt like she didn't need to be wary of this man at all.

Without thinking, she stepped outside. Her movement must have caught his attention because he immediately flashed a smile her way. She felt a whoosh of butterflies stronger than any thrill she'd felt for that boy all those years ago. This was something more, something stronger, and more intense, yet oddly stable at the same time. Like they had a true connection.

Maybe it was because of their shared experience earlier today, but whatever it was, their connection felt real. She smiled back, watching him approach until he stopped on the sidewalk right in front of her house. Her face almost cracked, she was so happy to see him.

He looked at her for a long moment. A surprisingly respectful look, too; his eyes only on her face when he easily could have given her a once-over.

"It's good to see you so well, lass," he said when he finally spoke, his accent moving right through her.

She blushed, grateful he couldn't see it in the dark. "Hi, Darach."

He motioned with his head to the Calder truck. "I don't want to get any closer without speaking to them first."

She nodded and watched as he crossed the street, grinning triumphantly. *See, Stan?! Would a bad guy do* that? She couldn't hear what he and the Calder men were saying, but after a moment, Darach turned and gave her a reassuring smile. Her breath caught a few seconds later when the back door of the SUV opened, but he looked over again, completely calm, and shook his head.

"It's okay, Celeste," he said loudly enough for her to hear before he stepped into the truck.

She nodded and watched as they disappeared down the street, feeling like he'd been pegged unfairly—like she was the one who needed to protect him.

CHAPTER 13

The drive in the Calder truck was relatively quiet, which suited Dar just fine. It gave him time to consider his interaction with Celeste tonight, how her mere touch had affected him. He wondered if Maggie had known this—had somehow known that Celeste would entrance him so? Was part of the reason she'd been so insistent on his being *really* ready for this quest because she'd foreseen how monumental it could be?

If he ever saw her again, he'd have to ask her, because when Celeste had looked his way and smiled, God almighty, it had gone straight through him. He'd wanted to close the distance between them then, but he knew, too, that he was being surveilled.

He wasn't surprised to see the Calder vehicle. Obviously with today's turn of events, they'd erred on the side of caution. Hadn't he had the same intention? So, instead of bypassing or ignoring them, he'd respectfully decided to let his presence be known and engage with them first.

"Smart call," the driver had said when he'd reached the truck's window.

From the passenger seat, another man who was on the phone said, "Wait here. The boss wants to see you."

While Dar was fine with that—was intrigued, actually, by this Montgomery fellow—he was a bit disturbed that they'd leave their station unattended. It's not as if *he* were the threat.

"What of Celeste's guard?" he asked.

"Right there," said the driver, pointing to another truck as it turned onto the block.

Ah, they *were* capable, these men. Satisfied, Dar nodded and called out to Celeste, hoping to assuage her fears. The last thing he wanted was for her to worry. Then, he climbed into the back seat, and a short time later, the truck pulled through large iron gates and down a long road. A fountain bubbled in the courtyard, and numerous cars and trucks lined the stone drive.

Dar was escorted inside, and then a hand was offered from the eldest Montgomery—the boss.

"MacKenna," he said, giving Dar a firm handshake.

"Montgomery," Dar returned.

He was taken to a large study, bright with computer screens and modern furnishings, and offered a seat at a long table. Three men were already there, including the other brother and the man whose woman was taken. They'd obviously interrupted a tense conversation, which ended now with the other brother saying, "You have a week reprieve, Stan. The moment we return, I expect answers."

Stan gave a curt nod and since they seemed done, Dar asked, "Your woman? She's okay?"

"She is now," Stan confirmed.

"The brigand?" Dar asked.

Stan paused with a curious look, then said, "Dead."

Dar nodded. Not one bit sorry. Men like that didn't change, no matter the century. "Well. Why am I here?"

"That's a great question, Darach," Stan said. "Let me ask you —why *are* you here? In the Hamptons? Tailing Celeste Lowell?"

"What makes you think I'm tailing her?" Dar asked, offering no more than they had.

Stan let out a sigh and gave him a point-blank stare. "I'm tired, Jenny's been through hell, and this back and forth is pissing me off. Thing is, you don't check out, Darach Grifud MacKenna. I've done a thorough background search on you and have turned up absolutely nothing—nothing, at least, beyond the past four-and-a-half weeks since you were somehow able to source legitimate identification. In my book, that's enough for you to be a liability, regardless of how upstanding you appear to be."

Dar raised a brow, taken aback that Stan knew his full name, but he remained silent. Less was always more, in his century and most definitely in this one.

The table suddenly lit up, startling Dar, though he tried not to let it show. When he recovered, he saw that the table was now covered with images of his government issued ID, his bank account information, all of it, and every electronic transaction he'd made thereafter, down to the receipt from dinner earlier this evening.

"You've existed for all of thirty-six days, Darach," Stan said, leveling him with a stare. "Quite a feat for any man. And imagine our surprise to find out your permanent place of residence is listed as none other than Celeste's home."

Aye, Dar could see how that was a problem. Willing to admit he was at a disadvantage, he calculated his next move, deciding to ferret out their possible reactions with an admission of sorts. "I haven't a plausible explanation. And I'm not sure you'd believe me if I tried." He gave what he hoped was a sheepish smile, but was met with Stan's stern expression.

"You're wrong there, my friend," Stan said. "There's very little you could tell us that we'd find inconceivable. Though you'll have to take my word for it."

Without thinking, Dar swore, a few choice phrases, none in English.

Up to now, the brothers and the fourth man in the room had remained silent, letting Stan take the lead. Now, the fourth man spoke up. "Latin?" he asked, eyebrow raised.

Dar shrugged. The language seemed to be a constant throughout the ages. Let them think what they wanted. He might have even managed to keep his placid expression had there not been a commotion at the doorway.

"Hands off, man," came a familiar voice.

Dar gave a nod to Montgomery, impressed by his acumen, how quickly they'd zeroed in on Nick. In truth, they'd had mere hours to piece together much of nothing, yet here stood his only real contact in the future.

"*Duuude!*" Nick said as he was frog-marched into the room.

Dar did his best to suppress a smile, Nick had that effect on him. "Hello, my friend."

Nick's expression changed as he suddenly seemed to realize whose home they were in. "Wait, these are the guys you had me look into," Nick said, doing his signature mind-blowing gesture with his hands.

Montgomery raised a brow. "Do tell, MacKenna. *You* had *us* looked into?"

"I saw Celeste dining with you last week," Dar said with a shrug. "I was curious."

A welcome distraction again, Nick looked down at the table then, his mouth agape as his hands spread across the images. "Oh man, this is *so* cool."

Dar shook his head and smiled. Though it was Stan who thus far seemed to be in charge when it came to asking questions, he knew who the real leader was, and looked at Montgomery.

"He's a nice boy, leave him alone," he said, gesturing to Nick.

"I can assure you, he's safe from harm. From what I've heard, he enjoyed the car service as well as the plane ride. According to Trevor, I may even have to employ Nick one day, as it seems he's quite resourceful and quick on his feet. Look what he's accomplished on your behalf," Montgomery deadpanned, gesturing to the tabletop.

Dar wasn't sure who Trevor was, but despite the situation he was currently in, he knew the Calder group was one of honorable men through and through. He wasn't even upset at what they'd unearthed about him; they were looking out for

Celeste. He'd been unsure of how to reveal himself, if at all, but it seemed the universe was forcing him to show his hand.

"I don't know what the problem is, but I swear, Dar is good people," Nick chimed in.

"Good people don't lie," Stan returned.

"Did he *lie* or did he withhold the truth?"

"Oh, for Pete's sake," Stan huffed.

Dar smirked. He really had made a good friend.

"Hey, man," Nick said, turning to Dar. "Brutus says hi."

"My warmest regards to our hound. Again, Nicholas, I can't thank you enough for your help and kindness." *And don't hate me when the truth comes out.*

"See," Nick insisted, as if this proved everything. "Give him a break, he's from a sleepy little town in Scotland."

"I see," commented Stan dryly. "Did he tell you where this 'sleepy little town' might be?"

Dar maintained his calm composure, for really what did it matter what town he was from? Still, he wondered how he might address this new question. Dunhill wasn't really a *town*, per se.

"No," Nick said, with a shrug, "but Celeste has family in Scotland, and she told me her cousin might be coming by, so..."

"*Oooh*, he's Celeste's family now, is he? MacKenna, why don't you tell him the truth."

It was not a suggestion.

There was a pause in which Dar tried to figure out how best to reply. Up to this point, he'd managed to avoid actually deceiving Nick, save the one initial untruth about being a cousin, which had been before he knew Nick would become a friend. Since then, he'd just agreed with his assumptions.

"Dar?" Nick asked, seeming uncertain for the first time since he'd arrived.

Though Dar was confident it was impossible for these men to know where he truly came from, he surmised at the least they'd ruled him out as being a relation of Celeste's.

He sighed, loath to tell another lie, and certain he would fail if he did anyway. "I'm sorry, Nicholas. Celeste is not my cousin," he said, noting only then that this was a monumental blessing in disguise. "I used it as a ruse to find her."

"*Duuude.*" Hands to his heart, Nick gave a look Brutus often wore when downtrodden over not getting a table scrap.

Dar winced. Nick was his closest friend in this time and he hated that he'd lied to him. "My apologies. My sincerest apologies. I hope one day you'll realize I treasure our friendship, and—"

"Yeah, yeah, yeah, we get it," Stan interjected, "you love each other. Say it with flowers next time or get a flipping room. You've got about three seconds, *Dude,*" he intoned, then paused, momentarily distracted by his phone vibrating. "Look, I need to go see my girl. So, out with it already. Why did you need to find Celeste?"

Now was as good a time as any. "I've come to deliver a message," Dar said, with all the import that the task required.

"Lovely. To Celeste?"

"Aye."

"Well, seeing as you've been here close to a month, what the hell are you waiting for?"

Dar shook his head. "I assure you, I was sent with the most noble of intentions, from her kin, no less. But what I thought would be easy, now seems fairly complicated," Dar admitted with a bit more frustration than he'd intended, but once he'd started, 'twas difficult to stop. "Frankly, I'm not sure the best way to proceed." Dar directed this toward Montgomery, who he noted had a keen interest in what he was saying.

"Wait. Wait just a minute," Stan said. He rubbed his eyes, and Dar could tell they'd all been hard-pressed by today's events, but were regardless determined to carry on and see to Celeste's welfare. A noble mark in his estimation. Especially as Stan's phone buzzed again.

"As you can see, we'll decide if your intentions are noble or not, but what I want to know is *who* in Celeste's family sent you here? Not to be harsh, but what family does she even have?"

So, here it was. Would saying it register with them? He'd never considered sharing the ostensible reason he was here with anyone other than Celeste. Dar muttered a cross between a curse and a prayer, unsure where this turn would take him. "Margret of O'Roarke," Dar said at last, watching the men for signs of recognition, wondering if naming Celeste's vanished kin had added fuel to the fire.

Stan peered at him through one eye, his reaction inscrutable. "I'm not familiar with a *Margret of O'Roarke*. Sounds made up, if I'm being honest. Who is she? Some misbegotten royalty? A forgotten monarchy somewhere?"

Dar chuckled. "While her curtsy could put a queen to shame, 'tis merely a pet name that's caught on throughout the household." It dawned on him then that these men would not know

Maggie's married name. "Before she wed my dear brethren Callum, she was known as Maggie of Sinclair."

Stan raised his brow. "Maggie Sinclair sent you here?" he asked, giving Dar a curious look.

"In truth, she didn't send me, I offered," Dar said with a shrug.

"You've spoken to this Maggie…recently?" Stan asked, again narrowing his eyes at Dar in a way that made him shift uncomfortably.

"*Recent* is an interesting word to use," Dar said, realizing the odd disparity between what was recent to him in memory and what would be recent to these men, given the historical timeline.

"Right. So, why, exactly, is it that Maggie couldn't deliver this message herself?"

Dar did not want to lie to these men, but he also did not want to be branded as a lunatic. He chose his words carefully. "Yes, well *traveling* to these parts is not as easy as it sounds."

"If she *traveled*…" Stan paused and a peculiarly odd look crossed his face. He glanced to his boss and then back. "…there, why not just *travel* back?"

Dar gave him a pointed stare, treading a bit further into unknown territory. "All I can say is she alighted to our homeland, and now it appears she is there to stay."

Stan's wide-eyed, "God *damn* it!" served as a confirmation of sorts. He reached for one of the laptops on the desk and spun it around, keying something in. Dar watched, wondering if they had a dungeon on the property or would instead render him to the city jail.

"Trevor, why don't you show Nicholas the billiards room," Montgomery directed to the young man who'd walked him in.

Trevor nodded, and gestured for Nick to follow. Nick glanced back at Dar and gave him a questioning look, but Dar just nodded. There was no reason for Nick to get further mixed up in this. Once they left, Stan closed the doors and turned to Dar, a new intensity in his eyes.

"Darach. Do you know Esmerelda Morgana—or, I guess she sometimes goes by Millicent?" he asked, and suddenly, everything Dar thought he knew about the twenty-first century shifted.

Dar took a moment to right himself from the shock. "I've never met her personally," he said carefully. But, aye, he knew her. The enchantress. Most knew of her. At least most in his circle. But his circle existed seven-hundred years hence. "She's here? The enchantress? Close by?"

Stan gave him a curious look. "If you're talking about the psychic who insists *Maggie's in the time that suits her best*, then yes, she's here."

Well, wonders never ceased. This shed much in a new light. If Stan was aware of the enchantress, then these men had to know that there was some sorcery at play. Perhaps his admission, if he made one, would not be met with disbelief after all.

"Maggie *is* happy now," he said, choosing his words deliberately. "In a time that suits her very well, yes. She is married to my brethren Callum O'Roarke. They have a babe on the way."

At this, Stan groaned and rapped his head against the table, muttering something about not wanting to do this again.

"Bloody hell," the younger Montgomery said, then turned to

his brother. "Bring up the Abersoch property," he said before looking at Dar. "I just remembered why your name is familiar." He then pointed down at the table and an image of a castle appeared. Montgomery used his hands to spin the image around, then enlarged the area by the foundation.

Dar sat in confusion. How did they know his name? And what did it have to do with this castle that, yes, looked more like anything from his time than he'd seen in weeks, but was otherwise completely unknown to him? "This was the original entrance of the estate—our estate at Abersoch. Look here."

Curious, but tight with apprehensive excitement, Dar leaned in close, as did Stan and the elder Montgomery, as the younger pointed to a stone. It took a moment, but Dar saw there, the names chiseled upon it and his heart leapt to his throat: Gavin Montgomery, Lachlan MacTavish, and, at the bottom, Darach MacKenna MacTavish.

Uncertain of what he was looking at—and sure he had never seen this stone before—Dar shook his head. "I don't understand. What are you showing me?"

"This is your name?" the elder Montgomery asked.

Dar nodded. "Yes. Or, it could be. Where is this property?"

"Today it's in Wales. When it was built, England."

"This is yours?" Dar asked, struggling to put the pieces together. For a moment, he reeled, wondering what this meant, if somehow, someday, he would carve his name there—would take Lachlan's name and etch it so permanently with his own—and if that meant he *would* one day return to his time, if...Then something else caught his attention. His thoughts splintering, he honed in on the one of least disturbance, the brothers' and Gavin's shared surname. "Wait a moment," he said, speaking slowly, "are you related to Gavin Montgomery? The Montgomerys of Lincolnshire?"

"You know of him? Them?" the elder Montgomery, Alexander, asked.

Dar didn't correct him. He didn't know *of* him, he *knew* him. "How are you related?"

"We're descendants, by four-hundred years."

Dar did the math, then looked back at Alexander curiously. "That doesn't add up, my friend."

The elder Montgomery smiled. "No, Dar, it does not."

His brother spoke up then, telling him to tread lightly. Though he did so in French, a different dialect, but still recognizable to Dar.

"I'm not sure that's necessary," Dar said, in his version of French, which he surmised they would be able to interpret.

"You speak *old* French?" their almost-silent friend asked.

Dar shrugged. "A commonality in my friend's home."

Alexander gave him a curious look. "You know these names, don't you?" he asked.

Dar nodded. "Aye, Gavin is the best friend of my brethren. I know him well."

"Gavin Montgomery is responsible for building our estate in Abersoch."

This was all getting stranger and stranger. "Well, as far as I know, he hasn't," Dar said. "At least not yet. He's been too busy tupping his wife and filling his castle with offspring."

Alexander chuckled. "The joys of love and life."

"Can you tell me what's going on?" Stan interjected, and Dar realized that they'd been carrying on in French.

"My apologies, Stan," the elder Montgomery said in English, then pointed to the names again. "Darach. Is this you?"

Dar was truly at a loss. "I know the other men listed, and this is nearly my name—could be my name, I suppose, but I do not know this rock, nor this estate."

"Construction began at Abersoch in 1431, Darach MacKenna MacTavish," the elder Montgomery said, and *that* gave Dar pause. He'd just left 1431, and no such building existed, at least that he knew of. And especially not one erected by his hand.

Dar shook his head. "I am sorry, I don't know it," he said.

"But you know my ancestor," Alexander said, "so let's just call a spade a spade."

"Funny, since we're all dancing around it," Stan grumbled, clearly still perturbed about being left out of part of the conversation. Just then, his phone vibrated on the tabletop again.

The Montgomerys both said, "Go," and Stan nodded. His woman needed comfort from her man.

At the door, he turned. "Look, Darach. I don't know all the details, but I'm starting to work the root of it out. Just a word of advice: cut your hair. It makes you stand out more than you should. First rule of blending in—especially if what I think is true is the reality. Don't draw undue attention to yourself."

Dar chuckled. That he could do. "I was angry, distracted. Mayhap I let it grow to irritate someone."

"Let me guess, your dad?"

Dar laughed again. It felt good to release some of the tension that had been building. "How could you know?"

Stan rolled his eyes. "Textbook. Typical power struggle. But take it from someone—me—who'd kill to have his dad back: the resistance? It's not worth it. And hey, welcome to the twenty-first century."

With that, Stan left, leaving Dar dumbfounded. Yes, the clues had been adding up, the suspicions in the room had been swirling, but Stan was the first to actually say it—to confirm that not only did they know, or somewhat know, who he was, but that his traveling through centuries of time was not so alarming after all. At least, not to these men.

After Dar told them everything—and how good it felt to divest of his twenty-first century posturing—the brothers and their friend Gregor shared their story as well. While they made it clear that traveling through centuries was *not* something one should share widely, it was still a great comfort to know that Dar was not alone in this fascinating but strange new time. Too, Dar's hope rose, knowing Alex and his wife were quite happy together, living in the present day.

"How did you tell her?" Dar asked, hoping some advice from his new comrades would aid him in his own necessary action.

"Tell her?" Alex narrowed his eyes. "Are you insane? What was I supposed to say? Gee, Amanda, I time-traveled from the eighteenth century to find you and our daughter. Hardly."

Dar paused, taken aback. His wife still did not know? For all his honor, Dar was surprised at Montgomery's deceit, small as he may think it. "Helpful, you're not," he said, perhaps growling a bit. "So, how *did* you sort it out?"

"I told her as much as I could without saying anything that would alarm her, or make her suspicious, and luckily, her memory returned."

"Ah. Well, that doesn't help. Celeste has *no* memory."

"Then I'll caution you to tread lightly in the meantime."

"I assume we have a truce then?" Dar asked.

Montgomery nodded. "Welcome to the fold, my friend."

A firm handshake later, Dar felt firm roots take hold in the twenty-first century, his new stomping ground fortified.

CHAPTER 14

The next morning, Celeste slung her bag over her shoulder, turned off the lights, and locked up the yoga studio. She was disappointed at how her visit from Darach had been interrupted the night before by the Calder guys, and wondered if they'd scared him off from contacting her again.

She was just about to start engaging in a bout of self-pity when she turned the corner and saw Dar leaning against the building across the street. He smiled at her and made his way over in that way he moved, like a lion leisurely traipsing the savanna, stopping when he stood right in front of her.

"Morning," he said, his grin widening.

"Hi." That was all for the moment and she just stared up at him, smiling. His eyes danced and she found her voice. "I see you've been set free. Tether?" she asked jokingly, glancing at his ankle just in case—she wouldn't put it past the Calder guys.

"If you mean a manacle, nay. However, there were a few conditions of my release."

"Oh?" she inquired, hoping he'd expound. He didn't, just grunted something unintelligible.

"Are you free?" he asked instead.

She nodded, trying to keep her face placid to hide her excitement. "I am," she said, "no plans until four and then just that hour."

He chuckled. She liked when he did that. When he smiled, or chuckled, his eyes seemed to light up from within, and fine lines crinkled around them. It was mesmerizing. It dawned on her then that there were very few people she paid attention to that closely. Maybe no one, truthfully, but with Dar, she was a hundred and ten percent dialed in.

"Coffee?" he asked. "Breakfast? Lunch? Dinner?"

She laughed and said, "Yes. Coffee first, and then the rest of it. But I can't miss my class at four. And I'd like to shower and change since you're looking all country club casual," she said, giving him what she hoped was a casual once-over.

He gave a nod and a wink, then gestured to her gym bag. "Let's get a coffee and I'll walk you back to your place," he offered, then slung the duffle over his shoulder before he guided her back onto the sidewalk and fell in step beside her. "Bea's?" he asked.

Oooh, Bea's Bakery and Bistro. Nice choice. "Yeah, I love their lattes," Celeste said. And their almond biscotti and their turkey and brie croissants. Okay, so she liked just about everything there, especially the pecan rolls.

Dar opened the door and when they stepped inside, Bea's

granddaughter clocked their arrival and called out, "Two medium caramel lattes" to the barista. Celeste hid a smile. Apparently, she and Dar had the same taste in coffee.

He leaned against the counter like he had all the time in the world, a stance she'd now seen him take several times. She really liked that about him, the seeming ease with whatever life threw his way. Inclining his head to the display case he asked, "Pastry?"

Not wanting to appear *too* eager, and hoping her eyes hadn't given her away, she shrugged nonchalantly. "I'll wait for lunch, I'm more of a savory person," she fibbed.

Celeste took out her wallet to pay, but Dar covered her hand with his and shook his head. She liked the feel of it, warm, and sure.

"Please, let me," she said, not entirely certain whether this was a date or not, and wanting to do the right thing either way.

"I'm old-fashioned," he explained, leaving his hand atop hers.

"It's good manners," she argued, but felt herself losing steam —and focus—the longer Dar's hand covered her own. "Besides it would be a small token of appreciation for saving me yesterday."

"I'd save you any day, lass, no matter the reward," he said, suddenly serious. Then the edge faded and he leaned into whisper in her ear, "And I'm *very* old-fashioned."

The heat of his breath and timber of his rasp sent a shiver down her spine like she'd never experienced in her entire life. She'd stood there for a moment, frozen, savoring the sensation.

Then, remembering where she was, Celeste managed a nod

and an *okay*, still feeling a little shaky when he let go of her hand to reach for his wallet. After paying and dropping a hefty tip in the jar, Dar handed her one of the lattes, then crowded her protectively from a large group coming through the door as they left. She liked that too.

As they headed down Main Street, Celeste tried to think of a normal thing to ask, something that would take her mind off his incredible closeness. It had been a long time since she'd been on a date, but she managed a pretty casual, "Do you live here? In the States, I mean?"

"I do now."

"But you're not from here." *Stupid question*, Celeste chided herself. There was no way that sexy accent was anything but Scottish.

"Nay, lass," Dar confirmed, chuckling. "My home is closer to the Isle of Skye, in Scotland, but I spent much of last year at my friend's home, near Wick. One's east, the other west."

Celeste didn't know where either of those places were, but now she wanted nothing more than to visit them. "I bet it's gorgeous. I've never been to Scotland, but I heard it's one of the most beautiful places in the world."

"Aye, it's that. But so too are these Hamptons."

Celeste looked up at him and grinned. He had such a funny way of speaking at times, but maybe that was just part of his Scottish brogue. "You know," she said, her eyes still on him, "I pegged you for a musician with your long hair, maybe even a bodyguard, based on, well..." She gestured, blushing, to his formidable figure. "Was either correct?"

Dar chuckled again. "Nay, lass, not as far as occupation. And

I'll admit, I've been told I need to visit the barber another block down to shed my rocker-boy persona."

She grinned and looked around, leaning into whisper, "What if you lose your superpowers? You *did* save my life, if you recall."

Dar took a moment to sip his latte, then nodded. "Ah, like a creature of mythical lore. Well, I've a talisman for that, so I believe we're worry-free." He reached into his pocket and pulled out a smooth stone and a disk, holding them out in his palm.

Celeste was surprised that someone like Dar—or someone like she'd assumed Dar to be, brawny, masculine, proud—would carry around things like this. She liked it.

Fingering the crystal, she noticed how small her hand was compared to his. She liked that too.

"Ooh, amethyst," she admired when she realized she'd been staring at his hand for a beat too long. "Protection, emotional balance, and confidence." She furrowed her lips and looked up at him. "I can't imagine *you* needing confidence."

She'd been joking, but he frowned, clearly taking her words to heart. "Everyone is shaken at times," he said with a serious-ness Celeste had not expected. "Even the strongest and most capable. How about the Greek gods, didn't even they each suffer at one time?"

Celeste liked his openness and vulnerability, so unlike most men she knew. She gave him a small smile and looked back down at his still open palm. "What's this?" she asked, tracing the wooden disk beside the crystal. When she really focused on it, her eyes misted. It reminded her of something that Derek might whittle. "Wow, that's really pretty," she complimented, though she heard her voice catch. "Look how detailed it is."

Dar put his hand over hers. "Celeste? What is it?"

She shook it off. Now was not the time for the my-brother-is-dead conversation. "It's nothing, I'm fine." She studied the image again. "Is that a…" She puzzled a moment, then said, "A griffin. Right?"

He smiled. "Aye." His thumb brushed over her fingers as she flipped it over to look at the back. "Blood of my blood," she said, reading the inscription. "Did your dad make this for you?"

An odd look crossed his face and he stared at her incredulously for a long moment. When he spoke, his voice was hoarse. "God almighty, lass. I think he did."

Celeste hadn't expected her question to elicit this kind of reaction. He stared at the talisman a moment longer, seeming to be in shock, then slipped both it and the stone back into his pocket.

More to clear the air than anything else, Celeste pulled out her own stone. "Look—I have one, too," she said.

"Ah, clear quartz," he said, rubbing it gingerly. He still seemed a bit dazed, then appeared to jolt out of it. "Wait, the barber," he said, indicating the storefront beside them.

Well, it wasn't really a barber, it was her yoga client Kathy's salon. When they entered, you'd think he really was a movie star or the rocker-boy extraordinaire she'd originally pegged him for. At least five stylists clamored for his business, women and men alike. Suddenly Celeste was feeling a bit possessive, another new one for her. Thankfully, Kathy seemed to understand what was going on.

"Okay, everyone, that's enough," she interjected, shooting Celeste a grin. "Celeste's man is with me."

The others backed off and Celeste was so relieved, she decided then and there to comp Kathy's next few classes. Until now, Celeste hadn't known she was the jealous type. Note to self: *I am.*

Celeste looked at Dar, whose amused expression clearly said, *You didn't object to me being called your man.* Celeste blushed and looked away. *No, Dar, I did not.* Then she shook her head. Was she seriously having an entire conversation in her head? *Yes, Celeste, you are.*

A wash later, Dar was in a chair as Kathy did that stylist thing with her hands, feeling up his hair. Celeste tried not to be too jealous.

"Are you sure you want to do this?" Kathy asked, looking at him in the mirror.

His nod was all Kathy needed. She was really good at what she did and right before Celeste's eyes, Dar went from hot rocker-boy to just hot. Like, *hotttt.* Oh mama.

He paid with cash and left another generous tip. "Many thanks, Kathrine," he said, and Celeste saw the other stylists all sneaking a look at *her man.* She stepped a bit closer to him.

"See you at four, Celeste," Kathy called as they headed out the door.

Outside, Dar gave her another amused look and said, "I take it you approve."

Ok, so she was goggling a little bit, and standing closer to him than she had on the way in. Was that bad? It was true, she couldn't stop admiring the new cut. She originally thought she'd miss his long hair, but… "Wait, who told you to cut your hair?" A hand flew to her mouth, *Shut up Celeste, it's none of your business!*

He chuckled. "Stan, though the rest of the men agreed. First condition of my release, cut hair so I don't stand out. And," he said, reaching forward and gently pulling her hand away from her mouth, "*you* may ask me anything, lass."

Her breath caught as she noticed him focusing on her lips, an instant before he brushed his thumb across them. She froze, and after a moment, Dar's eyes widened and he looked at her a bit gobsmacked before stepping back and murmuring a sorry.

Celeste slowly shook her head in wonder. She was so enthralled by his touch and the rush she'd felt, it took her a second to gather a thought, any thought. Blushing, she peeked up through her lashes, secretly thrilled by his boldness, and even more so that it seemed he'd reached out unthinkingly, on pure instinct. But all that aside, Stan was correct, Dar fit right in now with his new cut. Still on the majorly attractive scale, but the long hair had been a beacon. She wondered if they cared so much because they were considering hiring him based on his quick response to danger. He certainly fit in with those men.

Dar seemed to have regained his senses because he looked at her almost playfully—or, as playfully as she imagined was in Dar's capacity—and said, raising a hand to his newly cropped hair. "Well? *Do* you approve, lass?"

Celeste grinned. "That'd be a solid, aye, Dar."

By the time they got back to her place, she'd worked herself into a snit of sorts. Here she was, bringing a man home—just so she could change, yes, but still. Between her insecurities and inexperience, Celeste was so nervous she fumbled with the lock. She'd initially taken Dar's "coffee, breakfast, lunch, and dinner" suggestion as a playful joke—and had responded in kind—but now it seemed like he'd actually meant it. Not that she was complaining, she just wasn't used to this kind of attention.

"Celeste?" Dar placed his hand over hers, stilling her nervous fumbling, then deftly helped her unlock the door.

Embarrassed but grateful, she turned to face him. "Thanks," she mumbled, feeling suddenly exposed.

"'Twas no trouble at all," he said, his gaze on her. His dark eyes were soft with understanding. "Celeste. I would die before dishonoring you. Why don't I stay out here and wait for you?"

First of all, *wow. I would* die *before dishonoring you? See again, Stan! I was right!* But now, she felt foolish. Her nerves stopped doing the roller coaster whoop-dee-do in her stomach, it was silly not to invite him in, right?

Watching her closely, Dar shook his head and made the decision for her, handing over her bag before taking a seat on the large deck chair in the corner. He leaned back, clearly getting comfortable, and cast a smile her way, like nothing could be better. When she offered him a drink, he held up his latte and she turned a few shades of red before hurrying inside.

Ugh. Would you like a drink, come on, Celeste!

Breathing a sigh of relief at having a moment to collect herself, she sagged against the door then shot a text to Stan, telling him she was spending the day with Dar. A not-so-subtle test to cover her bases just in case. If there was any doubt or a problem, she'd know in a heartbeat. It may have taken two, but she got the reassurance she needed: *You were right, Dar checked out. We're heading out of town this weekend, but we're a text or phone call away.*

Satisfied, she hurried through her shower routine and changed six times before settling on a belted shirtdress and flats. *Take that, country club casual,* she thought, admiring herself in the mirror.

When she stepped out onto the porch again, Celeste felt herself blush. She hadn't actually expected him to wait around while she got ready, but it was nice that he had. It was nice to have someone at her home again, someone who was happy to see her.

"You look nice, lass," he complimented; and as his gaze traveled the length of her, the corners of Celeste's lips lifted.

"Thank you, it beats yoga clothes."

He grinned. "You look nice in those too."

Celeste laughed and asked, "What's next?"

"Lunch on the water."

Those parameters could have applied to any number of popular eateries in the area, but Dar had picked the trendiest, nicest restaurant right on the pier. Celeste had offered to drive but he'd already called a car service—she found that the chauffeur looked vaguely familiar, and she wondered to herself if he was one of the Calder guys.

When they arrived at the restaurant a short time later, the maître d' made a big fuss, falling all over Dar like he was royalty or something before apologizing for a slight delay as they prepared their table. Dar seemed oblivious to the special treatment, and what Celeste noticed from the whole exchange was that while he was in control and polite, smiling affably, his real smiles, the ones that reached his eyes, seemed to be for her and her alone.

At the news that they'd have a bit of a wait, he informed the staff they'd return shortly, then took her hand.

"Come, we'll walk the pier."

Celeste had never held hands with anyone before—well, besides family—and kept looking down at them, joined together, enjoying the feel of her small hand in his large one.

"What?" he asked, taking note of her glances. He lifting their intertwined hands. "This?" He grinned. "Too much?"

She laughed at this new playfulness in him and blushed as he brushed her palm with his lips before letting go.

Celeste couldn't remember the last time she'd had so much fun. Between the sunshine, the fresh open air, and Dar himself, she felt like the noise in her head had finally subsided.

As they strolled, he reached across her many times, pointing something out to be sure she didn't miss it, and Celeste relished the brushing of his arm as he indicated a school of fish, jumping dolphins, and even a few boats. At one point he stood behind her, tucking her between his arms to show her a lighthouse in the distance. Taking a chance, she leaned back, then wasn't sure if he nuzzled her head or if she'd imagined it. She tried to remember the last time someone had done this for her, taken an interest, and cared about her to such a degree. She'd kept to herself for such a long time, that until now, the sensation had been elusive.

It was all a bit intoxicating—and so was he. He smelled so good, like *g-o-o-d* good. Celeste couldn't quite describe it, but his scent was purely masculine, and despite their only having met a few times, she felt it was so embedded in her senses already that she could pick him out of a blindfolded lineup in a nanosecond.

After they returned to the restaurant and were shown to their private table, he pulled out her chair, winking at her as he tried the wine before nodding his approval to the sommelier. When she declined a moment later, he'd pushed his glass to the side and joined her in an iced tea. Maybe a bit lame, but she did still have a class to teach.

"You've done this a lot haven't you?" she asked, gesturing around her. He seemed so in his element.

He grinned, eyes dancing as much as she imaged her own were. "Never."

"Well, you're very well-seasoned for a novice."

Dar nodded and kept her gaze. "I wanted to make sure I did everything properly, so I watched a few videos on the internet and accepted some advice from a new friend."

"Oh, come on," she said, laughing. He laughed with her and she figured he was kidding. "Very funny."

He said no more, but reached over to refill her iced tea from the carafe on the table.

"I would have been happy having a hot dog on the beach," Celeste admitted, feeling suddenly vulnerable.

Dar looked up at her, and the seriousness in his gaze told

her she needn't have worried. "We can do that tomorrow," he said, holding up his glass. She clinked it with a smile, surprised that the thought of tomorrow sounded so wonderful. And that he wanted to see her again.

Just then, lunch was served, and not only was it delicious, but the experience of eating a meal at a place like this with Dar was wonderful. He was so easy to be with and there was this level of effortless familiarity—almost a closeness—that she'd never experienced before.

First of all, Dar loved to eat, and he obviously liked good food, but *everything* he tried he wanted to share with her. "Lass, you must sample this" was repeated throughout their entire meal, accompanied by charming stories and comparisons to foods from his homeland. Celeste found herself eating things she never would have considered trying before, just to keep the light dancing in his eyes as he practically spoon-fed her.

Never mind that he was correct, the ewey gross mussels *were* amazing, simmered in a delicate tomato broth with a hint of garlic and fresh herbs, and his Caesar salad, seriously, one bite and she realized she'd ordered wrong. She obviously didn't have a poker face, at least not with him, and he'd immediately waved the server over and had her Bibb lettuce hydro-some-thing-or-other replaced. Both of their entrées were outstanding. He loved her shrimp, and his steak practically melted in her mouth—and she melted, too, from the look he gave her as she gently bit down on his fork. She mmm'd as she took it.

As she sipped coffee while they waited for dessert, she was struck by something. This—this just *being* with someone new, enjoying their presence, opening up. It was easy somehow;

where before it had seemed impossible. So, why now, and why Dar? It wasn't like there hadn't been people in the periphery of her life who wished to do the same, who had tried to reach out and offer their company. Well, maybe not like this, but still, she'd never even considered letting them in. Never.

With the nonstop commentary in her head, she had missed the dessert order, but was grateful he'd opted to share—though, seriously, this lunch could have covered her meal intake for at least two days. When the server returned to their table, she realized he'd requested the special, a gooey brown sugar and cinnamon pecan roll with a large scoop of vanilla bean gelato. Celeste realized then that she hadn't had ice cream in years— not since Derek—and suddenly here she was, being spoon-fed her kryptonite by the man who had literally broken through her invisible defenses and set up shop inside; who she might, she realized as gelato melted on her tongue, be falling in love with. Was that crazy?

"What's wrong?" Dar asked, and Celeste startled. Jeez, he was observant.

She shook her head, and put a finger to her lips, hoping he'd get the message. Not now. Not as she was at this very moment floored by the irony of Dar finding a way through her emotional wall, while for the first time in years experiencing the cool creaminess of gelato slipping down her throat. It was bittersweet.

He looked puzzled for only a moment. "You wish me to ignore it? Whatever it is that's suddenly interfered with your good humor?"

She gave a small smile. "Yes. Thank you."

"That's very clever, Celeste."

"What?"

"Thanking me, as if it's settled."

"It's just..." Celeste sighed. He could read her too well. "I haven't had ice cream since my brother died."

He reached across the table, clasping her hand. "I'm sorry, lass. I didn't mean to upset you."

Celeste shook her head. "It's not upsetting at all, not really. It's just that ice cream was a family tradition," she explained, feeling safe and comfortable enough to share with him. "Once they were gone, I just...I never..." She let the words hang in the air. The look on Dar's face as he put his spoon down and took her other hand almost leveled her right there. Like he actually understood the enormity of what she'd been holding onto.

"Celeste. I never meant to open such a wound, but perhaps we may start a new tradition, you and I. Mayhap we can face a few demons together and put them behind us once and for all."

It was like he could read her better than she could read herself. And more than that, here he was again showing that side of himself that was human and needed work too. It took much of her initial sadness away, and she smiled softly, squeezing his hand.

"I think I would like that. Very much. To be honest, I've never spent the day with someone. Not like this, Dar."

Dar gave a soft smile in return. "If you're enjoying the day but a fraction of what I am, then all's well. Now, we'd best be on our way. You have to help me pick out yoga clothes so I can attend your class this afternoon."

Oh mama, she was in trouble.

CHAPTER 15

Just when Dar thought he was done feeling like an idiot, here he was in some ridiculous pose with his whole arse in the air, grunting and sweating more than anyone else in the class.

That being said, Celeste's choice of exercise was efficient *and* effective. She had quite the following too. Men and women alike. A few cast looks her way that were a bit too appreciative for his liking, and Dar may have growled like one of his hounds back home, but it seemed only Celeste noticed. When she sent him a chastising glance, he'd smiled sheepishly, thinking she should at least be grateful that was all he'd done. It's not like he'd pounced. And sunk his teeth in their jugulars. Yet.

Ah, but who was he kidding. A mere day in her company and it was he who was sunk.

He was happy he'd taken the brothers' offer to secure an "impossible to get" (their words) table at the exclusive eatery, as well as for the private ride over. It had given them an opportunity to talk easefully in privacy.

As Celeste directed the class into another pose, this one involving balancing on one leg, Dar grimaced, both from the effort and from the realization that he had yet to broach the subject of Maggie and the letter.

He'd been thinking of it as they'd lunched, but when she'd asked, "What *do* you do?" he'd been a bit taken aback. He should have been more prepared for that question because he'd learned from his observations that this was a common question in this century. Instead, he'd just stared at her for a long moment while he tried to remember what the brothers had advised him to say last night.

So, he'd told her he was in construction, or that he had been. It wasn't even a stretch. Dar had always had a penchant for building, and had even helped Gavin in the demolition and reconstruction of his keep.

Celeste had grinned and waved her hand casually. "Oh, if you wanted to, you could do that here. I think you just need to pass a test and pay for your license."

"Truly?" Dar had asked, wondering if he'd be in the present long enough to need an occupation.

"*Aye*, Dar," she'd said with a twinkle in her eye. "Truly. People do it every day. I was certified to teach yoga after a training course. Every state is different, but you can get a building license, or whatever it's called, for sure."

Perhaps a future endeavor.

Looking up at Celeste at the front of the room, Dar realized that while his mind had wandered, the class was now a few moves ahead. Uncertain how to get into the current position, Dar looked around, confused, until Celeste noticed and came over to him, grinning. When she placed her hands on his hips to show him what to do, his heart skipped a beat. Sure, he'd seen her adjust other students, too, but never with that twinkle in her eye.

After class, he walked her home; at the door, she turned, a nervous look on her face.

"Would you like to come in?" she asked.

He raised a teasing brow. "You're sure?"

She blushed a deep crimson and nodded, bashful despite this brazen move, and stepped aside to let him enter her dwelling.

Not that he'd been expecting anything in particular, but once inside, he felt a warm rush of energy, much like what he'd felt in her actual home. Celeste had clearly taken this temporary space and made it her own, Dar thought as he looked around and noted candles and crystals and a stack of DVDs, which Nick had shown him how to use his first week in this century.

"Would you like something to drink?" she asked, heading toward the kitchen.

"Nay, lass," Dar declined, realizing he was just as sweaty as she was, if not more. "Why don't I leave you to your shower and make haste in doing the same." He looked at his watch. "Say an hour, I'll pick you up and we can walk to dinner? I'm famished already."

Celeste grinned. "Okay, but let me grab you a snack to hold you over."

He followed her, leaning against a counter just as she turned with a napkin full of, "Cookies!" he said in delight.

She chuckled. "They're almond butter, only three ingredients and filled with protein. For a healthy treat, I think they're pretty good."

Dar took a bite and had to agree. He popped another in his mouth as she pushed an odd-colored drink his way. He took a sip, excited to sample another of her fares, but this was briny and gritty and tasted of the sea, nothing like the cookie.

"*Egads,*" he said, trying not to grimace. "Why would you ruin such a lovely experience?"

The beautiful imp before him shrugged. "It's good for you."

"I care not if it's the elixir or life, lass. Spare me its awfulness."

"Hey! It can take up to eight tries of something to get a taste for it," she said, giggling.

He pulled her close, liking how readily she came. "I can assure you, lass, I won't get nearly that far. But I thank you for looking after my welfare."

She smiled sweetly, and he reached out, tracing the side of her face. She took a sharp intake of breath, and Dar he hoped this wasn't going too far, but relaxed when she covered his hand and smiled up at him.

"That feels nice," she whispered.

He needed to go. Now. Keeping his voice light, he pulled his hand away slowly and told her that he'd be back in an hour. *After I douse myself with cold water*, he promised himself.

He thought of nothing but Celeste on the walk home. How lovely she was, how beautiful, sweet, and vulnerable. He wished to solve her every problem, soothe her every wound, and experience all that this life had to offer *with* her. "Bible" as Nick would say. The thought of Maggie and her letter lingered at the periphery of his mind, but for now, he just wanted Celeste for his own. He could deliver the errand later.

WHEN DAR RETURNED after his shower—and, to his embarrassment, after trying on three different shirts to wear—he knocked on Celeste's door. She opened it almost immediately, appearing before him in another fetching dress. This one had a beautiful sheen, eye-catching, yet not ostentatious.

"I believe on the proposed coffee, breakfast, lunch, dinner manifest, we're just about complete," he said, pulling his gaze up to meet hers.

She smiled. "I really wish we could have squeezed breakfast in, not that you haven't fed me enough today."

"Speaking of which, is there somewhere in particular you would like to eat tonight?" Dar asked. Lunch had been a planned extravagance, but he hadn't thought as far as dinner—hadn't expected, maybe, that she would truly want to spend the whole day with him.

Celeste paused in thought, then her eyes lit up. "Do you eat sushi?"

"Sushi?" he repeated, unfamiliar with the word. Then, pretending to check for a message, he "Googled" the word on his phone, just as Nick had shown him, and tried not to balk. "Raw fish?" he asked dubiously. Aye, he'd eaten it, but only when sustenance was necessary and fire unavailable. More of a meal of survival than of pleasure. This new century never ceased with its surprises—and oddities.

"Never mind," Celeste said, and Dar gave a small sigh of relief. "We'll try that another time. Let's do Thai."

Dar didn't know what *Thai* was, either, but it was bound to at least be cooked. "Yes, let us," he agreed, eliciting another bright smile from Celeste. He liked those very much.

After a short walk through town, and agreeing they'd prefer the outside patio in front of the establishment, which was aglow under strings of light, they were shown to a secluded table, tucked away in the corner.

"Mmm," Celeste said, looking over the menu of offerings. "I haven't had Thai in *forever.* Let's split a few things, so we can try a lot. What do you like?"

Unsure, he shrugged. "I'll leave it to you."

"Ooh, okay," she said, eying the menu again. "We'll have the soup special, and…" She looked him over rather appraisingly then said, "Wagyu beef fried rice and prawn pad Thai."

Dar had no idea what to expect, but at least he recognized most of the words she had said—no need for a surreptitious "Google."

The soup special turned out to be a rich beef-based broth, with slices of pork, noodles, and vegetables floating in it. It smelled divine. The server put the large terrine between them, then ladled portions into each of their bowls. The rich flavors were deep and complex, practically dancing on his tongue. Eager to let Celeste in on the sensations, he lifted a spoonful her way. Her eyes gleamed as she leaned forward and supped, chuckling around the spoon before pulling back and reminding him that she had her own bowl of the exact same. He shrugged, but laughed too. He cared not; he was enjoying their evening so much.

"Tell me about your family, Dar," she inquired before taking another bite of soup.

Dar paused, spoon halfway to his mouth. 'Twas only fair, he supposed. "Ah, opening *my* cauldron of demons, I see."

"Oh," she said, sitting back, clearly surprised by his response. After a moment she reached for his hand, a comforting and encouraging gesture. "Have I stumbled upon the demons you mentioned earlier, at lunch?"

Dar sighed. "It seems you have, my sweet."

He could tell by the curl of her lips, and how her hand squeezed his before pulling back, that she was happy about that.

"Well?" she prodded.

Dar took another spoonful of his soup, ruminating on what to say, how to express his complex history—and how to do it without revealing any alarming secrets. Finally, he settled on, "I have a very dear circle of friends, but as far as family is concerned, all save Lachlan are gone now."

Celeste nodded. "And, Lachlan? He's your father?"

"Well, that's the tricky part," Dar said. "I was reared by Ethan MacKenna, but Lachlan MacTavish is my…my father of birth, I suppose."

She scrunched her face prettily as she worked this out in her head. "So, you were adopted? How did you find Lachlan? Was it, like, on one of those genealogy websites?"

She said it so casually that Dar wondered how common a

predicament like his was in this century. Whether many sons and daughters were passed off as belonging to another.

"I learned of my parentage when my mother passed last year," he said, choosing his words carefully. He accepted her apologies for his loss and then told her of his mother calling for Lachlan in her final hours, her confession, and their subsequent goodbye at Remshire. He told her, too, about his feelings concerning Lachlan since, as well as their altercation at Dunhill.

Celeste stared at him, rapt, for the entirety of it.

"Oh my God," she said when he'd finished. "That's so sad. You had no idea? Did you know him?"

He grunted. "Aye, I knew him. I admired the man for the entirety of my life."

"Well, then at least you have him left. Did you see him before you came to the States?"

He nodded slowly. "Aye, we spoke," *had words,* "the day before I left."

They were interrupted then by the waiter bringing their next course. Before taking a bite, Celeste held up her goblet, a nice wine suggested by the server, and said, "Here's to family."

Indeed. The conversation was mercifully light through the rest of dinner, even flirtatious at times. The rest of the food was as good, if not better, than the soup. Celeste delighted in sharing with him a fried rice mixed with thin cuts of tender beef, and the other dish, one comprised of noodles, sprouts, and prawns spiced with flavors he'd never tasted before.

After paying for their meal, and agreeing he wished to come back, they walked through town, milling about with a plentiful crowd of families and couples. At one point, Celeste stopped to listen to the pleasant music wafting from a bar. They peeked inside to see couples dancing, and when Dar glanced back at Celeste, he saw a wistful look on her face.

Thinking of nothing he'd like more at the moment than to make Celeste happy—and to hold her in his arms in the modern way the couples were dancing—he bent to whisper in her ear, "Dance with me?"

She turned and her eyes shot to his, filled with marvel, as though she'd never imagined doing so. This was an indulgence that he was more than happy to entertain. Needing no further motivation, he clasped her hand and led her inside, finding a nice spot to join in. Amidst the other couples, he tucked Celeste in the confines of his arms and rocked her back and forth, liking how she felt there.

They stayed for two more songs, and when the tempo turned upbeat, headed out the door. A storefront on the next block was brimming with activity and as they got closer, Dar saw it was an ice cream parlor. He gave her a look, wondering if perhaps she might like dessert.

She smiled softly, and said, "I don't think I'm ready to slay that particular dragon, at least not yet."

"We'll try again another night," he vowed and she nodded appreciatively. "We can stop at the coffee house instead," he offered, pointing to Bea's across the street. "We'll have a treat there, unless you still stand by your savory preference," he teased.

She blushed and admitted, "I hope they're not out of pecan rolls."

They were not, and they shared the confection before leisurely strolling back to her home.

When they reached the top of the porch, he turned her, gently pressing her back to the door. He'd thought he'd be a gentleman and say goodbye to her this evening with nothing more than a chaste peck on the hand, but that had been a foolish expectation. Besides, after the small but profound intimacies they'd shared over the day, and the way she was looking at him, arching toward him, a brush of the lips to the hand would not satisfy her either.

"I need to kiss you, lass," he said, his voice low and insistent.

She lifted her chin, her eyes pleading as she nodded yes, and he leaned down, cupping her head to fit his mouth atop hers. He coaxed her lips ever so slightly, taming his hunger when he noticed how stiff and shaky Celeste was beneath him, how her hands resting on his chest never moved. It dawned on him then that she hadn't done much kissing. He pulled back.

The look in Celeste's eyes was one of embarrassment. "Was I that bad?" she asked, seeming to shrink away from him.

He shook his head. "Nay." He tsked away her doubt. Rubbing his thumb across the contours of her mouth, he said, "You have the lips and demeanor of an innocent."

He'd intended no insult and actually found himself a bit heady at the thought. When she neither confirmed nor denied, he knew it for the truth and shared with her a look of under-standing. He'd just begun thinking about how he would have to take things slow with this intoxicating woman when her arms wrapped around his neck and she leaned up toward him.

"Show me, Dar," she whispered against his mouth. "Please."

Dar needed no more provocation.

Celeste proved to be a quick study. Given a bit of encouragement, she took to it all easily, leaning into every move he made. Aye, they were fully clothed and doing not much more than kissing, exploring one another as best they could this way, but it wasn't long before all semblance of timidity was gone, and their kissing took on a new vigor. Celeste gave as good as she got, and after he'd suckled her bottom lip, she returned the favor. He'd nearly begun to pant, *him*, from the kiss of an innocent, and took a step back. Her eyes went wide.

"Hey," she pouted, that look of hurt and embarrassment back again. "What happened?"

"I need to go." Christ, he *was* panting. He pressed his finger to her lips. "I confess, that was the most amazing kiss I have ever experienced in my life."

"Will you kiss me tomorrow?"

Oh, aye, lass. God help him, yes. And every day thereafter.

CHAPTER 16

Celeste practically bounced her way home after class the next morning. It had taken her a while to get to sleep the night before, after the way Dar kissed her—after the whole day, really.

But, she had to focus, onward and upward... to tackle her list of errands. First, she needed to go to the club and pick up some things that she'd left in the dressing room.

Becky had called her earlier that morning with news that the band's singer was back, so they didn't need her this coming Saturday night. By her tone, it was clear Becky had thought Celeste would be upset at the news, but she wasn't. The performing had been fun for her, but that was all, and it was probably only fun *because* it was temporary. Plus, now she was wide open to explore this new thing, whatever it was, with Dar.

Thank you, universe.

She shot a text to Dar, letting him know she was running

out briefly, and his reply came quickly: *Then I'll come by around noon.*

Celeste allowed herself a moment to wonder how he was spending his morning. Not that it was her business, but he'd mentioned something about the Montgomery compound and some kind of lessons when they'd spoken earlier. Yeah, he'd called her this morning. Early. She grinned just thinking about it. She'd never understood what people were talking about before, when they went on about just wanting to hear someone else's voice, or leaving the phone line open just to be connected. Now, however... she got it.

Given their interest in him, she figured the Montgomerys might be training Dar to join their team, which she thought was a good idea—besides, it would mean she'd get to see the whole crew more often too. When she'd told him to tell everyone she said hi, he'd asked about her history with them, which had prompted her to ask if *he* had any good friends in the States. He didn't, he'd explained, but told her about the boys, men he grew up with, brethren, he called them, and she could feel how important they were to him. She loved their unusual names too. She kept rolling them over in her head as she got ready, thrilled to be seeing Darach soon.

With very little mid-morning traffic, Celeste made it to the club in no time, grabbing her extra makeup bag and the two blouses she'd left hanging in the closet. She looked one last time into the vanity's rectangular mirror and big bright lightbulbs. It was cheerful, and she liked that.

"Thanks, that was fun," she whispered, brushing her fingers across the top as she headed for the door.

After making small talk with a few servers and a bartender who was stocking a delivery, Celeste spotted Stuart hurrying toward her from the office.

"Hey, Celeste," he said, looking at his watch. "Listen, Becky and I are having an impromptu lunch at the house today. I know it's last minute, but we wanted to include you, if you're able. Bring Dar too. You guys can hang at the pool and even go riding."

She looked at him, confused for a moment. "Dar? *My* Dar?" she asked. When did Stuart get to know Dar?

He chuckled. "Yes, *your* Dar. Well, I didn't know he was *your* Dar until recently, but news travels fast around here. Anyway, he's something of a regular at the club—and last week, Dar and I were talking while you were warming up with the band and I told him he could come out and ride anytime."

"Wait, you and Dar were talking last week?"

"Yeah, he's been coming around since you started on the patio. I just hadn't put two and two together. If my opinion means anything—I approve," Stuart said.

Wait. What? "Since I started on the patio?" Celeste questioned, trying to work it all out.

"Yeah," he said giving her a concerned look before getting pulled away to sign for a delivery. "Lunch is at one," he called out behind him. "See you guys then."

Not sure what to make of any of that, Celeste shot Dar a text to give him a heads-up about the plan and make sure he was okay with it. She didn't want to ambush him or anything. It took longer than usual for the reply (not that they'd been texting one another for *that* long, but Dar had always been very prompt before), which made her nervous. She had just begun to second-guess herself, wondering whether she'd misread the whole situation, when her phone finally buzzed.

She grinned at seeing: *Lunch at the Adelman's sounds great. As long as we sup together.*

She checked her watch, ninety minutes and counting. What a turn this summer had taken. Seriously. Here she was surrounded by *friends* and busier socially than she'd ever been, even when Maggie was around. And she had a boy—jeez, a *Man* with a capital *M,* who she couldn't stop thinking about.

Thank you, Madam Fate. For once.

CHAPTER 17

"Celeste."

Looking through the screen door of Celeste's porch, Dar was barely able to do more than breathe her name when he spotted her, in what he'd learned was called a bathing suit, one that left very little to the imagination. Hearing his voice, she looked his way, and her eyes widened before she covered herself quickly with whatever garments she had in her hands.

"Hold on a sec!" she cried before disappearing down the hall.

Hold on to what, he'd like to know, because presently he could use a brace, and a bit of cover himself as his body responded to the sight of her exposed body.

A moment later, clad in a frock, she was opening the door, red in the cheeks and looking a bit flustered. *Aye, me too, lass.*

"Hi." She smiled. "Come in. You arrived just as I was just trying to decide on a cover-up."

Not only was he unsure how to respond, he wasn't sure he

could, if he wanted to at the moment. Still entranced, he gave a noncommittal grunt, hoping it passed for communication as he re-arranged himself and stepped inside.

"Are you okay?" she asked with a concerned frown.

Was he?

"Dar?"

He shook his head, snapping himself out of his revelry. "Morning," he said and bent to kiss her cheek.

This flustered her even more, but clearly pleased her, too, as she pressed her hand to the place his lips had just touched, eyes dancing. He swore then, perhaps out loud, given how her eyes widened and a knowing smile crossed her face. He went back in, this time for her lips, the only thought on his mind, *I need to kiss you now, lass.* Thankfully, she seemed to be in complete agreement, because she stood on tiptoe and wrapped her arms around his neck as he gave her a slow and poignantly heated good-morning kiss.

"Wow," she said fanning her cheeks. "I guess you like the suit."

"I like *you*," he said, finding his breath. And the suit. "Did you pack clothes to ride?"

She nodded. "I did. Are you sure I can't drive?"

Only if he wanted to cram his long legs in her passenger seat footwell for an hour each way. "Nay, our service is already waiting outside."

She peeked around him. "Isn't that a Calder truck?"

"Aye, it is," he confirmed. The Montgomerys had offered one of their drivers to him whenever he was in need, which meant he no longer had to fiddle with the Uber application. "We've reached a mutually beneficial agreement," was all he told her. Leaving out the fact that their agreement included driving lessons from their man Gregor.

After helping with her things and locking up, he led her to the truck. The ride that followed was beautiful and showcased scenery that Dar had not seen before. He liked how Celeste pointed out landmarks and farm animals along the way. They were sitting close together in the middle row, and each time she pointed, her other hand would rest atop his thigh, and her hair would tease his chin.

After she'd leaned over to excitedly show him the fifth "just gorgeous" vista, he turned to her and smiled. "You like it out here, don't you?" he asked softly.

She fell quiet. Her permanent dwelling was nice, as was the surrounding town, but he somehow couldn't imagine her living anywhere but where she was right now.

"I prefer it. It's open and quiet." She shrugged, deep in thought.

"If you could live anywhere you wanted, where would it be?"

She gave him a curious look and he suddenly pictured a life they could have together—one they *would* have together, he was sure of it now. The future and Celeste were his destiny. He cared not where they lived as long as they did so as one. She stared at him a moment longer, and for the briefest of seconds he feared she did not share his desire.

He gave her leg a gentle squeeze and kissed the top of her head. "Indulge me," he said.

Celeste sighed wistfully. "Well, I'd love to have a big piece of property somewhere."

"On the ocean?" he wondered, picturing the Montgomery estate. He didn't think he had the means for something quite like what they had, but they could definitely have a beautiful home on the water.

She shook her head, and her face took on a dreamy expression. "Honestly, I'd rather be tucked away somewhere. Like almost, *almost*, living off the grid, you know? But, with electricity and running water, all of that. Obviously. I mean, I'm not *crazy*!" She giggled and Dar held his tongue. "Kind of a compound of sorts but with a big sprawling ranch and pool and maybe even a barn."

"And stables?" he asked, picturing it too.

"Aye," she grinned. "Stables too. Wait 'til you see Stuart and Becky's place. I'd love something like that."

A short time later, Dar realized he and Celeste had very similar dreams for the future. The Adelman's property was perfect, save for the lack of a barn. After they'd supped, he spent an exhilarating hour riding the land. It felt good to be atop a horse again, even more so because Celeste was with him.

Dar had taken his time preparing their mounts, something he missed doing, while Celeste eyed him curiously from her perch on the front porch. After leading their horses from the stables, Dar checked their hooves, a habit, but also something that caused Celeste to raise a brow, though he didn't know why. He gave her a steady stare in return, then went about saddling, and adjusting the reins and stirrups. At this point, Celeste had begun to make her way over.

She stopped beside him and looked into his eyes with a

warm, gentle smile. "Have you ridden long?" she asked, stroking the horse's face tenderly.

"Aye, as long as I can remember. You?"

She shrugged. "I learned years ago at a church camp. My—" She paused, her gaze fixed intently on the horse. "My sister taught me."

"You have a sister?" he asked, not sure if she was speaking of Maggie or if there was indeed another Lowell sibling somewhere.

"Well, as good as," she amended. "She was my brother's girl-friend. We were very close."

Celeste said no more and he didn't press—Dar knew this was not the time to blurt out anything about Maggie. Besides, her letter was in his room at the inn, and he dared not reveal himself without that letter as proof. Still, he had a feeling that the time for sharing that information was fast approaching.

After he helped Celeste mount her mare, they spent a long stretch riding the property. 'Twas exhilarating to be on horse-back again, and he suspected she enjoyed it too.

After their ride, and after seeing to the horses, they went in search of their hosts. Stuart was tossing a baseball with his son, Robby, a strapping lad who was home from college for the weekend.

"Dar," Stuart called out when he spotted them approaching. "Join us."

Dar turned to Celeste, who gave him a bright smile. "Go on," she prodded.

He kissed her forehead, and called out, "Gladly," as he went to join them, catching the ball, and turning it in his hands to get a feel for it.

HE FOUND Celeste asleep by the pool a short time later. She'd changed back into her swimsuit and he couldn't help but reach out toward her. The back of his hand skimmed her shoulder and he found her soft skin hot to the touch.

"Celeste?" he murmured softly.

She made a sound, still half asleep, and he smiled at the thought that even her subconscious self liked the feeling of his touch. A moment later, she startled and sat up.

"I'm sorry," she apologized, squinting in the sunlight.

"For what? I was merely trying to wake you."

She blushed and reached for her coverlet, though he wished she hadn't.

"We have just enough time to get to the yoga studio," he said.

She jumped up. "Oh my gosh! I have to teach! Dar. We have to go. I completely forgot."

AFTER PATTING himself on the back for a class well done, Dar had gone home to shower before meeting Celeste for another meal and evening stroll down Main. He'd come in after dinner, and though he told himself it was merely to see her safely inside, if he was truly honest, it was mayhap also to steal just a wee bit more of her time. A few kisses too. When she alighted to her washroom, he flipped idly through the pile of DVDs on her console, not that the titles meant anything to him.

"Old school, I know," Celeste said, coming back into the room.

He turned to face her, enjoying her sheepish grin. "Well, lass, old school is exactly my speed," he returned.

She giggled. "Mostly I like watching them at night when I can't sleep."

"Pick one," he said, surprising even himself. He wasn't sure what watching a DVD really entailed, but if it meant he could sit beside her for a little while longer, then he wanted to do it.

She smiled. "Really?"

"Aye."

She lit up then. "Okay, well, first—forgive my selection. You can probably tell from all the titles when my life took a wrong turn."

He wasn't sure what she meant by that, but his heart constricted nonetheless.

"Really, it's okay," she said. "It's just, these movies make me feel like I still have a family."

She threw in what she explained was her favorite version of *The Parent Trap*, because apparently there were many others. It was a sweet movie and he held her close through all of it, hoping it would help her feel complete again. Because she *did* still have family. Mayhap not here, but Maggie was well. Guilt gnawed at him at the thought of her letter, but the longer he waited to deliver it, the harder it was to broach the subject.

When she laid her head on the armrest, he stretched out behind her so she could lay all the way down, using his arm as a pillow instead. He liked holding her like this and did his best not to nuzzle the sensitive skin behind her ear.

She enjoyed his touch, he could tell, and turned for a proper kiss a few times, which he gladly bestowed upon her. Each time, he swiftly flipped her back around after a moment or two, lest he be tempted to do more. He was obviously courting her, but was also trying to move slowly in deference to her chastity. He was afraid if he was too arduous too quickly he'd scare her off. And, aye, it was gentlemanly, he supposed, and sort of nice to have a slow build up. But still, for him, there was no doubt that Celeste was *his*.

And he would make it so.

Each time she arched against him, adjusting herself to keep comfortable, it all but interfered with his resolve, and each time, he rectified that with a grunt and shoved another throw blanket between them.

Finally, it was too much.

About an hour into the movie, he broke down and turned her toward him, staring deeply into her eyes before pressing his mouth to hers and playing it like a hummingbird on a nectaring flower. Her throaty moans confirmed her pleasure, and he was gratified that she did not pull away.

He suspected that her need for more was growing stronger every day, and hoped he wouldn't need to be patient for much longer. He growled, giving in for a blissful second, gently grinding his body against hers, before, God almighty, he stood abruptly and left.

He'd just reached the end of her drive when he turned back for one last look. Celeste was standing on her front porch, gloriously disheveled, and when she saw him turn, she narrowed her eyes and pointed at him. "You'll be back, mister," she called out.

It was all Dar could do to turn around and continue on his way.

Oh, aye, lass...I will indeed.

CHAPTER 18

"And, pressing back, feel that stretch all along your hamstring and into your hips."

After three back-to-back days of the *Dar and Celeste Show*, Celeste was doing her best to concentrate but it wasn't easy with Dar in her class again. It wasn't that he was a guy—though yoga generally appealed more to women, there were always plenty of guys at her four o'clock—they just weren't the guy who'd been kissing her at night, and sometimes during the day.

And those kisses. *"Mmm."*

She heard Dar chuckle and her head whipped up. Oops, she must have said that out loud.

"And deeper," she guided, then mmm'd again, hoping it provided cover for her faux pas.

Dar laughed. Guess not.

"I have to say," Kathy spoke up as Celeste shifted them into another cool-down stretch, "this has been the most electrically charged week of classes we've ever had. Makes your hot yoga pretty tame, Celeste, just saying."

Everyone laughed at that. Celeste rolled her eyes and directed the class into savasana.

In the silence of the deep relaxation pose, Celeste did the opposite of what she instructed her class to do and mulled over Kathy's comment. Okay, so it was obvious she and Dar had a thing going on. Which in and of itself was great. Right? Great guy, gorgeous guy, stupid respectful, approved by Stan and the Montgomerys, and so much fun to be with, he was like her new best friend and boyfriend all in one.

The problem was, Celeste really didn't know how to handle it. She was flustered and trying to hide it. This was all so new to her. How was she supposed to be levelheaded when she felt like her head was in the clouds and she had this constant rush strumming through her veins? She found herself at a loss.

"Okay, that's it for today," she said, literally throwing in the towel. "See you guys tomorrow." When she rolled over, Dar was there, holding out his hand to help her up.

"That was different," he said and she whacked his chest.

"You're messing with my concentration."

"Aye, I know the feeling."

After she closed the studio, Dar walked her home, which was becoming a routine, one Celeste looked forward to—a quiet moment after class holding hands and brushing up against each other.

He left her at the door with a brief but satisfyingly toe-curling kiss, one that ended with a look that said, "I want ye all, lass." Okay, so maybe she made that part up in her head, but there was something in his eyes when he looked at her that just spoke of more. What on earth was he waiting for? Celeste bit her lip nervously. Did he think she was too inexperienced? That she couldn't handle it? Because she was here to say, "Yes, Dar, I can." She wasn't the same nervous door-fumbling imp she'd been just days ago. Really, she wasn't.

Now, she watched him walk down the street, turning a few times to smile her way before waving at the corner and moving out of sight. Celeste stared at the spot where he'd disappeared a moment longer then sighed and headed inside. She capitalized on her pre-shower condition and did a little cleaning, and a bit of dusting and scrubbing later, she hit the shower and preened, hoping for more tonight.

She wasn't sure exactly what, but she was having dinner with him at the inn where he was staying. At the least, maybe they could sit on his sofa and watch a movie or something. A little more of the barely PG-rated cuddling he was famous for at this point, she thought, somewhat begrudgingly.

Only last night he'd come in after dinner, and Celeste had relished being able to lie down with him, to lean into him and feel his body against hers. He'd awoken so many new sensations in her over these last few days that she felt like her nerve endings were live wires on constant zing. Forget the rush she'd first felt from his presence earlier in the week, this was high def. HIGH—*DEF*.

Celeste grinned, thinking about how, in a fit of boldness, she'd arched against him a few times, hoping he'd get the hint, and later, after he'd *finally* kissed her, like *really* kissed her, she'd wrapped her arms around his head to keep him there as she moved her body closer, her need for more growing stronger. He'd left abruptly after that, and Celeste was hoping that meant he was close to giving in to the desire he so clearly felt.

She was surprising herself with her own thoughts and feelings—how *she* seemed to be the one who wanted more. But it was true. She wanted—needed—more of Dar. With that in mind, she chose a pretty slip-on pencil skirt (formfitting, but not too tight) and halter top. The front was cut a tad lower than what she usually wore, but still appropriate. The back, though, plunged, leaving her bare from her neckline to her waist. The fact that she was able to go braless made the effect that much better, in her opinion.

Take that, Darach MacKenna. I'll see your chaste line in the sand and raise you with a bit of provocation.

AFTER A SHORT WALK THROUGH TOWN, Celeste met Dar in the lobby of his inn. She noted his subtle, yet unmissable look of appreciation and suppressed a giddy grin. Yep, score one for her.

Dar had told her all about the owner's incredible attention to detail and as the night progressed, Celeste found that she agreed with him wholeheartedly. From the décor to the ambiance and the service, dinner was amazing, and as they'd gotten in the habit of the last few nights, they had a glass of wine.

After dinner—during which Celeste made sure to touch her collarbones a lot and play with her wineglass, tips she'd picked up from some online articles she'd read on flirting that afternoon—Dar took her up to his suite.

When they arrived, Celeste scanned the nice-sized living room and kitchen, nerves jangling inside of her. She commented on how lovely it was, wondering how obvious she should be about what she wanted to *do* in this very nice room. Besides being sparkly clean, it was terribly neat, even the large books open on the cocktail table appeared staged. When she went in for a closer look, though, she saw that they weren't the typical decorative fare. Architecture, building, as well as a few literary classics. Smart man, she thought, even though she knew this.

"Major?" she asked curiously. At his confused look, she clarified. "Did you study this in school? Architecture, construction, engineering?"

"It wasn't taught at St. Andrews, the university I attended, but I did study it with a private tutor, it was one of my favorite subjects," he said, clearly proud of his education. Then something changed in his demeanor. "Christ," he whispered, almost to himself. "He paid. 'Tis because of Lachlan I even had that opportunity."

"Your dad?" she said, purposely trying to humanize Lachlan for Dar. It was clear he still loved and respected his father—no matter what he said, it was in his expression whenever he spoke about him. *You're welcome, Lachlan.*

"Aye," Dar said, still lost in thought.

"And is that such a bad thing?"

He grimaced. "Merely another realization," he conceded, his voice laced with regret.

She sat there, heart breaking, then recalled what Dar had told her about their last interaction. "Wait. You didn't make up with him before you left, did you?"

He shook his head. "Nay, lass. I walked away and haven't spoken with him since."

Celeste observed Dar for a moment, the pain and anguish clear on his face, though she could see that they were tempered with something else—something more open, forgiving, perhaps.

"Let me see that disk?" she asked, pointing. "The one in your pocket."

Wordlessly, he handed it over, and she rubbed the mythical creature again like she had when he'd first shown it to her. She was so fascinated with it, she'd done her due diligence on the subject. So, now she used it as a prop.

Holding up the talisman, she looked Dar in the eyes. "Where's the griffin, Dar? That powerful and majestic creature? He doesn't run from things, he faces them head-on."

Dar held her gaze for a moment, then something changed, like a fire lighting behind his eyes.

"He's guarding a treasure like he's supposed to." Dar's eyes continued to bore into her, and she knew his thoughts were on her, and not his father. And, as much as she wanted to explore that path, she knew something else needed to be resolved first.

Still, she was blushing when she said, "That's sweet, but back to the real subject."

"You're right," he said with a sigh. "I was so angered, then disheartened. I admired that man with every fiber of my being —until I found out he was my father. Then, I showed him no compassion, no understanding for what he went through. Lachlan's the real griffin."

She shook her head. "No, everyone starts somewhere. Only someone open and evolved would even admit their mistakes. You *are* admitting that, right?"

"Aye, I can see a bit more clearly now."

She turned the medallion around, rubbing it again with her fingers. What she wouldn't give to have a family tradition like this, something to hold on to. How could she help him see just how wanted he clearly was?

"Blood of my blood," she said, turning the coin around. "That's not something that one inscribes lightly. Don't you see, that means *you're* the real griffin, too. You always have been, Dar."

He took it from her hand, fingering the lettering, nodding slowly. After a minute, he spoke, his voice soft. "I believe you're right. You know, until you read these words to me last week, it never occurred to me that Lachlan was the one who'd made the medallion. I don't know how, but now I know it's from him. Not Da, not Ethan, like I always believed. It was Lachlan who made this for me."

There was so much affection in his voice when speaking of Lachlan, she could only imagine the potential capacity for love he had for his birth father. "Will you call him?"

The look he gave her then was one she could not describe, but told her that there had to be more to the story. Still, his stubbornness in this hit a nerve. He clearly loved this man, Lachlan, even though he'd only recently discovered he was his biological father. It wasn't as if Lachlan had truly hurt him in any way. He was still out there, and Dar was just... blocking him out.

"I'd kill to have my dad back, Dar," she said, with more bite than she'd intended. Her eyes teared up and she swiped one when it fell. "Sorry," she said, collecting herself. "It's just that I don't have my family. I never will. I can't imagine having an opportunity to fix things and not taking it."

"I can't, Celeste."

"Can't or won't?"

Something in his eyes changed then, gone was the sure, levelheaded man who remained at ease even in times of difficulty. He stood up, paced a bit, and came back.

"I need to tell you something, Celeste," he said, seeming nervous.

Tamping down her own nerves at his sudden seriousness, Celeste grasped his hands. She wanted to prove that she was someone who would support him, who would be there for him in a way that she'd never had, at least not as an adult, and not in what already felt like a relationship. She just wanted to help, the way he'd already helped her feel confident and bright for the first time in so long.

"What is it?" she asked, searching his face for any kind of clue.

"I've been keeping something from you."

Celeste nodded, trying to ignore how her heart started pounding, trying to keep her breathing even. She focused on the last week with him, how real it had felt, how real it *was*, how real it still was, right? She held tight to all the incredible feelings and amazing times they'd shared. The dreams of a life she'd begun to imagine with him. A life together, as one. A life where she finally felt whole. She could feel it, she *had* felt it. Had she gotten too far ahead of herself? Or had she missed something because she was too caught up in these crazy emotions that she'd never experienced before?

She kept her eyes on Dar, who himself seemed to be working up a courage, and willed him to just spill it already. Had it all been too good to be true? Given her history, Celeste wouldn't be surprised if that was the case.

What Madame Fate giveth, Madame Fate always tooketh away.

CHAPTER 19

Dar stared at Celeste, watching a myriad of emotions swirl in her eyes. He knew he had to tell her about Maggie—it was the whole reason he'd invited her to sup at his inn tonight after all —but now he found he was unable to speak.

"You...you don't have a girlfriend do you?" she asked, her voice impossibly small.

"Don't I?" he replied, hating that he'd made her doubt his feelings for her, and fearful, too, that this might change everything.

Celeste let out a sigh and noticeably relaxed. "Well, you're acting all weird now and it's freaking me out."

"I'm sorry." He rubbed the amethyst in his pocket and walked to the bedroom, deciding it better to just show her.

"Where are you going?" she asked, following him.

"The safe."

"What's in it, Dar, your alias? Stacks of IDs? Is that what

you've been doing with the Montgomerys and Calder guys? Are you on a secret mission from Interpol or something?"

She kept throwing out guesses, each more ridiculous than the last, until he finally pressed a finger to her lips, and gave her a serious look. He couldn't think with all her nervous rambling.

"Well, that's rude," she murmured against the digit.

He chuckled. Even in the direness of this situation, he liked when she got a bit feisty. He liked all of her nuances. God almighty, it was more than that, wasn't it? Even though he had already begun to plan their life together, it hadn't dawned on him until this very moment that he loved her. He'd come forward to a time he now knew was his future, but that future was because of Celeste. And, if they were ever to have a chance together to build a solid foundation, he needed to be honest with her.

He cupped her face before pressing his lips to hers, pouring all his love into that one small gesture.

"If you'll give me a moment, I will explain," he said, pulling out of the kiss. "But first I need to grab a few things."

"As long as it doesn't include rope and duct tape," she muttered.

He chuckled again, though he didn't fully get her joke, then bent down to grab the ledger and the letter set inside the cover. Those in hand, he led Celeste back to the living room where he sat with her on the sofa. She looked at him expectantly, eyes glancing down to the ledger, then back to his.

Dar took a deep breath. "Right. Celeste. Some time ago, I made a pledge. My traveling here, to the States, was to deliver a message to you."

That took her by surprise. "You did?" she asked, giving the ledger an even more curious look.

"Aye."

"Not someone's last will and testament, I hope," she said, pointing. "Whatever you've got there looks serious."

"Nay." Not truly, but in essence…perhaps. He fingered the ledger, then pulled out Maggie's parchment missive, which was sealed with the O'Roarke family insignia.

He handed the letter over to Celeste, who fingered the thick paper, tracing the wax letters.

"This is for me? It's beautiful," she said. Celeste looked up at him hesitantly, and he nodded, watching as she then turned it in her hands, brushing her fingers over the script of her name. Her eyes darted to his again, this time filled with tears and confusion. "This is Maggie's writing."

"Aye." He nodded. "She wished for you to have some closure. Leaving you behind was something that tore at her heart."

Celeste tried to retreat, not literally, but inside herself, he could almost see her mind sorting through his words and whatever little information she already had. After a moment she looked at him again.

"You know Maggie?" she whispered.

"I do. I met her the day she was wed to Callum."

Celeste held up the letter, and when she spoke, her words caught. "This is really from Maggie? Maggie's actually happy in the place that suits her best?" She paused and took a shuddery breath. "The crone was right?"

They were questions and statements both.

When Dar nodded, she closed her eyes and mouthed something, pressing the missive to her face. Then she slowly flipped it over and carefully broke the seal. She brushed her fingers over the lettering, whispering Maggie's name as she started to read. Dar watched her face as she read, as emotion after emotion flickered across it. When she finished, Celeste let the letter fall and covered her face with her hands and cried.

"She's okay," she choked out in between sobs. "She's really okay."

Dar wasn't sure what kind of tears they were, but he gathered her in his arms and pulled her onto his lap, feeling a burden lift off of him as Celeste's comforting weight settled in. He'd delivered the message, there were no more secrets. She held on to him in a way he'd never been clutched at before, like he was her lifeline, her last and only stronghold after a cascade of tragedy. Or maybe, it was just the opposite, and she was his.

Moments later, she pulled away, her eyes swollen, her dark lashes spiked from tears. He'd never known a more beautiful sight. He waited as she stared at him, her eyes searching his. Then she reached for the letter and slowly raised it.

"This is true?" she asked, whispering, though her voice was stronger than it had been before.

"I haven't read her words, but if she explained the hows and whys of it, 'tis true."

She thrust the parchment toward him, wordlessly urging him to see the script, her look imploring that he do so, now. Touched by her trust in him, he took it from her hand and began to read.

As he carefully scanned the parchment, he found himself

grateful Maggie had left nothing pertinent out. There it was before him, before Celeste. The truth.

My dearest Celeste,

I pray my letter finds you well. Oh, Celeste, I'm so sorry for the pain my disappearance has caused you. I wish I'd had even a shred of control over what happened. If so, I would have done things so differently. I'd at least have made sure you knew where I was going. That I would be okay.

That day I found the sword under my bed—you remember, the one Derek must have purchased—I was out of my mind with grief, and when I saw it I was so filled with curiosity, obsessed really, that I didn't think about the effect, the immediate effect, my actions would have. How could I have, though, really? Never in a million years would I have guessed.

When I was on the phone with you, I noticed a divot in the hilt of the sword, and I just knew the jewel the crone gave me went there. It was instinctual. Still, I never imagined that when I placed it inside the fittings, the sword would literally transport me to another time.

Yes, I said that out loud. Or, wrote that in ink. You get what I mean.

I'm living in the fifteenth century now, Celeste. That price I had to pay, the price for begging the crone to have Derek back, well, this was it. And in a way, I do have him back. The crone told me that Derek and Callum, my husband now, share the same soul.

I know this sounds crazy and ridiculous and weird all at the same time, but I swear to you it's true. It has to be given the connection we have. Actually, the sword was first Callum's! It's like Derek sent me back to another version of himself.

When Darach offered to give this to you, I was so stunned, but grateful. I don't think I'll ever be able to come back to the twenty-first century, and it breaks my heart that I left you (and running water, but it's pretty astonishing the things you get used to!). While I can't be there, I couldn't think of anyone I would trust more to see to your welfare and to let you know that save from being separated from you, I am well. I have even found happiness.

I love you and miss you so much.

Eternally yours,

Maggie

P.S. Not only do I trust Dar with my life and yours, but the crone is here too. She prophesied that Dar was fated to come to the future and promised that you were waiting and ready. Make of that what you will.

ONCE HE'D FINISHED, hiding a small smile at Maggie's note about his character—and about the crone's prophecy—he handed it back, then looked deeply into Celeste's eyes, making sure she could see as he nodded and said, "Aye."

Her expression unreadable, she looked down at his ledger and asked, "What's in the journal?"

Glad for some direction, Dar slid her off of his lap and sat her next to him, relieved when she sunk into his side like she belonged there. She already did in his mind—belong there, that is—but he'd be telling himself an untruth if he didn't admit that he feared she might shrink away after ingesting information that anyone would find absurd. Too, that he had kept this knowledge from her. That she leaned into him now of her own volition spoke volumes.

Putting one arm around Celeste, he opened the ledger with the other and showed her the notes he'd taken. Pointing to each, he explained how Maggie and Gwen had spent hours coaching him and preparing him for any obstacles he might encounter. Celeste listened intently, nodding as she brushed her fingers down each page, looking carefully at the illustrations. It was only at this moment that Dar realized she couldn't actually read more than the headings that Maggie and Gwen had penned in English, given that he had written everything else in his native Scots Gaelic, which he always found easier to slip into when he had to write quickly.

"Is this the safety deposit box?" she asked, her finger stopping next to the heading "Safe."

"No," he said, shaking his head. "This is about the safe in the cellar of your home."

Her forehead furrowed. "Wait, I have a safe?" She shook her head. "I didn't know," she murmured softly, sounding almost like she was in shock. Likely, she was. Her fingers continued down the pages, and despite not being able to read most of what was written there, Dar watched as she soaked up every word she could until she reached the end.

When she reached his sketch of her likeness, her breath caught, and her eyes shot to his.

"You did this?" she asked.

He looked at it now, nearly having forgotten he'd done the drawing. This was the first time he'd seen it since he'd arrived, and Dar was struck by not only the detail, but the *depth* of his sketch. Seeing it now, the true care and, well, it couldn't have been love, not then, but whatever it was, it shone from the page unmistakably. It was all there, plain as day. As if fate had already known.

Dar met Celeste's gaze and nodded, keeping his eyes locked on hers.

After a moment, she whispered, "Why did you come here, Dar?"

It was curious, not accusatory, and a question he himself had turned over many times.

"Why did you leave everything you knew behind?" she pressed when he did not answer straight away.

"I came here for you, lass," he said, eyes back on the drawing of her that he'd made. There was no doubt in his mind now that this was true.

Celeste nodded, but broke his gaze. Carefully, she laid the ledger down beside her, then stood to face him. Instinctively, Dar started to rise, too, but she shook her head. For a moment, he was confused, but then she lowered herself down onto his lap, straddling him.

God almighty, Dar had not been expecting that, and with a sharp intake of breath, his hands covered the bare thighs that were revealed as her skirt rode up. From there, everything happened in a rush. He grasped her flesh, dragging her closer, and either at the same time or in response, Celeste's fingers swept through his hair and their mouths fused together. Caught in their fiercely passionate embrace, Dar couldn't get close enough, and they rubbed against each other unabashedly, bodies gripped tight.

He knew in that moment, he was but a hair's breadth from giving in tonight and making her his, and it was this last thought that spurred him on, pressing into her thighs to glide her center along his length, intense even through their clothes. He groaned as her body shuddered against his, awakening to this new sensation. It was all the better knowing that she'd never felt this before now, at least not from another man. Cupping her bottom beneath her skirt he brought her forward again. He was pressing himself harder against her heat, imagining what was to come, when a nagging thought popped into his mind. *What if...*

Dar froze.

What if he had to go back? What if a return to his own time was inevitable, if it happened without him even knowing? What if he had to leave her? What then? He'd have made Celeste his, and then would never have her—never have anyone—again. The worst fate he could imagine was making the same mistake Lachlan did and putting Celeste through the same pain as his mother.

Griffins mate for life.

It hit like a blow, and with lightning speed, Dar shifted underneath Celeste, set her on the sofa, and stood, all of it happening so quickly, the sound of their mouths separating lay thick in the air as she tumbled to the side before righting herself. He could feel her moisture atop his trousers and smell the sweet scent of her arousal as he pressed a hand to his erection, so hard now it pained him. He tried to focus on the artwork above the fireplace, needing both a distraction and to avoid her expression, hurt and murderous both.

"Right. Of course. So, where's my jewel?" she spat, sitting ramrod straight and smoothing her skirt out over her knees.

It took him a moment to gather his wits. "What jewel?" he asked, once he'd regained himself.

"The jewel the crone gave Maggie. Last I saw her, she told me it was mine now."

This was news to Dar, but he knew better than to start an argument right now, not when Celeste was smarting from what she surely saw as rejection.

"It's in the hilt of the sword," he said, trying to work out what this meant—what it would mean if Celeste took ownership of the jewel, whether it truly belonged to her now.

"Where?" Celeste pressed.

"At your home," Dar stated, believing that simple, straightforward answers were the best course of action presently.

Celeste folded her arms across her chest. "Well, I want it back. Now."

Aye, that he could see.

CHAPTER 20

They drove through the night, Celeste in the passenger seat, seething the whole way. At first Celeste had balked at Dar taking the wheel, based on what she now knew—that he was fully *from the fourteen hundreds*—but he'd assured her he'd been taught by the best, AKA the Montgomerys. Really, at this point, who cared.

She was still angry and hurt, and maybe even a bit embarrassed, at how Dar had unceremoniously dumped her off his lap earlier, right out of the blue, with no explanation. Again, yes, she was inexperienced, but God, she wasn't *that* bad. From a man who had no problem wooing her and cuddling her, he sure had high standards when it came to anything more.

Thinking about it again now, as she glared out the passenger side window, Celeste stiffened, and had a hard time reining in her impulse to snap at him, to ask him *what the HECK was that?*

Now, about halfway through the drive from the Hamptons

back to her house, Celeste snuck a peek at Dar, who was read-justing his large frame behind the wheel.

"When this is all sorted out, we're getting you a larger car," he said, noticing her attention.

Still feeling overwhelmed and snappy, Celeste rolled her eyes. "This is a nice car, Dar. And perfect for me. You can get your own."

At the crestfallen look on his face, she apologized. The longer they sat in silence, the more her anger waned, and she really had meant it as a compromise of sorts, though it clearly hadn't come out that way, since she left off the part that when he got his own car, they could take his. Whatever, she was dealing with a lot right now. But, she supposed, so was he.

He'd said, *I came here for you, lass,* and that had to mean that he wasn't breaking up with her, he obviously wanted her, despite his *literally pushing her off of* him earlier. But Dar, she knew, never did anything without a logical reason, and so she relented and eyed him warily, knowing he probably needed as much reassurance as she did right now.

"Dar," she said, then with more strength in her voice, continued, "if you pull over, and I come over there, you aren't going to push me away again, are you?"

Relief filled his eyes as he shook his head back and forth. Immediately, he pulled over to the shoulder, and Celeste climbed over the center console to fit herself across his lap. It was a really tight fit, but Dar wiggled her into just the right position, then wrapped her in his arms and pulled her in, expelling a deep breath. Yeah, they both needed this.

She heard his heartfelt apology as she burrowed into his

neck, peppering his skin with quick, comforting kisses as he did the same to her brow, each releasing a bit of the tension they'd felt for the past hour.

Owning the *sexual* tension that had been building between them all week, their quick kisses soon turned open-mouthed, and Celeste relished the shift. Crazy, unbelievable, wild revelations aside, this was still what she wanted—*Dar* was still what she wanted. And his response now assured her that this was what he wanted from her too.

Soon, their kisses were nothing near quick; instead, their mouths fused together, tasting and smacking as they pressed their bodies somehow even closer together. Celeste felt his thick erection pulse beneath her for the second time that day, and thrilled at the prospect—until he suddenly and unceremoniously deposited her into the passenger seat.

Fuming, Celeste righted herself, panting. "What the hell, Dar?" she yelled, her shock and anger taking over her senses. "Again?!"

As if he *wanted* to infuriate her further, Dar merely gestured for her to put her seatbelt back on as he turned the key in the ignition.

"I don't think it's fair that you're standing on some stupid hill of honor, or whatever it is that you're standing on, willing to fall on your proverbial sword," she announced as he began to drive.

Staring straight ahead, Dar said, "Hill of honor? Honor is all I have left, Celeste." He gave a quick glance behind him before he used the indicator to change lanes.

She had to admit, he was a surprisingly good driver and paid close attention to the directions plugged into her CarPlay. "I told you, I made a pledge."

"A pledge?" Celeste snorted. "And that's supposed to explain anything? Sounds archaic and stupid if you ask me."

She looked over at Dar, and saw his jaw clench. Yeah, he didn't really like that, did he? At this point, however, Celeste didn't care. She was sick of not understanding.

She sighed. She'd humor him. "Okay, fine. What kind of pledge did you make, anyway?"

"I pledged to see Maggie's message safely to you, lass. I pledged to look after your welfare, as your closest loved ones were now gone. I am bound by a blood oath to honor and protect those brought into my care. It is a pledge I made to my brethren and, most importantly, to myself."

Celeste shook her head. "I get that, blah blah blah you're so great. But you said yourself, the reason you came here changed, and your quest turned into something else." *You said,* I came here for you, lass. "Didn't you just tell me you came here for...for me?"

Celeste hated how small her voice suddenly seemed, how filled with doubt. It caught slightly and Dar noticed, his eyes darting toward her, his look scary intense.

His hands flexed on the wheel, and she could feel his tension from her seat.

"Don't ever question that," he warned, his voice low, eyes fixed on the road ahead. "I did come here for you. I want you, Celeste. I want every inch of you. I want to bury myself so deeply inside of you, you'll bear that mark forever. I want to be the only man you know. Ever." He paused. "But the griffin mates for life and I don't know if I'm here to stay or not."

She said nothing, just stared at him as she broke down his words into small bites she could ingest and make sense of. Ninety-five percent of what he'd said had been good, more than good—exciting, even, especially his delivery—but the last five percent gave her pause.

"*Wait,*" She gawked at him. "So you don't want to sleep with me because you *might* go back, and if you did, you couldn't be with someone else *just because* you slept with me? That's messed up, Dar."

He gave her the most incredulous look, then turned back to the road, "You're daft."

"*Daft?* Where did *that* come from?"

"Apparently it's a future affliction of women."

She scoffed. "Well, speaking as one of them, it's not appreciated."

He muttered something about her not being the only one, but said nothing more. *Well, two can play that game, Dar.*

When they pulled into her driveway two hours later, having glared at each other through a fast food and bathroom stop with nothing further resolved, Dar got out to open the garage door before pulling in between the Harley and Mustang. He grabbed their bags from the trunk as Celeste collected the wrappers and debris, and then they both headed toward the side door.

She usually felt a sense of satisfaction and ease when she came home after a long trip, but she was too angry to feel anything else at the moment. All she could think about was what *wasn't* happening and why—Dar didn't want to be stuck in another century, forced to be celibate because he'd already chosen her here. It was so backward and messed up.

Though, she grumbled to herself, what else could she really expect from someone whose social standards were seven-hundred-years old?

After he put down their luggage and made another trip for her guitar, Celeste plugged in her phone to charge, then whirled to face him, finally ready to continue their discussion.

"Look, Dar," she said, with enough force that he stopped in his tracks. "You can't make all the decisions. I know you have feelings for me. And I have them for you too."

"Feelings?" he snapped, which set Celeste back momentarily. Dar usually held it together, while she was the one who devolved into a tantrum. "Feelings," he repeated with increased force. He did this thing then, like his whole body got bigger, and he stalked toward her, pointing at her with his big beefy arm. Uh oh, she'd awakened the beast.

"I *love* ye, lass, with every fiber of my being," he all but shouted, getting right in her face. "If I haven't already made myself clear, the thought of taking your innocence and of burying myself deep, *deep* inside ye, 'tis a fight I have with myself every day. It drives me mad. And if not for possibly being separated from ye afterward, I would do it right now."

He was shaking when he finished. In an intense desire to soothe him, she stepped forward and wrapped her arms around him, *I love ye, lass* on repeat in her head. She didn't care about the future at the moment, she just wanted to live in the now.

Right away, Dar pulled back, but Celeste decided this was it

—the moment she would take control. It was high time she took charge—in this, and every aspect of her life. Taking a deep breath, she looked up at him, making her gaze as steely as possible.

"Take me upstairs, Dar," she commanded. "Make love to me. Please."

Yeah, she had him then and they both knew it. He hesitated only a second before closing the gap between them in one long stride. He lifted her up, and she wrapped her legs around his waist, crossing her ankles behind him. She felt his erection pressing against her as he took the stairs and walked them into her room.

Desperate though she was for him, Celeste had a sudden thought and abruptly put her hand up to his chest, stopping him. "Uh uh, I've been sitting in a car for six hours—bathroom, shower, *then* the bed," she whispered. There was no way she wasn't going to present her very best self to him, at least this first time.

After a quick visit to the water closet, they brushed their teeth side by side, staring at each other in the mirror. Celeste enjoyed the easy intimacy of the moment, how natural it felt. When he finished, Dar leaned against the counter, waiting for her to rinse her mouth before pulling her in front of him.

"I want to wash you," he said, his voice low and hoarse.

Celeste shivered. The thought of his hands on her, *really* on her, was intoxicating.

"Me too," she said.

Dar needed no further prompting. He took off his shirt, then reached for hers, dropping it beside them before tracing his fingers along the straps of her bra and the lace cups covering her breasts. His hands hovered there, playing, pressing and circling until she was arching into them and her nipples were firm, hard buds.

He slipped off the straps and she rushed to unhook the forward clasp. Breathing hard, Celeste watched his pupils dilate, his nostrils flare. She'd never felt so fully exposed and yet entirely comfortable, powerful at the same time. Then she reached for his jeans, tracing the bulge of his erection with her fingers before pulling against the button closure.

His hand gripped her wrist, tightly. "Not yet," he told her.

She nodded and let him take her capris off, his large hands, hot and shaky, like her, shimmying the material down her hips as she held on to his shoulders. He let her unzip his pants then, but held her hands back from doing anything more, and Celeste thrilled at knowing how her touch affected him, how it had to be rationed.

When he stepped out of his jeans, she ran the backs of her fingers along the waistband of his boxers, careful to play by his rules and not make contact. Instead, she pulled them away and down to free his member from confinement. *Oh mama.* He was a spectacular specimen of a man. She sure did know how to pick 'em...not that she picked him over anyone else, just...*oh shut up, Celeste.*

Trying to tamp down the chatter in her head, she focused on Dar, who was leaning into the shower, turning on the water. His eyes drank her in as the water warmed. When the glass steamed over, he led her inside, letting her take the lead when she reached for the soap first.

He shampooed his hair then stood in front of her as she washed every inch and crevasse of his body unabashedly, using both hands to wrap around his erection. She looked up at him, imploring him to show her what to do, what he liked best. He understood immediately, and covered her hands with his own, squeezing with just the right pressure as he stroked from base to tip. Groaning, he stilled her after a moment, then removed her hands, tucking himself out of her reach and rinsing off before he took the bar of soap from her.

He kissed her soundly before stepping back, then gently but thoroughly soaped her from top to bottom and everywhere in between, leaving no part of her untouched from his lathering ministrations. Lifting the handheld showerhead from its cradle, he used the water and his fingers to whisk away the soap that the main showerhead couldn't reach. She shuddered when the water hit her clitoris at just the right angle, and he stared, giving her a look of pure male awareness, like he'd just found Christmas, and adjusted the stream to a light spray.

"Dar," she said, with an urgency she hoped he'd pick up on.

He did. The look in his eyes gave her pause, in a good way. She was so turned on by the way he'd cleaned her, touched her, and now, the determination in his eyes as he watched her reaction to a pleasurable touch was just plain hot.

He placed her foot on the shower bench, then palmed her mound, his fingers gliding across and through her parted lips. She shuddered again, and this time, let her head fall back as he rubbed her, giving in to another onslaught of sensations as he whispered against her ear, "You're so wet, love. I'm going to make you release and then I'm going to have you. I'm going to

171

bury myself so deeply inside of you, you will never doubt you are mine forever. Aye?"

She made a sound, but clearly he needed a more verbal reply.

"Aye," she breathed, and Dar smiled in a way that made her shiver.

His fingers played with her entrance, teasing and barely darting inside before sliding up to circle her swollen bud. He spread her apart a bit more, using the water stream to pulse against her exposed pleasure point. She gripped his arms tight, panting, trying to stay upright as he kept up his assault on her senses. Then, his fingers went deeper inside her, and it felt so good, until she felt a pinch that caused her to cry out.

"Shhh. 'Tis done, love," he soothed, holding her against him.

Ah, she thought with clarity, he'd broken through her hymen. Celeste had always wondered what that moment would be like, and she was grateful it had been now, here, with Dar. The pain was fleeting and soon forgotten as his fingers lapped gently at her entrance again while at the same time, he increased the pressure of the water on her clitoris.

It wasn't long before she felt herself coil inside.

"Dar." She panted his name, opening her eyes as she clutched his biceps to get his attention. She wanted him to see what he was doing to her. When his eyes locked on hers, a deep groan rumbled from his throat as his finger pistoned inside her. Her mouth fell open as she came in a rush, crying out as her body pulsed around his fingers. He held her up as her knees buckled, kissing her open mouth as his touch softened.

Afterward, he dried her off and wrapped her in a towel

before carrying her to bed. She mmm'd appreciatively as he laid her down, cupping her bottom and pulling her to the edge.

"Your turn," she murmured.

His erection lay hot and thick across her thigh and she reached out, wanting to touch him, wanting to feel him inside of her. He wrapped her hands around his width, growling at the contact, showing her again how to touch him and what to do. She must have caught on because his nostrils flared again, and he made that sound she liked so much.

She was so turned on from watching him, she felt herself pool with moisture again, moaning as Dar pressed himself just inside of her, his heat and this restless feeling it evoked causing her to wiggle and moan. She moved her hips, beckoning him closer, and he used his manhood to spread her juices over her opening. Then, he cupped her bottom with both of his hands, bringing her right to the edge of the bed before thrusting himself deeply inside.

Her eyes closed as she cried out from the sheer intensity of the pleasure combined with a hint of pain. When she caught her breath, she opened her eyes to see Dar staring at her with an expression that surely mirrored her own. A mix of triumph and a need for more.

Just when she thought it couldn't get any better, he pulled back and thrust himself forward again. The friction as he pumped his hips harder and faster was unlike anything she had ever experienced before, and it wasn't much longer before she felt him reaching a crescendo. He shouted her name as his body went taught, then he held her tight, whispering words she didn't understand.

He collapsed on top of her, and Celeste reached her fingers up to play with his hair, loving the feel of his full weight. She rubbed his back next, her legs tightening around his waist to keep him close. When he rolled to his side, he took her with him.

She pulled back then, tracing her fingers along his brow and down his face before whispering, "You weren't...disappointed, were you?"

He chuckled. "Disappointed? Lass, ye almost killed me," he rasped.

That made her immensely happy.

"Maybe we should have saved the shower for afterward," she whispered.

Dar chuckled, but indulged her a few minutes later, leading her to the shower where they slowly, leisurely cleaned up. Then, they fell back into bed, and he held her tight, hugging her and kissing her everywhere his lips could reach. She smiled as she drifted off to asleep, his raspy whispered, "I love you, lass," the last thing she remembered.

CHAPTER 21

When he knew she'd fallen asleep, Dar pulled Celeste closer, rubbing her back as she sighed pleasantly and burrowed deeper into him. Aye, he was off to a good start, especially after their earlier debacle. Now to make sure he made her happy for everyday hereafter.

Nothing had ever felt so fulfilling—not their lovemaking, though that it had been—but just being together with her, like this. The intimacy of holding her close and knowing she was his. He loved it. God almighty, he loved her.

In this moment, all worry about what *might* happen in the future left him. It didn't matter. Odd how they'd lived without each other for the entirety of their lives, and yet now, the mere thought of not being with her was unthinkable.

With Celeste wrapped tight in his arms, he felt a peace he'd never known before, coupled with the enormity that having made her his, he was now solely responsible for her welfare.

Archaic, perhaps, considering the times, but in his mind, she was his gift from the gods to love and nurture and keep sound and happy.

She woke him in the wee hours of the morning with soft open-mouthed kisses upon his chest. Nothing had ever been so welcome as his woman in his arms, her touches coaxing his response. He lifted her to the pillow, since she'd used him as her resting place, and what a different Celeste she was—or, a more honest version, perhaps. There were no shy smiles this time, just need, raw and unmasked. He made love to her then slowly, gently. Gone was the urgency, what they shared now was piercing, emotional, and to his surprise, brought tears to his eyes.

They fell into a light slumber, waking in the early light to the sound of Brutus's excited barks.

"Ah. Nick's hound knows we're back," Dar said, pulling Celeste closer, finding it difficult to stop touching her.

"Did you meet Nick?" she asked.

"*Dude*, we're very close now," he joked, enjoying the sound of her laughter at his Nick impression. Not wanting to completely mock his friend, he told her how helpful Nick had been from the very beginning, while still remaining oblivious to his real origins. He also filled her in on the Montgomery exchange, figuring it best to lay bare every secret he'd been keeping, and that he and Nick had spoken shortly afterward and made peace.

"Good thing I told Nick my cousin might be coming in," Celeste mused. "From Scotland, no less."

"Good indeed."

"Coffee?" she asked, stroking her fingers over his brow.

"Aye."

Slipping into soft, comfortable clothes, they alighted to the kitchen, where he impressed Celeste with his coffee-making skills.

"My goodness, you've come a long way, haven't you?" she mused, then caught his eye and grinned at her unintended double entendre. Celeste turned toward the freezer, and jumped back when she opened it and several items fell out. Laughing she said, "I see you bought a few things."

Dar shrugged, and gave her a smile. He loved her attention to healthy eating, but needed more meat than she'd had on hand. He helped her dig out something she called a "breakfast casserole," then reorganized what was left. After putting the casserole in the oven, they took their coffees to the back porch.

"I love this backyard," she said wistfully, after settling into his lap in the large lounge chair.

"Aye, it's beautiful," he agreed, rubbing her back, struck by a moment of utter contentment.

"I bought a porch swing for back here, I just need to hire a handyman to put it together and install it."

Dar had seen his share of porch swings by now and was certain he could figure out their mechanism. "Consider it done, lass," he said, squeezing her shoulder.

A moment later, Nick appeared on his own porch, waving to them as Brutus began jumping at the fence.

"We didn't think you'd be back this early," Nick said in greeting, opening the gate when they called him over. "Hey, I need to run out for most of the morning, can Brutus hang with you?"

"Sure thing," Dar said, making Celeste giggle.

She looked up at him. "You sure have assimilated quickly."

Looking between them, Nick said, "Dude, good thing you weren't cousins after all."

"Good indeed, my friend."

They gladly took the hound into their care. Brutus enjoyed Celeste's casserole as much as Dar did. Then, she dared ask if he wanted to try another of her protein shakes, and Dar playfully swatted her bottom with a resounding no before making a quick call to Alex, informing him that they'd left the Hamptons and were back at Celeste's for the time being. At the same time, Celeste called the yoga studio to let them know an emergency had come up and she'd had to leave for the summer.

To Dar, Celeste hadn't mentioned the sword, or anything else for that matter, since they'd arrived, which suited him just fine for now. Better to bask in this moment of contented bliss before facing whatever it was that may come.

Watching Celeste entertain Brutus reminded Dar of the time they went riding at the Adelmans', the way she's looked into the horse's eyes and rubbed him affectionately. She was at home amongst animals, it was clear.

"You should have a pet, love," he said as he rose to begin working on the porch swing.

She smiled, Brutus curled up comfortably by her side, though it was the bittersweet kind. He remembered the look from their first lunch together, when he'd feed her a bite of gelato. It was her look of loss, of a painful memory.

He stilled, tools in hand. "Tell me," he said. "Unburden yourself."

Absentmindedly reaching to pat Brutus, Celeste sighed. "I've said goodbye to almost everyone and everything in my life, Dar. And most not by choice."

Ah. While loss was a part of life, Celeste had had more than her fair share.

"I understand," he said with a firm nod.

A small smile crossed Celeste's face and she turned to him, opening and closing her hand to beckon him as a child would. The innocence of the gesture paired with the depth of the life she'd lived, a depth she'd just expressed to him, highlighted the true juxtaposition of his woman.

He approached swiftly and knelt before her. She looked past him at first, brushing her fingers through his hair. After a moment, she inhaled sharply and looked him in the eye, placing her hands on his face. Under her intense stare, he held his breath, wondering what had caused her such gravity.

She whispered, "I love you, Dar."

Dar had already known this somewhere deep inside, but until now she had yet to say it.

He took her hand and kissed her palm. "And, I love you, Celeste. All will be well," he told her, hoping to give her some of his strength; for right now, his footing was more sound than ever. He added a few dogs and mayhap a cat to the list he was compiling in his head. A list of things he would give her when they made their home together.

She watched him as he built the swing, giving a hand when necessary, and beaming when he was done.

"The swing that Darach built," she said, sounding a bit triumphant, proud.

"Come, let's try it out."

They sat upon it, and he held her hand as he gently set the swing in motion with his foot. She giggled and he couldn't help gathering her in his arms. Brutus watched the motion intently, jumping up beside them when he figured out the timing. Celeste sighed as they all fell into a comfortable and companionable silence.

Aye, after an evening wrought with tension, this day was a welcome shift, and a splendid start to whatever was to come.

CHAPTER 22

"Will you show me the sword?"

Celeste had refrained from mentioning it—and if she was being honest, there were long moments over the past day that she'd even forgotten it existed—but Celeste had decided it was time. She wasn't ready to let anything interfere with the easy intimacy she had with Dar—an intimacy that had grown exponentially— but the sword was an inevitability. It was the reason they'd come back at all.

They'd taken Brutus for a long walk earlier that afternoon, which almost felt comfortably routine considering they'd been walking morning and night this past week. But now they were in her hometown, and to any passersby, they'd look like a regular couple with a dog; a family, even, dare she say...dare she? They'd even hit up the farmer's market on the way back, further cementing this picture Celeste imagined they made to outsiders. Cute couple, cute dog, strolling the farmer's market —it was almost too much for Celeste to handle.

When Nick had returned to collect Brutus, he'd surprised them both with his announcement that he was heading to a Calder Defense training facility. Celeste had grinned and congratulated him, enjoying how her world was knitting together.

After he'd left, Dar had fired up the grill, like he'd been doing it all of his life, and she'd watched him from the swing, strumming her guitar as he tended to the steaks he'd pulled from her freezer.

As he'd added corn to the grill, Celeste had flipped on the bistro lights and they'd eaten sitting at the table under the pergola. She'd turned on some music and they'd spent a long while stargazing on the porch swing, Dar using a long leg to rock them back and forth. Between the wine, the food, and the perfect summer night, she'd felt content, wholly content. She'd considered bringing up the sword then, but pushed it off, unwilling to shift the mood.

Later, they'd soaked in the tub together, and Celeste had noticed for the first time how Dar craned his neck uncomfortably. Eager to give him something, she'd gestured for him to turn and then dug in, rubbing at the knots while he groaned and sighed appreciatively. After, he'd taken her to bed and made her moan and sigh appreciatively. It was as she was laying in his arms afterward, drawing circles on his chest, that she knew the time had come, that she couldn't put off asking about the sword any longer.

Once it was voiced, the reality of their situation was out in the open again. But Dar didn't seem bothered, didn't grow tense. All he did was pull her closer, kiss her forehead, and say, "Aye."

They threw on their jammies and Dar held her hand as they walked downstairs.

In the basement, he turned on all the lights, pulled back a decorative rug that had hung on the wall for as long as Celeste could remember, and showed her the safe that sat behind it.

Celeste shook her head. Had she really never explored down here? How had she missed something as big as this? Something about it was comforting, though, finding a new piece of Derek, when she thought she'd already found them all. She had wondered before why she'd never come across any "go piles" in the house—Derek had always been insistent on having a plan, and something like this safe was so very him that it made her smile.

Watching as Dar keyed in the combination, she breathed, "I can't believe I didn't know this was here."

Dar nodded, opening the safe's door. "Aye, Maggie was upset they hadn't told you."

He stepped back, and gestured for her to do the honors. Feeling oddly nervous, Celeste reached in, and first pulled out a small stack of credit cards, but aside from one, they were all expired. Next was a large stack of currency, mostly American dollars, but some Euros and British pounds were in there too. She ran her fingers down a tower of American hundred-dollar bills.

"I knew something like this had to be somewhere," she said, shaking her head.

"Maggie said they meant to tell you," Dar shared, kneeling beside her. "She said that the safe had only just been installed when Derek…"

He trailed off, but Celeste didn't need him to continue. She nodded as he reached around her and took from the safe a cloth bag of sorts, almost like a jewelry pouch, but bigger.

She gasped when a pile of jewels tumbled out. "Where did they get *these*? Wow."

Dar smiled. "Ah, these are mine. I brought them with me, ten altogether to finance my time here. Nick helped me sell the smallest of the bunch. It fetched about half a million dollars, so I've yet not needed to exchange the rest. To be honest, I'm still trying to work out your currency here."

Celeste felt her eyes bug out. "For the runt? That's a lot of money."

"Aye, I think a few of these would fetch more than enough to secure that homestead you crave."

Her eyes shot to his at that, *that homestead you crave*. He was talking about making things permanent with her.

"Really?" she asked. "You're making plans for our future?"

He poured the jewels back into their pouch, then gave her his full attention. Grasping her hands, he said, "Aye, since the day you walked into me and plastered your face to my chest."

Celeste's cheeks warmed, and she knew she was blushing. "You know," she said, "I was so excited that afternoon for so many reasons, and it's hard to believe, but at the time, none of them included you. Still, I remember turning that corner and flying down the street like I had a date with destiny. And there you were."

"A date with destiny," he repeated, a slow smile spreading across his face. "Aye, I like the sound of that."

That settled, Dar, showed her the rest of the documents that were in the safe, things like the deed for the house (Celeste had been wondering where that was) and various financial investments Derek had made.

It was only after they had been through everything and locked the safe up again that Celeste realized the sword—the one thing she'd wanted to see—had not been in it.

"Where's the sword?" she asked, looking around.

Wordlessly, Dar walked over to a set of storage shelves her brother had built along the back wall, then shuffled some boxes around until he revealed a bulky object wrapped in fabric. Celeste stood and approached, curious. When Dar unwound the last of the fabric covering the sword, keeping the hilt covered so that his bare skin didn't touch it, she felt awestruck.

For one, it was big, beautiful, and shiny. She realized she'd been expecting something clunkier, something more medieval. But this was elegant, well-crafted. Eyes wide, she looked from the sword to Dar and back again.

"What is it?" he asked.

"I just…it's kind of crazy that that's your weapon of choice."

Dar's eyes twinkled. "I'd show you some of my more impressive sword-fighting maneuvers, but I fear doing anything that might alight me, you, or us both somewhere unprepared."

Unthinking, she reached out to touch it, but then hesitated, and at the same time, Dar tensed, tightening his grip on the fabric-wrapped hilt.

"Is it safe?" she asked, looking up into his eyes. "I mean, is it going to travel us back?"

He gave her a curious look then—not fear, but something she'd said had given him pause. She could almost see the swirling words in his head.

"What is it, Dar?" she asked. "Please. No more secrets."

Dar nodded, and, setting the sword down, he told her how traveling through time had worked for Maggie, and Greylen's wife, Gwen, and how their placement in his time was permanent.

"So, it *is* safe," she confirmed, nodding. "Right? You're here permanently."

When he didn't answer her immediately, she grabbed his hand, recalling his earlier fear, why he'd resisted temptation with her for so long. *He'd been afraid he might not be able to stay.*

Dar shook his head, looking uncertain. "We were never sure if I would be able to come back, and yes, we considered it possible that this future would be my permanent home."

"And still you came."

"Aye, and I did so for many reasons, but I can see now that they are all connected."

"So why the hesitation?" Celeste asked, willing him to just say it out loud, desperate to know once and for all what was really possible, and what was just unfounded fear.

He paused, clearly considering what to say.

"Please, just tell me."

He sighed. "When I was at the Montgomerys', they showed me something that leads me to believe I might one day return to the past. Or maybe that I *have* to."

Celeste's mind started racing and her eyes were drawn to the sword again, only this time in horror.

"Permanently?" she asked, pulling her gaze back up to his eyes. "Temporarily? Yourself? Or..." She trailed off. *Would you take me? Would I even want to go?* Oh my God, she was starting to panic. Suddenly she felt desperate, the prospect of life without Dar, a man she'd known for all of a few weeks was unbearable.

As if reading her mind, he reached out to touch her, calming her nerves slightly.

"I know not," he said slowly, "but I swear to you with every fiber that makes up my soul, being separated from you, even for a day, is unthinkable."

Celeste nodded, an idea forming in her head. She was surprised it hadn't come to her before—it was simple, really. She looked up at Dar and said, "I think I know someone we can ask."

CHAPTER 23

The crone greeted Celeste with all the warmth she'd come to expect from the old woman.

"Hello, my sweet," she said, holding Celeste's hands in her own and squeezing them.

Then she inclined her head to Dar. "Welcome, Darach," she greeted with a knowing smile.

Startled, Celeste looked at her curiously. "Wait. You know him?" Her eyes darted to Dar.

"Esmerelda," he said, returning the crone's smile.

Whoa, she had not seen that coming. "And he knows your *name?*" she cried, feeling a bit betrayed. Until now, Celeste hadn't known that. She wondered, briefly, if she'd ever thought to ask, but brushed the thought aside.

"There, there, child," the crone—no, Esmerelda—said, patting her hand, "Didn't Margret explain in her letter to you? Sit, sit, sit."

She bustled about in her comforting way, pushing Celeste into a chair and then disappearing into the kitchen before Celeste could say, *I didn't even tell you about the letter.*

Dar joined her at the table, a peculiar look on his face as he gazed out at the garden through the window.

"I know, it's like the enchanted forest or something," Celeste said, feeling suddenly awkward. How much more did she not know?

Esmerelda came back with a tray of steaming teacups and Celeste smiled inwardly when both she and Dar hurried to help her. At least *that* she knew to do. Esmerelda thanked them both, then disappeared again, returning a moment later and placing two plates down between them. Celeste grabbed one of her sandwiches, biting into it with gusto. Realizing too late how ill-mannered it was to just dig in, she pushed the plate toward Dar and said, "Wait 'til you try one."

But Dar was eyeing the other plate with a stunned expression, and Celeste wondered if the sandwiches were a favorite of his. She wouldn't be surprised. Actually, not much would surprise her right now.

"Go on," she said around another bite of cucumber, dill, and white bread. She watched Dar pick up the odd-looking treats piled in front of him and cautiously take a bite, watched as his eyes misted and he looked down on the little triangle in clear wonder. "Nostalgic, right?" she said. "Tastes like home, doesn't it?"

"My grandmère made a biscuit just like this when I was a boy. It harkens to a time of great joy in my life."

"Told you," Celeste said, grinning.

Dar gave her a compassionate look, but a moment later something changed in his demeanor. With his eyes still focused on her, Celeste had only a second to wonder what was going on before his head whipped around to the crone and Dar was up and out of his chair in an instant. In one swift move, he wrenched Celeste from her chair and shoved her behind him.

Celeste gasped, her hands flying to her mouth. The crone, to her credit, seemed unruffled.

"I mean you no harm Darach Grifud MacTavish," she soothed. "You and Celeste are safe from me. I swear to you on all the gods above, and even the few below with whom I deign to associate."

Celeste stared, heart in her mouth, as Dar digested the crone's words and, after a moment of consideration, he nodded, and took his seat again, hands flat on the table.

Celeste sat beside him and rubbed his leg, sending him a grateful smile, even though she'd never feared the crone, at least not lately. Still, she couldn't help but think, *my protector, the griffin guarding his treasure.*

"Why do you call him MacTavish?" Celeste asked Esmerelda, nabbing another cucumber triangle, and still feeling warm inside from Dar's grand gesture.

The wizened woman gave her a knowing smile. "Because Lachlan's blood runs strong through his veins, he's a MacTavish through and through. Blood of his blood. Soul of his soul."

"But I'm a MacKenna too," Dar argued. "I might even say first."

The crone shrugged. "Oh, pfft."

Dar raised a brow at her dismissal. "What precisely does that mean?"

The crone sighed dramatically. "Very well," she said, giving an eyeroll—and going a bit heavy on the histrionics, in Celeste's opinion. "Ethan was a good father to you, aye. No one would deny that. But your birth was already written, Darach, you were destined to be Ella and Lachlan's boy. It is *they* who should have had a lifetime together."

"How so?" Dar asked, leaning forward, clearly interested in this new piece of information.

The crone smiled and nodded. "When your grandda realized his daughter was in love with Lachlan, he had every intention to break the betrothal."

Dar shook his head, clearly confused. "My grandda? He knew? And tried to intercede?"

"Oh, aye, Darach. What is fated is impossible to change. You were always preordained to be the MacTavish who rose to succeed—and surpass—Lachlan."

"I was in awe of that man, Esmerelda. For most all of my life," Dar said, shaking his head.

"As you rightly should have been. But for Ethan's selfishness and the black magic spell he used to have his way, Lachlan and Ella would have had the life they were meant to—and you, Darach, you would have been raised by the man you so revere, even now."

Black magic? Celeste didn't dare interject—this was Dar's thing—but surely he'd noticed when the crone mentioned *that*. Celeste watched Dar, who nodded slowly at first, then recoiled.

"Pardon, but black magic? A spell?" he asked, shaking his head. "But isn't that what *you* do?"

Celeste grinned. "Pot meet kettle," she muttered.

"Oh, pfft," the crone said again. "Of course not. Contriving against the natural order is not something I meddle in. Helping what's *destined* to occur, now that's entirely different. In the end, Ethan got what he bargained for, but only that. He got his marriage to Ella, but never had her heart. And Madame Fate saw fit to allow your conception under tenuous, but honorable, terms nonetheless."

Celeste listened with bated breath as Dar explained to her then that Ethan had been thought dead for a time and how that was the only reason his parents were able to renew their love. This was truly like a tale out of one of the storybooks she'd read growing up.

"Timely, aye?" asked the crone, rolling her eyes. Celeste held back a gasp.

"That was contrived as well?" Dar asked incredulously.

The crone shrugged, smiling like she was enjoying this. "Was it? Or did fate take the upper hand? Your mother and Lachlan loved each other to the end. Ethan had her loyalty and your love, aye, he treated you as his very own, did he not? But he knew he'd bargained with the devil. Horace knew this too."

"Wait," Celeste interjected, unable to keep quiet any longer. "Who's Horace?" She knew she should let Dar have his moment, but she was also desperately curious.

"My uncle, who threw me out when news spread last year," Dar answered bitterly.

The crone nodded. "Ethan's brother," she added. "Who knew the truth all along."

"Oh boy," Celeste said, almost to herself.

Esmerelda reached forward and took Dar's hands in her own. "You have a job to do, Darach MacTavish," she said, her voice firm and her eyes fierce. "Your destiny still lays before you. You are the keystone and legacy of *two* houses. Never underestimate your place in this world again. The griffin was chosen for a reason."

Dar was silent for a moment, and Celeste dared not speak again.

"I must go back," he said after a deep breath, a steely determination in his voice, his hand gripping hers under the table.

At this, Celeste's world spun. Suddenly everything had gone from an intel recon mission to certain doom—when it came to her and Dar's relationship, at least.

"Aye, Darach, you will return."

"When?" he asked, and Celeste wished he would look her way, but he remained focused on the crone.

"This isn't the prophecy. I haven't an exact time," the crone said in her frustratingly cryptic way.

Celeste couldn't remain silent any longer. "So, are you saying he could just suddenly disappear and be gone? Back to the past? Forever?"

"I said nothing of the sort, sweet. I merely pointed out that Darach still has a date with destiny, no? There is still unfinished business he must attend to, and it's not just securing the Abersoch property."

Celeste was confused, but Dar nodded. "Lachlan?" he asked quietly.

The crone set her face into an emotionless mask. "Enough," she said, and stood to leave.

"Esmeralda," Dar called out. "Can we control the sword? The stone?"

That stopped the crone in her tracks. "Control it?" she inquired incredulously.

"What if we remove the stone?" Celeste asked, the thought coming to her suddenly. Hadn't the sword only worked for Maggie when she set the jewel in the hilt? It wouldn't account for Dar's experience, but she was looking for something, anything, to help, to give them some time.

The crone shrugged. "If it makes you feel better, remove the jewel from the sword."

Celeste shared a look with Dar.

"We never thought of it," he said. "Even back home, it had never been considered."

Celeste grinned, feeling good about contributing something to this. Something so obvious too.

The crone shrugged again, but said nothing more. Celeste thought she saw a small smile playing at the corners of her mouth, but not a moment later, all trace of it was gone, and she turned to leave.

CHAPTER 24

The crone's words rang in Dar's ears the entire drive home. He couldn't believe what she'd said about his da, about Ethan. Nor could he quite fathom that *he* was the keystone, and not one of his more impressive brethren. And her final words—her noncommittal response to Celeste's brilliant idea about removing the jewel. It was all too much.

Knowing he should focus on the road, and fully aware that he'd never work it all out before they arrived back to the house, that it was far too complicated, Dar tried to enjoy the drive, this moment with Celeste. He had to admit, it was *much* nicer being behind the wheel since Celeste had allowed him the use of her brother's car. He hadn't even asked, which had made the gesture all the more meaningful. Though it hadn't gone unnoticed that before handing over the keys, she'd run her hand along the frame, her eyes shiny with tears, though none spilled.

"I always wondered what attracted him to this car," she'd

said, gazing at her reflection in one of the windows. "I mean, I know it's a popular sports car, but he could have driven anything, really. He and Maggie did more than well together— financially, I mean—and we still have what's left of our parents' estate. Not that the money ever really mattered to Derek..." she said, trailing off, the rest of her thoughts going unspoken.

Wanting to offer some insight, to ease Celeste's burden even the slightest, Dar had thought back to what Maggie had always said, that Derek and Callum shared a soul. If that were truly the case, then Dar believed the answer lay here. Gently, he took Celeste's hand and brought it to the emblem on the hood of the vehicle, hoping his meaning was clear. She'd smiled brightly at him—it was.

"Oh, Derek *loved* horses," she'd said.

Aye, so did Callum.

When they arrived back at Celeste's, they made haste for the basement in an unspoken agreement to follow Celeste's suggestion.

"Ooh, I like that," Celeste said of his dagger when he retrieved it from its sheath.

"You may have it."

Celeste backed away, grinning. "It was just a compliment, I don't think I need a dagger."

Dar chuckled, and turned to the task before him. Making sure to only hold the sword by the cloth wrapped around the hilt, he carefully loosened the sapphire, working his way around its edges with the dagger. Once he dug it out, he handed the jewel to Celeste.

"Oh my," she breathed. "I'm not sure if I…it's just, I've never held it before. It's so beautiful."

They both gazed at it together for a few minutes, and Dar held his breath, waiting for something to happen. When nothing did, he let out a tentative sigh of relief.

"In the safe?" she asked.

"Aye, good idea." He secured the jewel inside and led Celeste back up the stairs to the kitchen, suggesting along the way that they treat themselves to a well-deserved glass of wine.

So, they settled on the porch swing, with Dar in the corner and Celeste shimmied up in between his legs, leaning against him. They stayed that way for a few moments in silence, each lost in their own thoughts until Celeste spoke up.

"You know, Maggie kept that stone in her pocket for months," she mused.

Dar nodded. "She told me about that day," he said. "Many times, actually. How she was on the phone with you one minute and in the next gone." He reached for her hand, kissing her palm, thinking of the unimaginable pain it had caused, especially compounded with everything else Celeste had already been through. She could have been so bitter, but she wasn't.

He could see in her all those parts of herself that made Celeste who she was; cautious but curious; mature and so aware, yet innocent. She had a keen mind, too, and was willing to accept almost any reality with the right evidence. Aye, for the most part, despite all that had happened in her life, Celeste remained untarnished.

"If not for that day, I wouldn't be here now," he mused, almost absently, though the second he voiced it, he was struck by how true it was. Having Celeste was only one of the many turns his life had taken this last year. Thinking back now to what Esmerelda had said about Madame Fate taking the upper hand, he knew destiny had set all of these acts in motion.

From before his birth until this moment—when he'd begun to feel its call, conscious of it in a way he had never been before. He had this restlessness in his bones, an aching need to attend to unfinished business back home. Unconsciously, he pulled Celeste closer, and breathed in the scent of her hair. He had to trust that if fate wanted the two of them to be together, they would be, no matter what course they had to take in the in between.

"You're quiet, Dar. Anything you want to talk about?"

Celeste's words jarred him from his thoughts. He shrugged, unable to express everything he was feeling at the moment. In truth, he'd been stuck in his thoughts since leaving the mystic's house, and there was still so much to work out.

"Not yet," he said softly. "I'm still sorting through it."

"I get it." Celeste reached up and snaked her arms around his neck.

Dar leaned back into them, relishing the sensation. "Why don't we order in dinner and watch one of your movies," he said, trying to push the inevitable aside, at least for now.

"I'd love that."

Aye, he knew.

DAR COULDN'T SLEEP that night. Of all the dilemmas he'd faced of late, 'twas this which affected him most. Just as he'd known that final night at Dunhill, he knew now: the time to leave had come. He could not ignore it. Destiny called. He felt its infernal pull. Yet he was torn.

Where before he'd been eager, perhaps even excited, to strike his own path away from the new uncertainty of his old life; now, he was conflicted, unsure. Aye, he felt an inner restlessness but for different reasons entirely. He knew he had to do what was right—he'd never rest otherwise—he just wasn't sure how Celeste would feel.

For hours Dar turned the dilemma over in his mind instead of sleeping, wanting two impossible things at once: to have Celeste and to fulfill his duty in his own time. Sometime in the wee hours of the morning, a thought came to him: Dare he ask if Celeste would come with him? The second he had the idea, his heart started racing with possibility. Would that even be possible? Would the sword allow it, if she wanted to come?

He couldn't be certain they'd see each other again if he went back without her. How fickle was Madame Fate? But if she were to come with him...well, that was something else entirely. Dar turned the idea over in his mind, picturing Celeste laughing with Gwen and Maggie, puttering around Dunhill while he tended to the business at hand. It was the first soothing thought he'd had all night, and soon, he felt himself drifting off to sleep.

She stirred as the sun began to rise, the movement of his restless sleep causing Celeste to turn his way. He'd slumbered while still sitting upright, which had made his neck stiff, and as he woke he realized that the lack of sleep must have given him a ghastly visage, for her brows furrowed in concern.

"What's wrong?" she asked, rising to her knees and studying his face. He loved looking at her, especially like this, void of makeup or other enhancements. "You've been so quiet, Dar." She smiled softly. "So good to me, so attentive, but I can see that you're struggling."

Aye he'd made sure they enjoyed a special evening the night before. Dinner under the pergola and the lights she loved so much, followed by much cuddling on the sofa before he made love to her like it might be their last encounter.

Not quite ready to say aloud what had kept him up half the night, he reached out, tracing his fingers along the curve of her face, wanting a moment to memorize her like this.

Then, her face muscles tensed under his touch and she gasped, eyes wide.

"You have to go back, don't you? That's what this is about." Celeste covered her mouth with her hand, a ghastly expression now marring her visage. "I had my head in the clouds. I couldn't see it, but of course that's true. It doesn't matter that we separated the jewel and sword. You're going to put them back together, aren't you?"

Marveling at her ability to read him, Dar took her face in his hands, trying not to imagine the possibility of never seeing her again.

He pulled back, and looked at her intently, then nodded, the truth weighing heavily. "I need to go back, Celeste."

There was a pause in which a thousand emotions crossed Celeste's face. When one settled, it was a calm, a determination he hadn't expected to see there.

"I don't want to be separated from you, Dar," she said, and

climbed on top of him, straddling his lap, hand on his heart, eyes searching his. "Do you?"

He made a sound, snorting at her ridiculous question. "Nay, I do not," he answered, shaking his head as he traced the straps of her nightgown. "Celeste, I wish to be here with you. Honestly, to *stay* here with you. But as Esmerelda said, I am fated to attend to things at home, things that must be addressed before I can move on. Even if not for her words, I would know it for the truth regardless. I feel it. So strongly."

"Wait," she gasped, clutching his head. "Could just you disappear, like right now?"

"Nay, love, I would need the sword and the stone."

He told her then what had happened the first time he'd touched the sword at Dunhill, how it had seemed as if it had revealed its power to him and foretold his journey, startling them all. How Callum had placed it on the wall in the great room shortly afterward, where it had remained untouched for months until its true pull had come that last night, impossible to ignore.

Over the course of his story, Celeste's grip had softened, and now she stroked his arm as she said, with fear in her eyes, "And you feel that now, Dar? That same pull?" Her voice held a marked acceptance of yet another blow fate was dealing her.

He nodded. "Aye, I am."

She hugged him then. "I don't want to lose you." Her tears wet his chest as she wept; he shed a few of his own.

"I love you, Celeste," he said, forcing the quaver out of his own voice. "I don't want to lose you either."

They held each other like that for a minute or two, and

eventually Celeste stilled. She leaned back a moment later and wiped her eyes, looking up at him searchingly.

"Can I go with you?" she asked.

Shocked, Dar shot upright, taking her with him. Had she read his mind, his dreams last night? "You would go with me?" he asked incredulously. "To the past?"

She nodded fervently. "Aye. Aye! I would rather be with you than chance being separated. Permanently separated." Her eyes roamed his face, waiting.

He barely knew what to say. He hadn't expected this from her, not really. "Celeste, I…" he trailed off, trying to find the words to encompass everything he was feeling in that moment.

She pulled back, eyes narrowed. "Are you unsure?"

At that, all the tension he'd been experiencing evaporated and he chuckled at her ire, feeling a spark of hope for the first time since their visit to Esmerelda.

"Aye," he said, "but not because I don't wish to be with you. That is something I'll always want. Always."

"Then take me," she said in earnest, staring imploringly into his eyes.

A million things ran through his mind as he stared back. His thoughts in the early morning hours had been pure fantasy, or, at least, he'd assumed they had been. But could it be so simple as to bring her with him?

"If we go together," Celeste said, interrupting his thoughts, "do you think we'll be able to come back?"

And there it was—the biggest question of them all. "I do," he said slowly, turning it over in his mind, thinking about what Esmerelda had said, and of how he was certain he was fated to be with Celeste, how he was beginning to feel about the twenty-first century the way he'd observed Gwen and Maggie settling into the fifteenth. "I believe our destiny ultimately lies here."

Her shoulders sagged in relief, and she nodded. "As long as we're together." She hesitated, and made a face. "I think."

While Celeste was a good sport, mostly, Dar couldn't quite imagine her adapting to his time like Gwen and Maggie had. He decided that at least for the moment, he would trust in fate, would trust that She knew what was best for the both of them, individually *and* together.

With renewed hope, he flipped Celeste beneath him, grinning down at her. She squeezed him tight.

"So, we have a plan?" she asked, giggling.

"Aye, but first I'm going to make love to you."

"Oh, I'd like that."

Aye, he knew.

Dar sent a text to Alex, updating him of their plans. Almost immediately, he received a "thank you and good luck" in response. Satisfied, he and Celeste spent most of the morning in heated and excited discussion. Celeste had a myriad of questions—about what life was like in his time, about how it felt to travel through centuries, about what Maggie did with her days—and he did his best to answer what he could. At times, he pressed a finger to her lips for a moment of quiet.

In one of her rare moments of silence, Dar watched as she

grabbed a bag and started rummaging through clothing, toiletries, and even the pantry.

"What are you doing?" he asked, picturing her loading up several suitcases for their travels; which was, of course, impossible.

"I want to bring Maggie and Gwen whatever I can," she told him, head in a cupboard. "Things from this time. Maybe we should go shopping."

Dar shook his head and suppressed his smile at imagining Celeste laden with bags and gifts full of twenty-first century treasures. At this rate, they wouldn't have a free hand to hold the sword or put the jewel in place.

"Celeste," he said, "as much I would love to indulge you, and Maggie and Gwen, too, I fear what might happen if we try to bring more than what can fit on our persons."

He told her then how Gwen and Maggie each had managed to travel with a few things that had been in their pockets, and that he, too, had carried a small bag. But now, with the prospect of taking Celeste, he needed to be sure it was Celeste who came with him— not unnecessary objects beyond what they could fit in their pockets.

He saw on her face that Celeste finally realized the tenuousness of their situation. From there, her many questions ceased, and they finished their coffee and cleaned up in silence. Hand in hand, they walked to the basement together and opened the safe to collect the jewel. Celeste was quiet through all of this but stopped him before he could reach for the sword.

"Wait. One more time: we *are* going to return together,

right?" she asked, even though they'd sorted through it many times, agreeing that that was their intention and firm resolve.

"Aye, once I've spoken with Lachlan and Gavin and seen to the start of construction at Abersoch, we'll return."

Celeste said nothing, but continued to search his face. For a moment, he wondered if she might change her mind, but then she nodded, and Dar released the breath he hadn't realized he'd been holding. As if she could read his mind, she patted his chest and whispered, "It's okay. I'm okay." He wasn't sure if she'd said it to reassure him or herself, but it was what they both needed.

The time was now. Dar retrieved the sword, again holding it through the cloth, and nodded to Celeste. They shared a look as she reached for the stone.

"It's going to be alright, isn't it?" she said pleadingly.

God, he hoped so. He chose to give her the truest answer he could. "I know without a shred of uncertainty that I will love you forever, Celeste Elizabeth Lowell."

She shot him a worried look. "I love hearing you say that, but it's not comforting right now, Dar. Maybe you should just make sure we're touching or something so we go together."

Aye, indeed. He pulled her tightly into his side, overcome with a feeling of certainty, and kissed her quickly but soundly. She gave him a determined look as she snapped the jewel into place and he let the fabric fall. The sword began to glow, his hand warming on the bare hilt. Dar registered one last thought before everything swirled and shifted around him: *never let her go.*

CHAPTER 25

SCOTLAND, 1431

Bright sunshine flooded Celeste's eyes, causing her to wince and turn into Dar's chest. She took comfort in his warmth, leaning in, listening to the steadying beat of his heart, which calmed her own nerves, still frazzled by the odd prickling sensation of spinning.

When she was able, it took her a moment to orient herself, to even remember *why* they had been spinning. And when she did, she clutched Dar tighter. Had it worked?

It felt like only seconds ago they were in her dimly lit basement, but there was no denying the blazing sunlight in wherever they had landed. She remembered snapping the sapphire into place, praying it would allow her to travel with Dar, whose arms held her like a vise. That's when the room began to whirl and fall away. When it started to seem like it was actually working.

"Are you alright?" Dar asked, his words piercing through her dazed feeling. When she didn't respond quickly enough, his tone changed to worry. "*Celeste?*" he asked, keeping her in his arms, but pulling back slightly to see her face while he patted her down soundly with his free hand.

Celeste kept her eyes firmly on his chest as she mentally scanned her body. She was still a bit disoriented, but felt whole and unscathed, and had to admit she liked the protective feel of his hand roaming her back.

Taking a deep breath, she looked up at him, and when she saw his face—real and solid and unharmed—she smiled, overcome with relief. She was here—wherever *here* was—and so was Dar. He had taken her with him. She'd been so scared he would leave her behind, whether for some duty-bound reason, or because the magic of the sword simply wouldn't allow her to come. But Celeste realized she needn't have worried. The moment she'd suggested it, he'd seized on the opportunity, his destiny. He'd seized *her*.

Celeste tried to answer his question, to say she was okay, but nothing came out. She hoped the gratitude she felt was reflected in her eyes. He smiled softly and kissed her forehead, nudging her face so he could cover her lips. She sighed, winding her arms around his neck and kissing him back with vigor. Something must have caught his eye beyond her because he pulled back with a sharp intake of breath.

"Oh, lass. We're here." He lifted his chin, indicating she look in that direction.

And suddenly, her trepidation was back. This wasn't just a

Celeste and Dar thing—this was a whole new country, a whole new *century* thing.

She was scared to look. It was one thing to *think* of coming to the past, to stand in the safety and security of her home, with the man she loved, ready to jump to another century, and quite another to actually do it.

Dear God, *had* they done it? Having no idea what to expect, she turned cautiously, keeping her eyes low to the ground until she worked up the courage to look up. When she was able to focus, she stared, confused at first. Whatever she'd been expecting, it surely wasn't this—a magical-looking castle, straight out of a fairytale.

In the pictures Dar had shown her online, Dunhill looked nice as far as medieval castles went—kept up well enough, but still, you know, medieval. It had looked worn and weatherbeaten, one side crumbling a little, the other fortified with modern beams and struts. Moss and lichen everywhere. So, considering it had been built more than seven hundred years ago, good, but nothing like *this* castle, which shone like a beacon on a hill. It *was* a beacon on a hill. And in front of it, standing on a lush swath of grass, was a woman who bore a strong likeness to Maggie, though at this distance Celeste couldn't be sure whether that was just wishful thinking.

All those feelings she'd locked away and pretended didn't exist flooded her. If she wasn't being held up by Dar, she may have fallen. He'd told her Maggie was here, the crone had said the same, but Celeste realized that until this moment, she'd never actually, fully believed that something like this was possible. Because it couldn't be…could it? *Was* it Maggie?

This woman's long wavy hair was pulled back, and she was wearing a cream-colored tunic over leggings. She had a sword in her right hand and seemed to be practicing some fancy sword-fighting maneuver. Then, a man appeared on the steps of the castle, holding a baby. The smile this man wore on his face was filled with pure love, Celeste could see it even from this distance.

A moment later, the man noticed them and waved before starting their way, baby still in his arms, gripping Maggie when he came upon her—because by now Celeste was sure it was her —by the shoulder. Celeste watched as he cupped her face with his free hand, before holding it out for the sword. She put her hands on her hips and waited, a stance that was so familiar to Celeste she almost laughed. Then the man said something, and Maggie shook her head. He nodded with a grin, and then she whirled to face them.

Oh my God, it *was* Maggie.

Maggie screamed, pushing the sword toward the man, then grabbed the material of her dress and took off at a run. Celeste did the same. Tears streamed down her face as they ran to each other, calling each other's names before crashing into one another and falling into a heap of a sobbing, laughing mess.

It was as she held on to Maggie, feeling her solidity, the evidence that she was whole and alive, that something just snapped inside Celeste. Like suddenly, this wall she'd erected and lived behind shattered, leaving Celeste raw and open for the first time in months, years, even.

She stopped laughing, and instead, sobbed and screamed uncontrollably. The feelings rushing through her were *good* feelings, the best feelings, really, but they were overwhelming and powerful. There would be no dismissing anything today.

"No. Nonono, shhh. I'm here," Maggie said, holding her tighter and rocking her in her arms. "Celeste, baby. Shhh, it's okay."

She felt Dar come up behind her then and saw the man who must be Maggie's husband—*Callum*, that was his name—approach with the baby, all of them cocooning her in an embrace. It was so comforting, their soft voices and the warmth they created, that gradually, Celeste calmed, her sobs slowly subsiding. She caught her breath, and, somewhat embarrassed at the scene she'd caused, darted a glance around to each of them. Thankfully, no one seemed upset or uncomfortable, and no one, for that matter, made a move to break up their little huddle.

Maggie whispered, "Better?" and when Celeste nodded, the men stepped back without fanfare.

"Thanks for that," Celeste said, turning to the guys, still feeling a little raw.

"Yeah, they're pretty amazing," Maggie said, grinning. "Take away all the modern-day psychobabble and you're left with plain old good men with solid intellect and simple solutions."

They shed a few more tears and sat on the cool grass for a while longer, Maggie practically holding Celeste in her lap, until the baby started fussing, and Celeste whispered, "Oh my gosh, Maggie, you have a baby."

Maggie nodded. "Aye. Come meet her, please."

Celeste hadn't realized how near the men had stayed until she and Maggie were lifted gently from the ground on the heels of Maggie's statement, helping their women up without being asked. Celeste leaned back into Dar, closing her eyes for a moment, enjoying the feeling of such security. When she opened them, she saw Maggie looking at her expectantly, almost a little nervous.

"What is it?" Celeste asked, standing up straight, but keeping Dar's hand in hers.

Maggie didn't answer right away. "Celeste, this is my husband, Callum," she said, glancing between her husband and Celeste, looking almost nervous, like she was unsure of what Celeste's reaction would be.

Ah, Celeste thought. Of course. But Maggie needn't have worried, Dar had filled her in on how Maggie and Callum came to be together and married. Besides, there was something comforting about Callum, something oddly familiar about his stance and his smile.

Feeling suddenly shy, Celeste sent a cautious smile his way and offered an awkward, "Hello."

He inclined his head, a sparkle in his eyes—that, too, familiar.

Celeste glanced at Maggie, who was watching the interaction with an expression of delight, before she turned back to Callum, who was holding out the baby in his arms.

"And this is Isla, she's six weeks old," Maggie said, smiling warmly at the infant.

Celeste shook her head, not quite ready to take the baby in her own arms, instead running her fingers down the side of her tiny, precious face.

An overwhelming feeling engulfed her and Celeste stepped

back toward Dar and wrapped her arms around his waist. She realized in that moment how much Dar had needed to adjust when he left this place for the twenty-first century. Now it was she who needed grounding in an unfamiliar world—and she had help.

How had Dar done it by himself? she wondered. It had to have been so difficult. She was struck with a newfound sense of compassion and empathy for him. She pulled back to tell him then just how incredible she thought he was.

"What's wrong?" he asked, searching her face.

"You were all alone, in a new world."

He smiled softly, his eyes full of understanding. "I think we both were."

Someone cleared their throat and Celeste turned to see Maggie and Callum watching them curiously. Waiting. Celeste realized that if anything, they would have expected Dar to return by himself, and they probably hadn't counted on them turning up together in any sense, let alone like *this* together.

She pulled back from Dar and turned to her friend. "Maggie, I'm sorry, it's just—"

Maggie put a hand up. "Nay, it can wait. You both obviously have much to tell us. And, Dar, you haven't said a word to me!" she said, making a face.

He chuckled. "My apologies, Maggie of O'Roarke. And I thank ye, from the bottom of my heart."

Maggie laughed, looking between Celeste and Dar. "Aye, I can see that, but I can't take the credit." Then her eyes fixed on the sword. "Just keep that thing far away from me, please." She pulled Celeste back to her side. "Come. Let's get something to eat and get you settled. Hopefully your arrival here will be less turbulent than mine."

As they walked toward the entrance and up the steps, Maggie told her the whole story of how she'd first come to this century, about how she had ended up on the grounds of an abbey where Callum's aunt was living, and how the old woman had gone all bug-eyed when she recognized Callum's sword with the jewel back in its place.

Celeste had so many new questions about the sword and jewel, but they'd just gotten to the top of the castle's steps and when she looked up at the massive doors, she was so blown away by their sheer size and beautiful craftsmanship that all other thoughts left her mind. Then they were crossing the threshold and Maggie was pointing. "Here she is now," she said, as a woman approached. Maggie explained that Calum's aunt had moved back in with them a few months ago. "Aunt Cateline, please." Maggie waved her over to make the introductions.

"Oh, Celeste, my dear. Come let me look at you."

Celeste was surprised to be so known by this lovely woman with a beautiful French accent, but welcomed the coming embrace. It was only when Cateline gave her the once-over, amusement dancing in her eyes, that Celeste realized how out of place she must look here. Yes, she'd worn her favorite yoga pants, top, and jacket.

"You're fine," Maggie chuckled, clearly sensing where Celeste's thoughts had turned. "I'll have Nessa and Rose bring you some of my things to wear, once you get settled." Maggie stopped right there in the grand entrance, a look crossing her face, "Wait, you *are* staying, right?" Celeste looked at Dar, who had been following close behind, and then back to Maggie.

"I think so," Celeste said, nodding. "For a little while at least."

"Aye." Dar nodded. "For a while."

Maggie seemed relieved, and pulled Celeste in for another tight embrace. "I have so much to tell you."

"Me too."

Aunt Cateline took the baby from Callum, and Dar passed the sword to him, saying, "I'll return this to your keeping for now." Callum took it, nodding firmly.

They all followed him into a large room with a humongous fireplace and oversized furnishings. If Celeste remembered correctly from the few historicals she'd read and the movies she'd watched, furniture from this time period was usually smaller.

"This doesn't look like I expected it to," Celeste murmured.

"Callum is quite the craftsman," Maggie put in, as Callum set the sword into some iron hooks affixed to the wall. "All I have to do is sketch it up and add a few explanations and voila, it appears a short time later."

Callum, who had finished putting the sword up, turned around and smiled at Maggie. Celeste saw the look they exchanged, the love so apparent between the two. If what Maggie had written was true—that Callum and Derek shared a soul—they had more than just a karmic connection, and it showed. For a moment, Celeste lost her breath at the realization.

Dar squeezed her hand to get her attention. "You're alright?"

he asked. When she nodded, he turned to Callum. "Where would you like us to stay?"

"Where?" Callum repeated, looking confused. "In your chambers. Upstairs."

"You kept my things there? I assumed..." He trailed off, and Celeste realized he hadn't been sure whether he'd return.

"Dar, this is your home," Maggie and Callum said at the same time.

"*And*," Maggie added, grinning. "Did you say *us*? As in you're sharing a room?"

"Margret," Callum said. "Of course they would share a room. Dar is a man of honor. Surely, he and Celeste have married by now."

Seeing how Dar winced at Callum's words, Celeste held back her laugh. Under his breath, Callum let out what sounded like a swear.

"I better stay out of this," Maggie said, taking a step back.

"Wait, is this because we're sleeping together?" Celeste asked. She'd meant to direct the question just to Maggie, but when Callum raised a brow and Maggie covered her mouth, she realized she'd spoken a bit too loudly.

"Celeste," Dar tried to interject.

"Well, don't blame *him*," Celeste said. "It's my fault. I mean, I pressured him. Like, threw myself at him and basically—"

"Celeste!" they all chimed in, clearly trying to stop her.

"What?" she protested in her own defense. "It's true. And it's only been, like, two days. What if we don't want to get married?"

Up until that point, there'd been an air of amusement

around the whole thing, but based on Dar's expression now, she'd obviously misspoken. Immediately, Celeste sobered.

"Oh. *Do* you want to get married?" she asked, feeling oddly put on the spot.

He stared at her for a long, uncomfortable moment. "I wouldn't have bedded you otherwise," he bit out.

Oh. "Oh."

"Right. *Oh.*" That was all he said, then he turned and left.

CHAPTER 26

SCOTLAND, 1431

Needing a moment to himself, Dar left the Great Hall and headed for the kitchens, feeling as though a cup of Ide's brew was in order. Had Celeste really not thought his intentions were honorable? he wondered. Were *hers*? Deep down, he knew that they were, but her reaction had jarred him. Let her stew on his words a bit longer, as frankly, he was in no mood. He thought she knew him better.

Call him foolish but after witnessing her reunion with Maggie, and how she'd caressed Isla's cheek, all Dar could think about was being wed, of he and Celeste having a babe of their own. He'd envisioned them beginning a family, the start of their legacy together. Between the two of them and their past and recent history, marriage should be of the utmost importance, yet Celeste seemed not to care. Bah.

Dar gave Ide a start when he came upon her in the kitchens, but quickly murmured an apology.

"I'm back," he offered with a sheepish smile.

"Aye, I can see. Timely, too, your favorite happens to be on the table," Ide said, pointing to a pitcher of tea.

It was only when he sat down at the wide wooden table that he realized this was the first time that he felt like he was on solid footing. *Felt it.* Here. In the century from whence he came. It was a rather odd feeling considering the strife he'd gone through this past year.

"I was pondering on a main for super. My decision's now clear."

Dar chucked, aye, he was partial to red meat and Ide knew it. She made an outstanding roast with root vegetables; he couldn't wait for a taste. Then he wondered—and felt badly for doing so—if it would taste as pleasing as what he'd become used to in the future. Of course, the fare Ide provided was better than most. He conceded that it was a matter of apples and oranges, to use a phrase Celeste had taught him. Each was good, merely different. After taking a long pull of the tea Ide had poured for him, he offered thanks and went to settle things with Celeste.

He'd really only needed a few moments to calm down and collect himself. But they were well taken indeed, considering that he and Celeste had now had heated words on more than one occasion. He was halfway down the hall when he saw her rushing his way. When she reached him, he could see that she was close to tears. His heart wrenched at the sight of her anguish.

"I thought you went outside," she said, reaching a hand out to cup his face.

Thinking now he'd acted hastily, he sought to soothe her. "Nay," he comforted, putting his hand atop hers. "I thought it best to take a few moments to compose myself."

Then, he offered her a sip from his glass and she drank, looking up at him the entire time. When she swallowed, hard, tears awash in her eyes, he brushed a finger down her cheek. "I'm sorry," he said, and she threw herself against him. At this, he gathered her close, feeling even worse.

She pulled back a moment later, looking up at him again. "I didn't mean to upset you. I just didn't know."

He put a finger to her lips, and she rolled her eyes, as had become her custom—he had to admit he'd become rather fond of it. "Let's discuss this upstairs," he suggested when he noticed Maggie and Callum peering at them from down the hallway.

Celeste nodded, and Dar led her upstairs, gently guiding her by the elbow. He realized, as they rounded the landing and made their way down the hallway, how desperate he was to be alone with her. He opened his door and stepped aside, allowing her to enter first then watching as she ran her hands along the furniture, the tapestries on the wall, the draperies, and stone windowsills, taking great interest in each. Dar let himself see his quarters through her eyes, and wondered what she made of the space, the furnishings, the things he'd accumulated over time. When she was done, she turned and smiled softly.

"This is really nice, Dar. You lived here?" she asked.

He went to her, brushing the hair from her face, just to touch her. "I've lived with Callum and Maggie since they married. Save for one short trip to Remshire, which happened to be my last."

Her eyes lit up then. "Oh, I would love to see where you grew up."

Dar hesitated. In some ways, he would also love for Celeste to see his boyhood home, but now, knowing the duplicity of his da and Horace, he had mixed feelings. His residence with Callum and Maggie felt almost more like home than Remshire did for him now. It was no longer the ancestral home he'd once taken it for.

"It's best we stick to our plans," he said. Besides, he had a feeling that Celeste's enthusiasm in being without her modern amenities wouldn't last the three days' ride to Remshire.

When she frowned, he rubbed his thumb across her lips. "Nay. I've found my place, and it's with you," he said. "Not just here or in the future, but in the universe." He stared at her a moment, needing again to broach the subject of marriage, but suddenly almost nervous to do so. He'd been shocked at her reaction downstairs, having never thought she'd have been opposed to a union. "I know the subject hasn't arisen before now, but marriage *is* something we must address."

Celeste nodded, and was quiet for a moment. When she spoke, her words were tempered, even. "It's just...usually couples take their time. Years, even."

"These are unusual circumstances, Celeste. And I must tell you, being wed, for me, was always a given. I'm afraid now you haven't a choice."

Celeste balked. "Did you really say that?" she asked hotly, stepping back from him, surprising Dar with her intensity. "Because I happen to *like* choices. In case you've already forgotten, I'm a twenty-first century woman, and there are rights that we've fought hard for and won."

Dar nodded. "Yes. A twenty-first century woman who is now in the fifteenth century. We need to be wed, Celeste." He was beginning to understand Celeste's reaction—that perhaps it wasn't that she *never* wanted to be married to him, but that she just didn't understand how things worked in his time.

She made a face. "Was that a marriage proposal? Romantic."

He chuckled. "I'll try again. Celeste, my love, I wish to spend the rest of our lives together. Under God. Legally. Bound. Forever."

Though he was quite certain she'd say yes, Dar found himself growing nervous as Celeste stared at him intently, scrutinizing his face.

After a moment or two, she nodded, as if a deal had just been made. "I'd like that. All of it. Now, will you show me where the bathroom is?"

Dar chuckled, relief flooding him as tension he hadn't been aware he'd carried released. Celeste was used to making her own decisions. He knew if they'd stayed in the future, they would have gotten there, eventually, but now, being here, he needed to secure their union.

It was her request for the bathroom that had him spinning. It was a simple question, but had launched him headlong into the next challenge at hand. Although Dunhill was more modern than most castles in this era, and he'd forewarned Celeste of the luxuries she'd have to forego, he wasn't sure she'd truly understood how living without modern amenities would work. And with that thought, he realized with a start that he was looking forward to finishing their business and taking her back home—to her home, in her time, with him. He had a feeling, oddly deep and instinctual, that Celeste was not cut out for the fifteenth century.

It wasn't a matter of strength, emotional fortitude, or capability—lord knew she had all of that in spades—but it was so clearly, simply the wrong fit. Celeste was a woman of the future, and nothing would change that. Frankly, Dar didn't *want* to change it. He wanted her exactly as she was. What he was afraid of, he realized now, was that being here too long *would* change her, especially if she started to feel trapped, unable to make her own choices, less like herself. Her reaction to his assertion that they needed to get married would only be the start, Dar knew.

He worried, too, that she would begin to despair from leaving the safety and sanctity of her beloved routine back home. He didn't consider her delicate, but she'd been through much in her young life, and he knew she found comfort in her surroundings and her routine. There would be routine here, of course, but again, it would not be the same. Dar silently reaffirmed his vow to keep her safe from harm, and get her back to her time—with him—as soon as possible once his task was complete.

God help him, he was already second-guessing his decision to bring her here.

AFTER ESCORTING Celeste to Maggie's chambers, Dar went in search of Callum. Alone again for the moment, he realized that not only was he on solid footing—traversing centuries aside— he was filled with confidence, a surety about what he needed to do. Whereas earlier in the kitchens he'd merely been aware of the difference he'd felt, now that difference felt like a strength. There was a bounce in his step, a sense of stability and fortitude, each new and welcome.

He wondered a moment of home and the significance he'd put on the word itself. Mayhap it wasn't the actual *place* that made a home, but the people he shared it with, the connections one made, that fortified one's place in the universe. He'd felt it with Celeste in her era, and he felt it now, here in the fifteenth century, amongst his dearest friends.

The home he'd known his entire life was no more, not without his mother alive. And though he knew he was always welcome at Dunhill, and had spent plenty of time here, this place itself wasn't truly his home either. He did, however, like the cadence he felt in being back. The underlying quiet and calm. It was a welcome respite after his time in the future. He was hopeful this time and place would provide what he needed to really evaluate what mattered to him.

Not finding his friend inside the keep, Dar took to the courtyard, greeting Andrew and Graham and a few others he saw along the way. He was pleased to see the progress they'd made on the place. They'd refurbished so many of the outbuildings on the property, and it was truly a wonder to witness it alive and bursting with action again.

Dar had searched the cobbler, the smithy, and was on his way to the stables when he finally caught sight of Callum walking inside the chapel. Dar noticed new window boxes and two large marble urns by the doors. Nice indeed. Unlike Seagrave, Dunhill didn't have a priest on-site for much of the year, but since they'd restored the small house of worship, Father Michael had begun to visit periodically.

Upon entering, Dar lit a candle, just one, and said a prayer for his mother.

Callum approached and nodded toward the single lit candle, raising a brow in question.

Dar shrugged. "I learned a few things whilst I was gone."

"Such as?" Callum pressed.

Dar filled him in on what Esmerelda had told him about Ethan and his uncle. Then, he broached the subject of Seagrave.

"I have need to speak with Gavin," he said, already thinking of how to next broach the subject of Abersoch, "and I thought we might meet there. And, if Father Michael happens to be in residence, I have need for the priest as well."

Callum gave him a wry smile. "Celeste has changed her mind, then?"

"Funny, Callum." *Not.* "If I remember correctly, your fair Margret didn't jump at the prospect of marriage either."

"Daftness is an affliction of the future," Callum chuckled, clapping him on the back as they headed back outside.

Gods how he'd missed this place, Dar realized, taking it all in. Aye, he'd enjoyed facets of the twenty-first century hamlet he'd summered in, but this, *here*, this was his hamlet. He smiled as they approached the stables, and his heart skipped a beat at the prospect of reuniting with his steed, of riding the expansive grounds—the freedom and power in it.

This was the one building that had needed no repair when

Dar came to live here last year. In fact, it rivaled those of modern times, large and airy with a vaulted ceiling and polished wood beams. In a word, it was magnificent, and as he stood there, breathing in the welcoming scent of fresh hay, he heard a familiar whinny, and his heart swelled that his horse sensed his presence. Dar quickened his pace until he reached his stall.

"Hello, my friend," Dar said, stroking his snout. "I can see you've been well cared for." He received a nicker in return, a sound saved for mates, or in this case, a sign of a deep abiding bond.

"We've taken turns riding him," Callum said, "but I've a feeling he's been waiting for you."

Indeed. After a few more nudges and sighs, Dar moved quickly to saddle his steed. He and Callum spent most of the afternoon riding the land, and speaking of Dar's time in the future. At one point, Callum said, "Lachlan's been out here every week." He shook his head. "I told him you were on a family errand for Margret, but I'll say this: that man won't give up. He's determined to make things right. He wants you with him, Dar."

Dar gave a curt nod. Things were far different now than when he'd left. Mostly, within himself, which affected how he took in everything and everyone around him. He was no longer a man adrift, a man without purpose. In fact, it seemed Madame Fate had turned that around entirely and given him purpose across *two* expanses. And, an errand to see it to fruition.

"Well, if history is correct," he said, referring back to what he'd already told Callum, "my father and I have a castle to build. At the least one we'll start together."

"I think that would please him. And 'tis an endeavor you're both well-suited for."

Dar looked up at the sky, gaging the time as the sun began its descent.

"We'd best get back," he said, pulling his horse around. "I'd like to check on Celeste."

CHAPTER 27

SCOTLAND, 1431

Celeste sat on the hearth in her chamber, which was more of a large apartment comprised of three connected rooms, with a private latrine built into the outside wall. She could tell Dar was worried she wouldn't be able to handle living without modern-day conveniences, but it wasn't that bad; besides, it was temporary, and a small price to pay to stay with Dar and be reunited with Maggie too.

Celeste had spent the entire afternoon with her, and it was absolutely glorious. Well, aside from one small oversight which had led her to where she was now—in front of the fire, dabbing a thick ointment on her hives, a result from an allergy she had to wool. It didn't reverse-skip a generation or thirty-five like she'd hoped. She was just as allergic in the fifteenth century as she was back home in the twenty first.

But, after a shaky and somewhat rocky start to the day, the tide had finally turned, and before she knew it, it felt like old times with Maggie. Almost like they were back at home, as inseparable as ever—only now they had to catch up on everything they'd missed.

More than that, they had both moved past the desperation and dread they'd been stuck in the last time they were together, and now it was only excitement that spurred them forward. Almost like Madame Fate had given them a clean slate, as if to say, *you've earned a bit of happiness.*

Maggie had shown her all around the keep, another name for their home, so proud of the work she and Callum had put into refurbishing things. It seemed that after Callum lost his wife a few years ago, things had fallen into disrepair. Celeste had a peculiar experience when Maggie told her what happened; though Callum was all but a stranger to her, the pain she felt for him seared through her. If not for Maggie's presence, Celeste would have found a place to sit and weep, her heart hurt for him that badly.

SHE WAS THINKING about how well-suited Maggie and Callum were for each other, how lucky they were to find each other, with a little help from some good magic, when she heard the knock on her bedroom door and hurried to open it. "You don't have to knock," she said, thinking it was Maggie. When she pulled the door open and saw that it was Dar, she grinned. "Oh, well, you especially don't have to knock. These are your rooms too."

Dar shrugged. "I hoped to give you a bit of autonomy."

She was glad to see him, but still rolled her eyes. "This, from

Mr. If-I-bed-you-I-must-wed-you." His eyes danced a moment before narrowing in concern when they honed in on the welts atop her shoulders and arms. "What's this?"

"Ugh. I have an allergy to wool, and totally didn't think about it when Maggie brought me some things to wear. I was mostly just excited to try on some fifteenth-century clothes," she admitted with a sigh. "Maggie is bringing more lotion and says that someone named Nessa will make me a shift out of a less offending fabric."

"Let me," he offered, reaching for the small pot and cloth she'd been using.

"I just need a hug, please," Celeste said, reaching out to stop his hand.

She got more than that. Dar gripped the hand she'd put out, picked her up, and carried her to their bed.

"Ah, I see. Our bed's been stripped of all offending fibers, too, and replaced with linens fit for a queen," he said, laying her down on the silk sheets.

When they sunk down, Celeste had to admit she was surprised at how soft and plush the bedding was in this era—the mattress especially. Thank goodness she wasn't allergic to down.

"Well, there is that, I suppose." She rubbed her face into his neck, inhaling deeply. "Why do you smell so good? You've been riding all day. And you're in nice clothes too."

Dar smiled. "Seeing how late it was, Callum and I stopped at the stream to wash before supper. I couldn't come back to you smelling of sweat and horses." His nose pressed into her hair. "You smell nice, too, lass."

Celeste laughed. "Yeah, well in my case, after I tried on one of Maggie's dresses and broke out into hives, Rose—everyone here is so nice, by the way—Rose ordered a warm bath with salts of some kind. I'm ashamed to tell you, I cried at how kind everyone was being. I'm usually a bit tougher than that."

He tsked and pressed his lips to her temple. "Even the toughest of us crumble when being taken care of—*especially* when we know we're in good company."

Celeste nodded, remembering how good it had felt to have someone else take over, to not have to make any decisions or wonder what to do next. After being isolated for so long, doing virtually everything herself, she was now surrounded by loved ones and family again—some were new family, but their care was genuine.

She took a deep breath, letting herself sink farther into the mattress. "That's true. It really was so nice how they fussed and fawned, and even washed my hair. Maggie was brushing it—we were sitting over there by the fireplace, helping it to dry—but then Isla started to fuss and she left to tend to her."

Dar reached out and ran his fingers through Celeste's still-damp hair. "Why don't I finish applying this balm to your shoulders and then help you dry your hair."

Celeste made a pouting face, raising her eyebrows. "You'd brush my hair… by the fire?"

Dar chuckled. "I can think of nothing I'd like more."

"You're just worried I'll back out of our upcoming nuptials so you're being *extra* attentive."

"I hadn't given it a second thought. Should I?"

She couldn't keep up the ruse and smiled. "Nay. Not even for a second. I love you, Dar."

A sound rumbled deep in his chest, as he gave her a gentle squeeze. "I love you, too, sweet. Come, let's see to your hair." He re-tied the belt of her robe, and looked her over. "This is nice too."

Celeste made a face. "I would have used yours, but they snatched it from my hands the second it was clear that the wool was the culprit."

He chuckled. "They were just seeing to your fair, delicate skin."

"I know, I just hate to be such a bother."

"Trust me, I've no doubt they love doting on you."

Knowing that was probably true, but having a hard time accepting it, Celeste followed Dar to the hearth where they sat down together. He picked up the brush, using long strokes and rubbing the strands between his fingers as the fire crackled and dried it. After a few moments, a knock rapped on the door again and Celeste called out, "Come in," at the same time Dar said, "Enter."

It was Maggie back with Isla nestled in her arms, Nessa just steps behind her.

"We come bearing a new shift and dress," Maggie said, motioning to the bundle in Nessa's arms. "And since *you're* ready for dinner," she said, taking note of Dar's more formal trousers, shirt, and boots, "why don't you go down and we'll join you in a few minutes."

Dar glanced to Celeste first, a silent ask.

She smiled and nodded. "Go. I'm okay."

He kissed her forehead and left her in Maggie and Nessa's care.

"Is it helping?" Maggie asked, gesturing to the lotion as Celeste stood and began to change into the new clothes.

"It doesn't itch or burn anymore, so yes." Nessa helped her into the shift and Celeste sighed as the soft, cool fabric glided across her skin. "Oh, this is divine."

"Gwen sent the fabric a few months ago. I didn't want to waste it on maternity clothes."

Celeste turned to her friend. "Oh, Maggie, I don't want to take this from you."

"Are you kidding? This makes me happier than you'll ever know." She stood back, smiling as Nessa adjusted the dress that slipped over the shift. "So pretty," she said, tearing up for probably the millionth time that afternoon. Celeste followed suit—it had been such an emotional day for everyone.

Maggie laughed, wiping her tears. "Would you look at us? Crying over a stupid dress! Come on, let's go to dinner. Ide made Dar's favorite. I promise you'll love it."

Celeste laughed, too, and ran her hands over the bodice of her new dress as Nessa fastened the back. It felt like playing dress-up, only ten times better because it was real.

Once the dress was done up fully, Nessa took Isla and Celeste and Maggie walked arm in arm downstairs. When they entered the dining hall, Celeste was taken with how pretty it was. Maggie had given her a tour earlier, but that was in the afternoon. Now candelabras and wall sconces lit the room, casting a warm glow across the long buffet and table that looked to seat eight or ten. There was a much larger table in the

Great Hall, but Maggie had explained that they liked to eat here in a more intimate setting.

Dar and Callum stood as they entered, each looking quite handsome in their semi-formals and the low candlelight. Celeste loved the way their black Hessian boots were polished to a shine and how the loose fit of their ivory-colored shirts tucked into trim-fitting trousers. The men pulled out their chairs, covered in fabric and filled nicely, Celeste noticed as she sat, before laying a linen square on their laps. *Nice.*

Callum was at the head of the table, Maggie to his left, and Aunt Cateline next to her. Celeste was to Callum's right, with Dar beside her. Moments later, a server came and poured wine, smiling broadly at Maggie, as if he were thrilled to see her so happy. Of course, Maggie would charm everyone, including the staff of her home—Celeste would expect nothing less.

Accepting a glass of wine, Celeste marveled over how well-appointed the table was. She had never been one to fawn over glasses or platters or anything of the sort, but it was all so stunning, she couldn't help it.

"These are beautiful," she admired, running her hand along the colored goblet.

"These are Margret's favorite," Callum said, eyes on his wife, filled with adoration.

"You know that?" Maggie seemed surprised.

"Aye, my love—my good humor rests on your happiness."

Right then and there, Celeste's heart turned over. Callum's sincerity was plain to see, as was the depth of their connection. He was the kind of man Maggie not only deserved, but one who suited her, like Derek had. Her brother—like Callum—was never mushy or over the top, but the deep love he'd had for Maggie was always clear. The formality of Callum's language made it all sound much grander, but really, it was the same as when Derek had grinned and told Maggie that he always made sure to wear her favorite shirt of his—the one she'd bought him for their first Christmas together—whenever she'd had a bad day.

"These glasses were my mother's favorites as well," Callum said, turning the green goblet around in his hand.

Celeste listened as Callum spoke of his family's history, Aunt Cateline interjecting occasionally to correct or add to his memory. Callum had clearly had a close relationship with his mother and father, and his aunt, too—one he obviously valued deeply. Again, so like Derek.

It was odd, really—at first Celeste had thought that she was only imagining her feeling of kinship with Callum, that maybe she was being swayed by Maggie revealing that he shared a soul with Derek. Celeste truly did believe such a thing was possible —she'd read a book on reincarnation once that had blown her mind—but the idea that one could actually *experience* that kind of karmic connection, the connection of a soul in real time, seemed as unlikely as, well, time travel.

But now, with each passing story and time spent in his presence, she felt it. Callum wasn't Derek, not exactly, but something in his being connected with her in a way that felt as real as anything she'd experienced before. And, sure, it might still be her imagination, might be an effect of this make-believe-esque setting, but after virtually being handed a family on a platter, she wasn't about to put her hand up and say no thank you.

Once their initial chatter died down, Ide came in, followed by others laden with serving dishes. Celeste couldn't believe how good it all smelled. She hadn't been sure what to expect, but it hadn't been this. A large tureen—as beautiful as the rest of the serving ware—filled with roasted meat and root vegetables was placed in the center of the table, and matching deep bowls filled with accompaniments surrounded it, including a thick crusty bread and fresh butter.

"A toast," Callum announced, once everything had been laid down. "To family. Old and new. Our table is full tonight, as is my heart."

Hear, hear! resounded around the table, and the meal that followed was delicious. At one point, Celeste noticed that Dar was watching her intently, eyes gleaming with excitement, eager to see her reaction to his favorite foods. Whenever she wasn't sampling fast enough, he'd send a filled fork her way. She realized then, with her mouth full of buttery roasted potato, that although Dar had adapted so well to the future, something about his being here had changed the him she'd grown to know. He seemed so at home, so comfortable in his own skin in a way she hadn't seen before.

They stayed at the table for some time, laughing and talking, just happy to be together. Before she was put down for the night, Isla made the rounds as well, and Celeste held her for the first time. As she looked down at her precious face and felt the solidity of her weight, Celeste had a flash of what it would be like to have a baby of her own. With Dar. She glanced his way, and from the look on his face, she could tell he was thinking the same.

They finally retired, all walking through the long hallway and up the stairs together, saying their goodnights first to Callum and Maggie and then Aunt Cateline when they passed her room. Once inside their rooms, Dar pulled her back against him, nuzzling her neck.

"You're feeling alright?" he whispered against her skin.

"Yes, my lord, I'm feeling quite well," she teased, a bit light-headed from the rich food and two glasses of wine. That sound she loved rumbled in his chest. "Take me to bed, please."

"Should I draw you a bath first?" he murmured.

"Good lord, no. It took long enough to fill the tub with tepid water earlier. I can only imagine the time it would take to fill it with hot."

Dar chuckled. "Not so long, there's a pump, and the fireplace is big enough in here to heat it rather quickly instead of bringing it up from belowstairs."

"Well, you'll have to show me where you and Callum wash in the stream and we'll save the hot bath for once a day."

"Never."

She laughed. "What do you mean, never?"

He turned her, lifting her chin. "No man may look upon your fairness but I."

"Okay, caveman," she said, rolling her eyes. Not that she wanted other men to see her, either, but sometimes his overly old-fashioned way of speaking just made her laugh.

"'Tis no boast. I think I might kill them, Celeste," he said, seeming suddenly deadly serious.

It struck her then, their fundamental differences, each products of their own times. And while Dar had seemed so amiable and easygoing with her in the future, natural even, they weren't there anymore. *This* was who Dar was, at his core. His possessiveness and authority shone clearly through in this environment, and there was a marked change in his eyes that sent a shiver down her spine. Not in a bad way, even though it gave her pause. Celeste knew she loved him no matter, she'd just recognized in this moment exactly who she'd gotten into bed with—and who she realized she was willing to share her bed with forever.

He kissed her then, and though he was gentle and coaxing, there was a harder edge to him that she'd never felt before. After carrying her to their bed, he removed her dress and shift, brushing his fingers lightly over her hives. "We'll reapply more salve later," he said, with a grin.

She nodded, then tugged on his shirt, feeling a need for him —*now*. She helped as he pulled it off, laying an opened-mouth kiss on his chest. That rumbling sounded at her touch, the noise cutting straight to her center. Dar excited her in ways she hadn't been aware existed. Now, just the thought of him touching her, making love to her with his hands, his mouth, his body, sent her nerve endings on high alert. She blushed, looking up at him as he smiled knowingly.

"Aye, I feel it too," he said.

He placed her on the bed, and she lay on her side, watching as he took off his boots and trousers. Then he was next to her, pulling her close, and all thought fled. She was overcome with emotions and sensations as Dar kissed her lips, playing with her body as his fingers worked their magic on her. She felt herself coil as he brought her to the edge, and he leaned back to watch as she tipped over. Then he entered her with care and made love to her slowly, gently, poignantly.

They washed by the fire afterward, using the basin of warm water on the hearth and the soft linen squares that lay beside it. Celeste was grateful to find the crude-looking toothbrushes in their bathing chamber as well. Then Dar dotted more balm on her welts and helped her into the nightgown Nessa had left for her.

"Ready for bed, love?"

She was more than ready. It had been an eventful and emotional day. As much as she loved seeing Maggie and meeting Callum and Isla, Celeste had to admit she, already missed home. The safety of its familiarity. Of her things. Of knowing what to do and where everything was. Really, that was all she'd had these last few years; her surroundings and routine had become her norm, her haven. Now, she'd been thrust into a new world, and even though she was encircled by people who cared for her, something nagged just beneath the surface, a sensation, almost like an omen. Too tired to address it now, Celeste pushed the feeling aside as Dar pulled her close, kissing the top of her head. Then, she fell into a blissfully deep sleep.

CHAPTER 28

SCOTLAND, 1431

It was mid-morning when Dar reentered the castle. He'd been out since dawn, enjoying his old familiar grounds, the scent of the air, and the sight of lands he'd loved since he was a boy. It all left him feeling fresh, alive, and emboldened.

If not for Celeste, he was sure he'd be halfway to Seagrave by now, but he worried over leaving her alone so soon after their arrival, before she'd had a chance to truly settle in. Instead, he'd sent word to both Greylen and Gavin, requesting that the three meet at Seagrave, which lay between Gavin's keep and Dunhill, in a week's time. He'd suggested meeting at Dunhill, too, for Celeste's sake, but wasn't confident the other two would be able to accommodate his request on such short notice.

Dusting off his boots, Dar caught sight of Celeste and Maggie sitting in the great room, Celeste holding Isla, and Maggie playing her game on the floor before the fireplace. The women were laughing, bright with smiles and red in the cheek. It was a good look on them both. Callum appeared from his study and caught Dar's eye as he walked down the long hallway to meet him. They glanced at their women and shared a smile, still standing just outside the room.

"Prepare yourself, my friend," Callum warned. "This is usually the day and time Lachlan pays a visit."

Dar felt his chest catch for a second, unsure how it would feel to see the man, now that he'd had time to adjust to everything he'd learned since their last meeting. "Noted," he said, steeling his nerves.

The women noticed them then and waved them in.

"We missed you at breakfast," Maggie said as Callum bent to kiss her.

Dar cupped Celeste's face and whispered, "I'm sorry I wasn't there when you awoke."

"You were the first time," she whispered back, a mischievous grin on her face.

Aye, that he had been. He'd pulled her close sometime before dawn, just to hold her, rub his lips across her forehead and temple. She'd sighed and done the same, which in turn led to a bit more kissing and holding. The rest, as they said in the future, was history.

He grinned and kissed her now, taken again at the sight of her holding Isla.

"Your hives?"

"Better. Almost gone. That lotion really helped."

"Good," he said, recalling how Lady Madelyn had always

had a way with ointments and healing. With Gwen's added expertise, he was sure it was much improved.

Maggie reached for Isla then, and Callum held out a pouch he must have been holding, hidden in his palm. "For you," he said to Celeste.

"Really? For me?" She smiled at him, a bit bashfully, as she opened the drawstring sack. "Oh! Jacks!" she breathed, tipping out the assortment into her palm.

Celeste had told him how she and Maggie had often played the game together on quiet evenings, so he knew she'd value the gift.

Callum smiled. "I thought you might like your own. I have a few spare sets now."

Celeste beamed, clasping the set in her hands. "Thank you, Callum. I'll treasure them always."

Callum nodded, and Dar noticed that he was blushing a bit under the praise, which he tried to hide by busying himself with the babe. Dar felt a rush of warmth toward his old friend. If Callum and Derek truly did, somehow, share a soul, then he was glad for Celeste to have a semblance of a brotherly relationship in her life again.

Just then, there came a ruckus at the front doors, followed by Lachlan's booming voice. "Where is he?"

Lachlan didn't wait for an invitation and stepped into the room, flanked by his men as Dar pushed Celeste behind him and Callum stood in front of Maggie.

If Lachlan took insult to their posturing, he didn't let it show, and instead looked Dar dead in the eye. "Darach Grifud MacKenna," he said, a bit of exasperation in his tone. "Finally."

Dar winced as the MacKenna name crossed his lips, reminded again of Horace and Ethan's plot. This was the first he'd heard it spoken aloud since he'd learned the truth. To his credit, though, Lachlan let it flow naturally. Dar admired him even more now for the effort.

Dar nodded. "I was told recently that I'm a MacTavish through and through."

"Och, son, that you are. If not for you and Ella bearing the MacKenna name, I'd have razed what's left of them to the ground—and Remshire, too—when they spurned you."

In Dar's estimation, this was another mark of profound regard from Lachlan. Deference to his mother and respect to the name that she'd carried. Dar was startled from his thoughts by Celeste walking toward Lachlan, something held in her outstretched hand. Seeing what it was, Dar's chest tightened. He'd been so lost in his thoughts that he hadn't realized Celeste had reached into his pocket and retrieved his medallion. It was one of the few things that they'd taken with them from the future. He was glad she'd chosen the medallion and not his amethyst, unsure how Lachlan or the others might react to something of the sort.

"Did you make this?" she asked Lachlan, holding it up for him to see.

Lachlan raised a brow, but reached out and took it, sighing deeply and turning it over in his hands. He rubbed the crest of the griffin and then breathed the words *blood of my blood* etched on the other side, caressing it as one would expect of a prized possession.

"Who are ye, lass?" he asked softly.

Dar answered for her. "This is Celeste Lowell. She is to be my wife."

"Ah, a Lowell. Of wolves." He looked at Callum. "Kin?"

"Aye," Callum said instantly, claiming their connection.

Dar noticed Celeste's smile at the acknowledgment.

Lachlan nodded in Callum's direction then gave Celeste his full attention. "Aye, Celeste," he said with all the warmth one bestows on a loved one. "I made this for Darach. I didn't know his name then, but I knew who he was—my future son, whose arrival I would celebrate for the gift it truly was. I haven't seen it since the night Ella told me that Ethan was found alive. I knew I had to let her go then, but I wanted our son—" he paused then and said, a little softer, "You see, I knew he would be a boy and I wanted him to know his worth, no matter his birthplace."

Listening to Lachlan speak, Dar was overcome with emotion. He'd never known any of this, his mother had been so weak at her end, unable to say much at all by the time she'd called for Lachlan. He realized now he'd been harboring ill will toward someone who'd only ever wanted him to thrive. If only he'd been able to lay aside a fraction of his anger, he might have found himself in different circumstances.

When Lachlan started to hand the medallion back to Celeste, Dar noticed his eyes narrow and he gently grasped her wrist, carefully examining the faint marks still visible from her hives.

"You have a salve for this?" he asked. "If not, I have a fresh pot in my bag from my visit to Seagrave."

Celeste blushed at his care. "I'm using it. Thank you," she

said, finishing with a curtsey, which was unnecessary, but, he supposed, endearing.

"We don't curtsey," Dar said, softly, trying not to roll his eyes, noting, too, that Lachlan still had the medallion in his hand.

"Maggie does," she said a bit defensively.

"Maggie lived with the sisters for nigh on two years."

"Well, I think it's nice," she said, straightening her shoulders. "Polite even. Would you like me to be rude instead?"

He tried not to chuckle but failed. Pressing his finger to her lips, he started, "I wish..." then stopped, realizing so many things as he stood there on what felt like newly hallowed ground. On the cusp of a silent thanks to Lachlan for his words but a moment ago, he stepped closer and said, for her alone, "I wish for you everything good, I wish for your happiness and your health, and that we are blessed by God forever."

He obviously hadn't been quiet enough, because Lachlan asked, "When's the wedding?"

Dar kept his eyes on Celeste, waiting for her assent. When she nodded, he grinned, then turned back to Lachlan. "Now, if you have you a priest with you?"

"Give me two days, mayhap three, depending on how long it takes Father Michael to get ready. He didn't seem to have pressing business elsewhere so I can't imagine a further delay."

Dar ran his fingers down the side of Celeste's face. "And so it shall be."

Celeste's eyes sparkled, and in them, Dar saw that this pleased her, too, thank goodness.

She turned to Lachlan. "You'll be there? Yes?" she pressed.

"Aye. I would meet your parents, lass."

At this Celeste faltered, but only for a moment. "My parents are gone, sir."

Lachlan nodded, understanding filling his expression, and Dar wondered how he'd ever questioned this man's true intentions. "Then I will fill their void," he vowed.

Celeste's eyes flooded with tears as she bowed her head. She glanced at Dar afterward, a look that clearly said *and you ever doubted this man?* He wanted to reply, to tell her that he'd already come to the same conclusion himself, but knew he'd have to save that for later, for when they were truly alone.

"Darach," Lachlan said, inclining his head. "I will assume you won't disappear on me again?"

"You have my word," Dar promised, meaning it as much as he'd ever meant anything.

Sensing that Lachlan held back out of deference, Dar initiated a warmer farewell and extended his hand. Once the gesture was given, Lachlan didn't hesitate, and somehow the simple handshake he'd first offered turned into a brief but meaningful embrace. Afterward, they stared at each other a long moment, each misty-eyed, then Lachlan and his men bowed their heads and headed for the doors.

Lachlan turned a moment later, and walked back to him, placing the medallion in his hand. "This is yours, son."

Aye, indeed. Dar accepted the medallion with a quiet, "Thank you," adding a silent *father*—a word he finally meant, but wasn't yet ready to say aloud.

CHAPTER 29

SCOTLAND, 1431

A few days later, Celeste was looking out the window in her chamber, watching Dar as he headed for the stables when Callum trotted up behind him and clapped him on the shoulder. Dar whirled around, his face alight, and they exchanged words, smiling and laughing.

It reminded her of boys back in high school. The popular ones at least, happy and confident, ready to embrace the day. She loved seeing Dar so carefree and boyish, even. It seemed silly to think of him like that, given his normal demeanor, but that's exactly what it was. He was clearly in his element here—powerful and assured, but at ease, too, with his lifelong friends and now his father.

Lachlan had returned just that morning, and as promised, with a priest in tow. Father Michael, she found, was friendly and kind, and had, thank goodness, seemed to have come willingly. If he had not, Celeste was sure Lachlan, based on what she'd seen of him, would have dragged him otherwise, but the mood would have been different.

Celeste had been so excited to see Dar standing with his father, warm smiles between them, that she'd run up to hug Lachlan in greeting. She wasn't sure why she did it, just that she couldn't help it—there was something about him that screamed "dad," and when he kissed the top of her head and said, "Morning, piseag," she didn't even care that he'd called her what she assumed meant a little piglet. When Dar corrected her later, and told her that *piseag* meant *kitten*, her smile almost broke her face.

Lachlan had also brought news that Dar's brethren, Greylen and Gavin, the men he'd told her about, would arrive with their wives and children before supper. At this, Celeste's happiness only grew. It seemed Dar needn't have worried about the allegiance of his brethren, who were quick to come to his aid. It did help that Gavin and his wife, Isabelle, were already in residence at Seagrave, and as it was only a bit more than a day's ride, Lachlan said that they were all looking forward to seeing the new baby, meeting Celeste, and attending the nuptials. Apparently, once a marriage was decided by one of these men, the ceremony was close behind.

With all the excitement, Celeste's previous reservations felt faraway and unnecessary. She *did* love Dar and truly had already envisioned their future together many, many times. In her heart she knew there was no one else for her out there—in this or any century—so why *not* marry sooner rather than later?

Besides, she was with Maggie again, which, in a way, made Dunhill feel like home. Not *her home*, but the *feeling* of home, albeit with a sprinkle of fantasy. Her best friend and constant companion was once again always at her side, or checking on her, or just available and nearby. And of course, there was Callum, who Celeste found herself constantly curious about, wanting to know what he was up to at all times. Fittingly, it reminded her how she used to follow Derek around just to not be left out.

Twice now she'd come upon him as he went this way or that, and on each occasion, he'd waved her along like she belonged there. The first time he was going to a building where they housed falcons and hawks. Who knew what an endeavor that was! She was fascinated by it, though, and Callum quickly began imparting her with his knowledge, whistling and bird-calling to ensure the animals did his bidding. After prompting her a few times to follow along, and Celeste demurring, he'd finally said, "You don't know how to whistle?"

Embarrassed, Celeste had blushed and shaken her head.

He'd given a curt nod and said, "Falconry aside, 'tis important you have a way to communicate should you get lost or find yourself in trouble." Then he'd devoted a fair chunk of time to just that. It reminded her of how Derek had made sure she knew the basics, and then some, of self-defense.

And then earlier today, when she'd been tasked with going along with him to gather some supplies that had been packed away just last year, Celeste had practically skipped behind him to a room they used for storage. She'd stood there, awed at the rows of wooden chests, stacked up as far as the eye could see, some more ornate than others.

"Oh, Callum," she'd said, brushing her hands along the beautiful wooden chests as he took a few down, "these are stunning. You made them, didn't you?"

He'd nodded and smiled, then opened a few up before digging around and retrieving a beautiful string instrument. It was triangular in shape and small enough to be held upon one's lap.

"My mother's psaltery," he'd said, extending it to her. "I have heard about your gift of music and would like you to have it."

Her bottom lip had wobbled and she'd tried so hard not to cry, but a few tears had spilled anyway. At least Callum didn't seem bothered by them. Instead, he had smiled, hugged her, then quickly got busy retrieving the things they were supposed to be getting in the first place.

So, being with Maggie again, coming to know Callum, being doted on by Aunt Cateline (who insisted on everyone calling her Aunt) and the staff, Celeste had felt this new sense of home. One she was deeply enjoying. And she was elated to hear about Greylen and Gavin's arrival, knowing how much it meant to Dar that his friends had come calling at once.

At once with the news of their arrival, Dunhill had been thrown into a frenzy of preparation. While the inside of the castle always seemed to sparkle, Celeste had been helping Maggie and the girls freshen up the guest quarters ahead of everyone's arrival, leaving piles of extra linens and fresh flowers. They'd need at least three rooms abovestairs, as they said, and chambers with enough space to accommodate babies and children. Lachlan had offered to bed outside with his men, but Callum had put his foot down. "We've plenty of room," he'd said, "and honestly, I can't think of a better way to test Dunhill's resilience than seeing her run at full force again. A true testament."

Thank goodness they'd started preparing when they had, because no sooner had they closed the last chamber door and heaved a celebratory sigh of relief did they hear riders approaching in the courtyard.

"They're here!" Maggie said, grabbing Celeste's hands, filled with excitement. "I can't wait for you to meet everyone."

Eyes wide, Celeste reminded her, "We're a mess, Maggie." Seriously, they'd been going at it most of the afternoon. To make her point, Celeste reached out and tried to tame Maggie's curls, brushing them back from her face.

"You look perfect," Maggie said, but straightened Celeste's neckline with a giggle anyway. "Besides, they've been traveling since yesterday, so we'll be no more disheveled than them."

While Celeste *was* excited to meet more people, she was nervous too. These were Dar's childhood friends and their families. She wanted to make a good impression on them, and felt most stressed about meeting Gwen, who was Maggie's closest friend here. Of course Maggie had leapt back centuries in time and managed to find herself a husband and a new best friend—she was just magnetic like that—and of course, Celeste knew that this didn't mean that Celeste meant any less to her, but still. She suddenly felt insecure.

But that wouldn't serve her, would it? *Come on, Celeste,* she chided herself. *Where is your newfound confidence?* Taking a deep breath, Celeste trotted after Maggie toward the front doors, then followed her as she dashed outside. For a second Celeste's heart sank—had Maggie forgotten about her? But the fear only lasted a moment, because Maggie quickly realized she'd left Celeste behind and whirled around, leapt back up the steps to grab her, all but dragging her down them again.

Introductions happened in a whirlwind. Somehow, in the flurry of warm welcomes and hugs and hellos, Celeste and Maggie ended up with a baby apiece as the men saw to their horses and Gwen and Isabelle helped their older children.

Gwen and Isabelle were quick with questions about the wedding and baby Isla as they piled inside and up to their rooms. If there was ever a day to have had hot running water, today would have been it—Celeste was sure she smelled at best of dust, but it was probably more likely that she'd sweated through her new shift and dress. Thankfully, the staff was well prepared, and, after leaving Gwen and Isabelle in their respective rooms, Celeste made haste for her own hot bath.

Now, clean and refreshed, Celeste turned her focus from her swirling thoughts to the men—Greylen and Gavin had just caught up to Dar and Callum—down on the grounds. Part of her wondered whether she would be able to tear Dar away from this. She was sure he would come with her—it was their plan, after all, and he was a man of his word—but she wasn't sure how he would feel about it when the time came.

Deciding it was a thought for another day—for after the wedding, after the brethren departed—she sighed wistfully and settled into watching the happy scene.

A few moments later, she was startled by a loud rap on her door, and almost tripped over her dress as she hurried toward it, then bumped her head as she pulled it open.

"I knocked a few times," Maggie said, giving her a concerned look. "Are you okay?"

Celeste winced, but nodded. "I was totally lost in my thoughts, then fell into the door as I was opening it."

"Of course you did," Maggie said, laughing and shaking her head. Celeste had also gotten a huge splinter stuck in her foot last night, so her injuring herself around the keep seemed to be a thing now. "Let me look."

Feeling sheepish, Celeste pulled her hand back, and drew a sharp intake of breath at the pain—the pressure had been helping.

"Oh dear," Maggie exclaimed, as her eyes darted to her face, "that left a mark."

Celeste blushed, then gestured toward the window. "Yeah, I was busy ogling."

Maggie grinned. "I get it. I can't tell you how many times I stared out of my window when I first got here, both shocked and delighted." Maggie looked at her face again. "Well, Gwen's here now, and she might have something we can use to conceal it. In any case, hopefully it won't get worse. But let's get something on it right now to try to keep the swelling down."

THE BRUISE WAS the first thing Dar noticed at supper, just after he strode into the great room—tonight's supper venue, a step up from the smaller dining room—with Callum, Greylen, and Gavin. All four of them had dressed for dinner, but their hair was still damp from what Celeste assumed was their dip in the stream. It was both a sign of how busy they were, and how considerate they still were, managing to be clean and dressed for dinner. She was disappointed Lachlan wasn't with them, but he'd left in the late afternoon to attend to some unnamed business, with plans to return later that night or early in the morning.

When Dar's eyes settled on her, his handsome face marred at once with a frown. He was all over her a second later, inspecting. Embarrassed by his thorough and obvious care, she wrapped her arms around his neck, and leaned up to brush her lips to his ear.

"Please," she whispered. That seemed to get his attention, and he pulled her into an embrace, murmuring an apology. He squeezed her tightly, concern still on his face. "I'm okay, I swear."

He nodded, but still said, "At this rate, you won't make the end of the year."

"Dar!"

He pulled back, gently outlining the bruise. Okay, so it ran from the top of her temple down to the outside corner of her eye. A solid door in the fifteenth century was apparently way different than those in her time. Celeste guessed it was true what they said: they sure don't make them like they used to.

"Don't you like my dress?" she asked to distract him. Nessa had made her another beautiful dress, one Celeste liked even more than the first.

Grey snorted, and Callum coughed on a sip of his drink. Dar didn't blink, just crossed his arms over his chest. "I'll remind you, we're not the daft ones," he said, though Celeste noticed that he eyed her dress approvingly anyway.

Heaving an exasperated sigh, Celeste turned to join Gwen, Isabell, and Maggie, grinning when she felt Dar's hands on her shoulders, pulling her back against his chest.

"You look beautiful, Celeste. You always look beautiful."

"She has a bruise the size of an egg on the left side of her face," Greylen interjected.

"We know," the women chorused, rolling their eyes, all three of them.

"Well, don't pretend that *we* don't," Greylen said, and Celeste giggled. She'd only just met him, but she liked his sense of humor.

"I think we should have a drink and celebrate," Celeste said cheerily, hoping to leave the subject behind.

"You trained her fast," Grey said dryly, looking at his wife.

"Well, it's not like we have *that* much to do," Gwen said, good-natured sarcasm dripping from her words. Gwen had just told her and Maggie about the last two days traveling by carriage with two children, and Celeste was exhausted from the retelling alone.

There was a palpable shift, then and everyone busied themselves with the meal. The men held out their chairs, and Nessa, Albert, and Rose, served one of the most superb dinners Celeste had ever had. Of course, the pomp and circumstance might have had something to do with it, but the meal was divine—perhaps even more so than the roast a few nights before.

It was like some formal affair right out of a storybook, but it was real and she was living it. As they ate (and Celeste noted the modern touches, which Maggie had told her earlier were due to her and Gwen's influence), Aunt Cateline regaled them with stories of Greylen and Callum's parents in their youth. When she started telling a story about Lachlan and Ella, Dar coughed on the wine he'd just sipped.

"You never mentioned them before," he said, gathering himself.

Cateline blushed. "Darach, until recently, the story of your mother and father was known and discussed between only a very few."

"So you all knew each other," he said slowly.

"Oh, aye, we did. Madelyn and Allister were well married by the time Fergus brought Isabeau and I along, but we quickly became close friends. It was only a year or two after Isabeau paid the enchantress with the sapphire that Ella and Lachlan grew smitten with each other. They loved one another very much."

Celeste squeezed Dar's hand beneath the table, and he shared a look with her, one filled with so many emotions she couldn't name them all. Still, it was all coming together for him, and she couldn't have been happier.

Dar cleared his throat and turned back to the older woman. "I was told Ethan used black magic," he said, his voice even.

Aunt Cateline nodded sagely. "I'm not surprised. Though if any of the MacKenna were to traipse that line, I would suspect Horace to be at the helm. He's a spiteful man, always was. He'd have filled Ethan's head with lies or half-truths, to be sure."

There was a grave silence as everyone around the table allowed Dar to absorb this information. After a moment or two, Dar gave a sharp nod and turned back to his plate, indicating that the subject was done for the moment.

Taking her cue from Dar, Celeste turned to Gwen and started asking her questions about how she'd learned to mix her ointments and medicines. Dar squeezed her hand again under the table in a silent thanks, and the conversation was much more pleasant as dessert was served. Cake eaten, and with a few fussing babies in tow, it wasn't long before everyone retired. With so much commotion and the busyness of the day, Celeste snuggled against Dar and was quickly asleep.

CHAPTER 30

SCOTLAND, 1431

Dar was awake before dawn. He usually slept deeply beside Celeste, but this morning, he felt anticipation humming through him. He drew her close, thinking about how the next time they found one another in this bed, it would be as husband and wife.

A formality yes, but securing this union with her, and doing so today, was paramount. A necessary step before he could begin to execute plans for Abersoch and ultimately return with her to her own time. And yet, though he couldn't quite put his finger on it, something else was lingering beneath the surface that gave the whole endeavor a bigger weight even than that.

He'd spoken with Gavin yesterday, explaining the importance of acquiring the land that would become his family's stronghold for generations to come, and its significance to the Montgomery lineage. With the realization of the task before them, came the need to make haste. And in fact, plans had already been set.

At Gavin's expression of gratitude for his aid on such a large project, Dar realized how odd it was both to be charged with something of such consequence and to be thanked for a deed he'd not yet done from recipients hundreds of years apart.

All of this contemplating brought Dar to his current dilemma. He hugged Celeste tighter as he thought it over for what felt like the thousandth time. No longer was he grappling with his sense of purpose or belonging—nay, Dar had no trouble finding that now. But with that confidence came the problem of choice. Of knowing he belonged in two worlds, two eras, of the awareness that, if he so pleased, he could find purpose and footing in both.

When he'd assured Celeste they would return to the future, it was a promise he'd every intention of keeping. In fact, he liked much of the twenty-first century: the way people interacted with one another, the closeness and informality between friends, friends he now had in the Montgomerys as well as Nick.

He liked the ease of life, too, not to mention modern luxuries, not essential but duly appreciated. If pressed, though, what he liked most was Celeste herself, that she was more alive there. And why wouldn't she be? It was where *she* had purpose, where she'd secured a life all on her own. So when they'd spent the morning preparing to travel back to his time mere days ago, he'd looked forward to returning at some point and creating a life with Celeste in the twenty-first century. It had seemed so obvious then—but, now, circumstances made everything a bit more complicated.

Now that he was here, it seemed with each day that passed, he fell deeper in step with his life in the fifteenth century. It wasn't just the familiarity, he was actually approaching his days with a different air than he had before he'd left—but then, that made it all the better, he thought with a sigh.

And this on the cusp of a new understanding and relationship with his father, a man who'd made every indication that he wanted Dar in his life. Lachlan had agreed without question or hesitation to help with the building of Abersoch. Dar had been surprised by the ease of it, but when Dar had heard him return late last night, he'd asked and Lachlan had just smiled. Then, looking him square in the eye, he'd clasped his shoulder and said, "Count me in. You can give me the details on the morrow. You have the heart of a young lady and the house of Lowell to secure."

Of all his relationships, 'twas this one that gave him pause. Lachlan had even offered his own home, Pembrooke, as a residence for Dar and Celeste after the wedding and once the business with Abersoch had been completed. How was Dar to leave him behind when the time came? Dar wasn't sure what the answer was, and spent much of the morning before the sun rose staring at the ceiling in troubled contemplation.

As the first light of dawn trickled in through the window, he moved to kiss the side of Celeste's face, and was surprised to see her staring at him, her own expression carrying something weighty.

"Are you alright?" he asked, searching her face when she

remained stoic. At once, Dar was filled with worry, though now it was for Celeste herself.

"Are you happy?" she asked quietly, as if just finding her voice.

Dar's heart plummeted. This was not what he wanted to hear from his bride the day they were to be wed. No wonder he'd awoken feeling anxious—Celeste had been radiating worry right there beside him. Mayhap he should have pressed Father Michael to perform the ceremony yesterday upon his arrival, when chaos abounded and Celeste was caught up in the excitement.

"Without question, I am happy," he assured her as quickly as he could, reaching out to brush her hair off of her face. "But *you* are obviously not, my love. What's bothering you?"

She swallowed. Hard enough that Dar could see it, then looked at him a long moment before speaking.

"It's...I suppose this is not how I imagined my wedding day." A pause, in which Celeste seemed to search for the words to say next. "But if I'm being honest, I didn't really imagine it all that much."

He smiled softly, understanding at least this. "Nor did I."

In truth, he hadn't. There had never been anyone who'd had his real interest or whom he'd been pressed to make a match with. Until he'd run into this whirlwind of a woman on a sidewalk seven hundred years in the future, he hadn't given it a thought. But she was light and depth swirled together in an impossible contradiction and ever since that fateful day, he'd thought of little else. Mayhap not marriage specifically, but of Celeste, aye. "I know this is a far cry from any event you may have envisioned, but I swear to you, Celeste, I will make you happy. Every day of our lives, I will ensure that above all else."

She frowned and shook her head. "I don't want you to think that you don't make me happy. You do. I feel whole and complete with you. In a way that I never knew existed. I didn't realize how empty I was before, how insulated, until you were there with me, and we were together. I've loved every second that we've spent with each other, Dar."

She cupped his face and began stroking his skin with her fingers, though he could feel that there was a nervous energy to the gesture. "It's just...I'm worried that you'll resent me for taking you away from your home," she said eventually, barely meeting his eyes as she spoke. "And your dad."

Dar was struck by how close Celeste had hit to the root of the matter, of what he'd been grappling with only moments before. It was as though she could read his thoughts.

But she was errored in thinking it was because of her that he held any doubts. Celeste was the one thing he was certain of. And with that realization, suddenly it was clear—no matter the century, she *was* home for him. Feeling a renewed sense of purpose, he locked his eyes with hers and said, "Home? I wouldn't say I'm rich in the 'home' department. But I plan on changing that, today, with you."

She gave a cautious smile, the first of the morn, and it allowed him to take his first deep breath since he'd awoken.

"Do you think that's why we're together?" she asked. "Because we know what that's like? To have it ripped out from beneath us all the time."

Och. He sat up and took her with him, staring deeply into

her eyes. Her visage grew haunted again, and he pressed his forehead to hers, as if he could pass some strength to her as his own mind reeled. She'd sliced right through the chaff to reveal the simple truth, and it struck him now that they'd found one another for a reason beyond what he'd previously fathomed.

There was no doubt in his mind that Celeste was his soul-mate. None. Theirs was no chance meeting. He thought of Esmerelda's words, and though he didn't need magic or fortune tellers to show him the truth, it all aligned. They'd found security in each other when they'd both been cast adrift.

There was a relief in the realization too. That the choice was not *here* or *there*, but *with* or *without*. He would always, always choose *with*. With Celeste. He tried his best to soothe her now.

"I think at its core, that's what's magnified our connection," he offered, holding her fervent gaze. "But nothing more has been ripped from beneath us, not since we've been together, aye?"

Celeste pulled away from him, and gave him a long look. "It's just…something usually is, Dar. Eventually. At least in my case."

He couldn't deny her words but refused to believe that this meant that they were somehow doomed. He shook his head. "Nay. We came together for a reason, Celeste. And if you look at our circumstances, it's a reason beyond comprehension. So, I, for one, cannot subscribe to the idea that this entire machination occurred to leave us with nothing."

This got her interest, it seemed, as she rose to her knees, eager to hear what more he had to say. He would show her, prove to her that there was nothing they could not accomplish together.

"At the very least you are this griffin's mate," he said with a fist to his chest, "and we are bound for life. But what if we look at today and our vows later as more than joining our houses together for as long as we both shall live? What if it is instead a ritual to bind our souls together as one? So that no matter, you and I will forever be secure in the knowledge that we have each other."

He watched as Celeste took this in.

"So, when we say our vows later," she began slowly, "we'll be affirming to each other that we will love each other forever? This isn't just a formality, or something we're being forced into by whatever rules you have in this century? You really want that with me?"

"More than anything," he said at once.

She smiled then, her whole face opening up. "Me too."

Aye, he knew. And it seemed that fate had laden him with several tasks. *Ask and ye shall receive, I suppose.* Not only was he responsible for the fortification of Abersoch, a vital portal between the past and the present, but it had become clear to Dar that he was also the gatekeeper of Celeste's soul, his indispensable other half.

CHAPTER 31

SCOTLAND, 1431

"And breathing in, two...three...that's it," Celeste guided, relishing how good it felt to be back in her element—finding something in the fourteen hundreds that was solely *hers*, and that *she* was the expert on—leading a morning yoga session. "Let's extend that arm a little farther, feeling the stretch all along your side."

"Oh my God, Celeste, this is *a*-mazing," Gwen gushed, going deeper.

Celeste smiled. Gwen was what Celeste would call an ideal student. Happy to exert herself, a stickler on form, and most importantly, *very* complimentary of the instructor. It was just what she'd needed after her moment of panic and doom this morning.

It had not been the ideal start to the day, but when she'd awoken, she'd realized with a start what a big day it really was

—or at least what a big day it *should* be. It was her first milestone without either her parents or Derek.

She'd been telling the truth when she'd said she'd never pictured her wedding day much, but she'd realized, too, that if she ever *had* imagined it, she'd always imagined her father walking her down the aisle, and after he passed, Derek. That would never happen, of course, regardless of the circumstance, but now her circumstances were unrecognizable.

She had time-traveled back seven-hundred years and was living in a castle with no modern amenities. There was nothing familiar to take the place of what her family would have been. And besides, the whole thing had felt like something to check off a list—a necessary, but unromantic, task to complete.

And then there were the smaller things. The things that she felt silly for even caring about, but to her, they were actually important. Celeste didn't consider herself spoiled, but seriously, a girl could want a hot shower and a grande latte without feeling like she was shallow, couldn't she? Even Dar missed those things and had joked only yesterday that he was running out to Beas to grab coffees and a pecan roll.

Poor Dar, nothing like making your lover and soon-to-be-husband insecure on your wedding day. Part of her wished she'd kept her big mouth shut. The other part loved his reaction.

It helped that he seemed to understand her fears—and more than that, respect them, maybe even share some of them. She knew this kind of understanding was one of the reasons their connection was so intense. Like twin flames, the most powerful soul connection to exist.

With his offer of elevating their vows to something more sacred, instead of looking at their ceremony as a mere formality, the wedding held new meaning to her. Dar wasn't placating her, she knew this, and even though Celeste understood their souls already were connected, there was something about the way he'd said he wanted to bind their two houses together that took it to a whole new level. It somehow managed to sound archaic and noble and hot all at the same time.

It had actually been Dar's idea for her to hold a yoga session this morning. He'd said Gwen would love it, and he thought it might help center Celeste a bit. So, after a bit of a redo, which included many kisses and cuddles (they'd decided to save the rest for later), Dar went to find the guys and Celeste went knocking on doors. Gwen and Maggie were quick to say yes, and Isabelle, who was busy with the twins, had said she'd come to Celeste's room when she could—not that she had any idea what yoga even was.

"Oh dear," she'd drawled, when she'd walked into their "class" a little late. "What on earth is this?"

"We'll call it 'yoga with babies,'" Celeste said, gesturing to Isla, who was cooing close by in a basket, which made Gwen and Maggie giggle—Celeste had come up with the name after telling the other women about the yoga with goats craze she'd begun seeing a few years ago.

"I haven't a care what you wish to call it," Isabelle declared, eyebrows raising at the sight of all three of them in downward-facing dog. "The answer is, nay."

When Celeste opened her mouth to explain, Isabelle put up a finger and shook her head.

"Nay. I'll come back. How long will you continue this torture?"

Celeste chuckled. "We should be done in about ten minutes."

"Lovely, for you then," Isabelle said, quickly exiting the room.

"Exercise was never her thing," Gwen told Celeste. "Anyway...yoga with *goats*? Really? That's a really a thing now?"

"Shhh, Gwen," Maggie groaned. "Oh my God, this feels so good. I wonder why we don't do this ourselves."

"Why would we have to?" Gwen questioned. "We have Celeste now."

At this, Celeste's head whipped up, eyes darting from Maggie to Gwen and back again. How did Gwen not know?

"Wait," Gwen interjected. "What's going on?" she asked, breaking form and sitting cross-legged on her blanket.

Celeste and Maggie followed suit, and Celeste looked at Gwen a moment, wondering just what Dar had or *hadn't* told his friends, because she for one had already told Maggie their time here was temporary.

"I'm not staying, Gwen," she admitted, feeling suddenly uncomfortable. "I mean *we're* not staying. Dar and I."

A flash of surprise crossed Gwen's face before she softened her features and seemed to grow thoughtful. "You're going back? Dar too? You can do that?"

Celeste shrugged. "I think so, that's the plan, at least."

She hadn't actually considered that it *wouldn't* be possible, but Gwen's incredulity was making her suddenly nervous.

"Huh. I don't even know what to say," Gwen went on. "Do you know when?"

Celeste shook her head. "It depends on how long it takes to start construction at Abersoch."

Gwen looked even more confused. "Abersoch?" she repeated.

Thankfully, Maggie jumped in and filled her in on the pertinent details and explained that Celeste would stay at Dunhill in the interim.

Gwen grinned. "So we *do* have a yoga instructor!"

Celeste smiled, glad the tense moment was over, but unable to shake the new fear that returning home would be more complicated than she'd initially thought. "For the time being, yes, I suppose so," she allowed, deciding to shove the worry to the back of her mind.

"Wait, did you say Abersoch?" Gwen asked. "As in Abersoch, the estate in Wales?"

Celeste's jaw almost hit the floor. "You know it?"

Gwen nodded, eyes wide. "I think I've been there." She paused, and a peculiar look crossed her face. "If I remember correctly, my aunt Millicent had a friend who was in the process of refurbishing it. We visited one summer when I was still an undergrad."

"Whoa, what are the odds?" Celeste wondered, marveling over how interconnected everything seemed to be. She didn't get a chance to ask any further questions because baby Isla started to fuss at the same time that Isabelle came back into the room, so she suggested Gwen ask Dar about it.

Feeling dazed, she leaned back against the wall, letting her mind drift back to the morning and her freakout. Combine that with this new possibility of not being able to return and Celeste was certainly having a day.

After Maggie had quieted Isla, she came to sit beside her, asking, "Are you okay?"

Suddenly they were all looking at her, even Isabelle, who had sat on the stool in front of Celeste's vanity.

Celeste scrambled for how best to encapsulate all that was swirling around in her head and decided to go with the simplest thing. "I think I may have told Dar I was unhappy this morning. I may have cried too." She placed her head in her hands. "I mean, it ended well, and good, and lovey and all of that, but *still*! On our *wedding* day!"

"Pfft, big deal," Maggie said. "I bawled like a baby before my wedding, and if I recall, I wasn't so pleased with Callum that day either. In fact, besides 'I do,' I think I barely said a word to him."

"I'll say," Gwen laughed. "It wasn't pretty. But, I think I have you both beat. I threw up *and* cried."

Celeste let herself laugh at that. "Well, seeing how happy you both are," she said, once her giggles had subsided, "maybe it's jitters like these that makes for a good marriage with these men."

LATER THAT AFTERNOON, Celeste sat on an upholstered stool in front of her vanity, having been fussed over and primped the entire day. Forget bachelorette parties, or even bridal showers. What she'd experienced today was nothing short of complete fawning.

Not only did the girls not let her out of their sight, they'd kind of had this private girl vibe, a "let's spoil Celeste all day" thing going on. Even Aunt Cateline had joined in. It had all made Celeste feel like she was surrounded by family and friends; truly like a bride.

After yoga, they'd gone down to the dining hall where Ide had laid out a special breakfast that included, thanks to what Gwen had brought along from Seagrave, a drink that rivaled any latte back home. This, Isabelle had been more than happy to take part in. Celeste had reveled in sipping the foam from the top and letting the brew slide down her throat. "Oh my God," she'd said, "this is divine." They all agreed on that point before digging into one of the most delicious quiches she'd ever tasted.

Afterward, they'd floated from room to room, while babies were fed and put down for naps and decisions were made on dresses. When they'd all piled into Aunt Cateline's room to see her choice, Celeste got the sense that the girls were up to some-thing—a sense that turned into a definite suspicion when they all gathered around Cateline's bed and dissolved into giggles.

Once they'd collected themselves, Cateline rose from her seat by the fire and said, "Celeste, dear. I had hoped you might wear the dress my sister wore when she married Fergus."

Before Celeste could even register what was happening, the girls stepped away from what they had gathered around, revealing a beautiful jewel-toned gown, sapphire, almost the exact color of the stone.

Celeste gasped. She'd been wondering what she would wear, and couldn't have imagined a prettier dress than the one before her. It had an empire-waist, long draped sleeves, and laced up the front. The outer part of the dress was a deeper blue, and beneath the lacing was a ruched bust in a lighter fabric of the same shade.

Now, sitting on the upholstered stool in front of her vanity in her own room, Celeste looked at her reflection in the mirror, feeling like a beautiful fairytale princess. Her makeup was subtle, but lovely—Gwen had done an incredible job enhancing her eyes and lips. Her hair was in a sort of half-up style, with a beautiful jeweled comb holding it back from her face, and just enough left down to hide her bruise.

"Well, it seems that three is finally the charm," Gwen sighed, looking at Celeste and her handiwork, baby on one hip and palette of makeup in her free hand. She cocked her head to the side, and then nodded. "Perfection, right?"

"It's perfect, Gwen." Celeste beamed, turning from her reflection to look at the other girls. How she got lucky enough to have a chosen family here *and* back at home in her own time was astounding. "But what do you mean by three's the charm?"

Gwen made a sound as the others chucked. "I'm just saying we've come a long way in the past few years. My wedding felt more like a sacrifice." At Celeste's horrified look, Gwen quickly corrected herself, "Not literally, sweetie, I was just caught off guard. I knew I loved Grey, but he'd been gone for almost two months and then sprung the wedding on me the day he returned, so I was both a suspicious bride and a hopeful one all at once. And then Maggie's..." She paused. "Huh, Maggie's was on the fly, too, and jeez, it was also tense that day, wasn't it?"

"Tenser than I was before the LSATs," Maggie confirmed, though she smiled as she said it.

"But you both seem so happy now," Celeste said, her mind spinning. What was she getting herself into?

Maggie laughed. "More than happy! And we were happy, then, too—the fifteenth century just takes some getting used to, you know?"

Celeste nodded. Was that ever true.

"Oh, Celeste," Maggie said, taking her hands. "You're okay, right?"

Celeste thought back to that morning, how strong her connection to Dar was, and how *he* just seemed right, even if the situation was crazy. She shrugged. "Well, I don't think we would be getting married so quickly if we were back home, but I think—I know—we would have gotten there eventually. I do love him, Maggie."

That seemed to be enough for Maggie. Tears filled her eyes, which made Celeste well up too.

"I'm so happy I get to be at your wedding," Maggie blubbered.

"Stop!" Gwen cut in, laughing. "You'll ruin your makeup, both of you. Buck up. I have to tell you, it doesn't take a brain surgeon to see that all these guys—all these *Lairds of the Crest*—marry women like us."

"What if the next one is?" Maggie asked, wiping her eyes and grinning.

"What, a brain surgeon? Hallelujah."

CHAPTER 32

SCOTLAND, 1431

Dar stood in front of the small house of worship with his brethren and father. Not only were Grey and Callum present, but Lachlan, *his father*—how strange and good it still felt to think of the all-powerful Lachlan MacTavish this way—had somehow gotten word to Aidan and Ro, who'd arrived only hours ago.

It had been a welcome surprise. Over the past few years, the full grouping of the Lairds of the Crest had only come together for the autumn festival, an annual celebration to commemorate the night Grey's and Callum's fathers had sworn them into their sacred brotherhood, and to also honor Allister and Fergus for doing so. Dar realized then that this year, that honor would extent to Lachlan, who he'd also since learned had been instrumental in its creation.

Dar's breath caught, watching now as the women left the keep. Maggie stopped Celeste atop the steps, brushing something off her shoulder before giving her a quick once-over from head to toe.

Even from afar, Celeste looked magnificent in the gown that he'd been told had been worn by Callum's mother, Isabeau. Blue signified purity, and although they were not in fact pure in the sense that he'd claimed her but days ago, Celeste herself was the embodiment of the word, pure as the driven snow—and as unpredictable at times too.

The women approached until they were but paces from them. There, they stopped, and Lachlan clasped his shoulder, indicating it was time to take his eyes off his bride and go inside. Dar inclined his head to Celeste, who smiled in return, then he turned to enter the chapel, the men following behind toward Father Michael, who waited at the altar. They took their places, and when the other women came in, they stood by their husbands, Aunt Cateline in the pew in front.

He smiled at Celeste standing in the doorway, her eyes going wide when Callum stepped up beside her and extended his elbow. Dar saw Celeste's telltale intake of breath, which meant she was getting emotional at the gesture. He caught her eye and mouthed "don't cry," but it came too late—the candle-light caught the big glittering orbs falling down Celeste's cheeks.

Dar couldn't take his eyes off of Celeste as Callum walked her down the small aisle. When she reached him, he grinned, cupped her face, and kissed her, placing her in the spot where she would become his wife, and the keeper of his heart and soul for all eternity.

It was a powerful feeling that swept through him as he

stepped back, taking his place next to her as Father Michael cleared his throat. And when Greylen handed him the tartan, the one Dar had retrieved from his mother's chest of personal belongings, the priest joined their hands and laid it over them. He glanced at Lachlan, who gave him a knowing look.

Father Michael spoke for long minutes on the sanctity of marriage, and Dar stood there feeling utterly calm. It was as if a balm washed over and through him, bathing him in what could only be described as supreme rightness in all that was happening.

When the priest began his recitation of marital promises, he commenced with Dar's name, which finally and rightly so was that of his father's. Celeste's eyes darted toward Lachlan as the words "Do you, Darach Grifud MacTavish," escaped Father Michael's lips. Her smile confirmed Lachlan's approval. As Dar said, "I will," he thumped his chest, as he had only hours ago in their chambers, then he stepped closer to her, cupping her face and pledging his soul to her for all of eternity; promising to safeguard hers in this lifetime and each that followed. She held his gaze as the words fell from his lips, then reached her hand out to cover his heart.

It was Celeste's turn next, and Father Michael repeated the vows for her, prompting her when he finished to say, I will.

"I will," she breathed, and then more loudly, "Forever, I will."

Aye, he knew. And on the heels of Father's Michaels declaration that, "You may kiss your bride," he bent his head, covering her lips as he sealed their commitment.

He'd loved Celeste before this moment, but it felt as if his bond with her grew tenfold.

Celeste and Dar stood together for a long moment, locked in an embrace. When they pulled apart, Dar noticed her blush when she remembered where she was. She giggled and turned to face the pews, and did one of her little curtsies—silly and sweet at the same time.

The ceremony over, Lachlan approached. "I'm happy for you, son," he said, his eyes warm, perhaps a bit sad, and fixed on the tartan Celeste was now holding.

"It was with her things," Dar said, realizing that he must recognize it as his mother's.

Lachlan nodded. "It was the tartan I wrapped your medallion in years ago," he said, then clapped Dar on the shoulder, hugged Celeste, and stepped outside.

After a round of congratulations from the rest, introductions were made between his new wife and Aidan and Ro, and they all trekked back up to the main keep, adjourning to the great room, toasting and drinking and feasting on a meal on which Ide had once again outdone herself. When they sat later for dessert and brandy, Callum and Lachlan each presented Celeste with a gift. First, a medallion of her very own from Lachlan, inscribed with "heart of my heart." The way she clutched it, beaming at the sentiment, you'd have thought she'd been given the Holy Grail.

Callum cleared his throat then and presented his gift next, a letterbox with a heart-shaped lock and two silver skeleton keys, each on their own matching chains.

"My parents had one of these boxes, and Margret and I as well," Callum said, casting a warm look at his wife. "A special place to leave a note to one another."

Celeste fit one of the keys into the lock. "A key to my heart," she whispered, clearly overcome with emotion, and Dar suspected it had something to do with the care she was receiving, how she'd been welcomed by this group as family.

As the hour approached midnight, and everyone started making their way to their rooms, Dar carried Celeste over the threshold of their chamber, giving into tradition and superstition. The room was softly awash in candlelight and warm from the fire, steam rising from the tub.

"Another hot bath?" Celeste asked, turning to face him.

"For my wife? Anything."

Celeste smiled, looking truly at peace for the first time since they'd arrived. "I can't tell you how happy that makes me, but I feel guilty at how hard everyone worked for me—for us —today."

Dar shook his head. "They were happy to be a part of it. And tomorrow will be a day of rest for most." He turned her around to unfasten the bindings on her dress, loosening the laces as he bent to kiss her nape.

"Mmmm, that feels wonderful," she breathed.

He chuckled at the sound of her pleasure, and continued with her undress, anxious to hold her and make love to her. Though, when he finally had her naked and beside him in bed, all thoughts of a bath gone from both of their heads, he took his time, kissing and petting her gently until she whispered, "More, Dar, please."

He brought her to the edge then, knowing exactly how to touch her and play with her. When she cried out, her fingers clenching in his hair as her body did the same below, he nearly lost himself in her bliss. Then he was on top of her, nudging her legs farther apart so he could enter her. "Dar," she breathed again, her hands moving to help him. Gods he suddenly felt frantic and desperate. She cried out again and gasped as he pierced her, feeling so hard he worried he'd caused her some discomfort. "Celeste? Are you alright, love?"

She nodded, but whispered, "Slow, just for a minute."

He did as she asked, watching her carefully, and when he felt her relax, he began to move inside of her, deeper and then faster, her body and her cries pushing him over the edge. He held her afterward, resting on his elbows, still above her as he kissed her face and played with her hair.

"I love you," she said.

"I love you too. forever."

"Forever."

CHAPTER 33

SCOTLAND, 1431

Celeste waved, feeling surprisingly steady as Dar left with Gavin, Aidan, and Lachlan two days after their wedding. Still, it felt surreal to be staring at their backs as they rode off in the company of twelve other men.

"Are you sure I can't go?" she'd asked again last night, even though she already knew the answer. She'd waited until after everyone had retired and she had Dar all to herself—which, at Dunhill, wasn't necessarily easy. Especially because all the boys —well, the brethren, as Dar called them—were still here. Apparently, there was a big annual autumn festival, and this year's was being held next month at Seagrave. Dar had said that, usually, it was the only time the Lairds of the Crest were together as one each year, and so it was a big deal—but with all the uncertainty around how long the Abersoch project would take, they'd decided to capitalize on opportunity and lit a bonfire, paying homage to their fathers, and this time including Lachlan.

So, though it was later than she'd wanted to have the conversation, it was also great timing—Dar was in such a good mood post-bonfire, after spending time with his closest friends and getting to honor the part that Lachlan had played in bringing them all together, that Celeste had her fingers crossed that maybe the conversation would go her way.

Dar had told her unless there was an emergency, they'd be out of contact. Because of the distance and borders crossed, a courier was out of the question, and based on their plans, this initial trip might take up to three months.

The thought of being separated from Dar for that long was terrifying, especially with no way to contact him, and no real understanding of just how dangerous it might be out there. More than that, Celeste had begun a daily second-guessing of her decision to come with him to the past.

Part of her wondered what she'd been thinking, though the other part knew she'd have been sick with worry if she hadn't made the leap too. She'd be sitting on her porch right now, rocking in the swing he'd put up for her, preoccupied with thoughts of his welfare and her fears of never seeing him again. After a week in the fifteenth century, though, Celeste was beginning to think that might have been the better option— especially now that Dar was leaving anyway.

"Celeste," Dar had said, softly shaking his head in response to her request. "It's days of riding without accommodation. I know it's already been an adjustment for you to be here, in my century, and you've experienced the best this era has to offer.

So trust me when I say, the road is no place I wish you to be. Would I keep you safe? Aye, with my life, but knowing you're here, safe and whole at Dunhill, will allow me to move swiftly and see to what must be done."

She'd nodded and buried her face in his neck, and he'd held her as he always did, like she was a prize above all others. But now, Celeste was faced with the reality of existing here without him. Sure, Maggie was here, and it was a temporary separation, but it was still another adjustment.

Celeste's biggest comfort was the knowledge that she wouldn't be here forever. Though Gwen's skepticism still worried her from time to time, she had to remember that fate had finally done right by her by bringing Dar to her, and she just had to hold on to the hope that it would continue to be so.

And things *were* okay for the first few days after Dar's departure. Gwen, Greylen, and Isabelle had stayed on, making the place feel full and lively. Gwen was so upbeat and effervescent that Celeste was hard-pressed to find time to be sad, especially with the two yoga sessions they had each day. But then they said goodbye, too, and Dunhill felt suddenly quiet. Silly really, Celeste chided herself, with all the staff and people coming and going, it was a metropolis of its own. Okay, maybe not a *metropolis*, but at least a, very, very, small town. But still, somehow, it was quiet, lonely.

She did whatever she could to make herself useful: help with Isla, follow Maggie and Callum on all kinds of errands, and when allowed, she even helped Ide in the kitchens. And still, there were so many hours to fill, she thought she might go crazy. Celeste hadn't realized just how much of a comfort her stash of DVDs were, or how much time she passed idly scrolling on her phone until she had neither a TV nor a device. Even reading was out. Unlike Maggie, Celeste didn't know any French, so the solarium filled with rows and rows of books *en français* was of no use.

About a week after Gwen and Grey left, she was in there, looking wistfully at the shelves, when Aunt Cateline came upon her.

"These were my sister's favorites," the older woman said fondly, running her hand along a shelf.

Looking at it more closely, Celeste saw that this wasn't like a normal row of books, but what looked like a collection of literature of all sizes and lengths, from a one-page poem on a thick piece of parchment or wood to a large tome.

"Pick one, sweet, I can teach you," Aunt Cateline said, and Celeste's heart swelled.

From then on, they spent time each day, heads bent at the table by the window, reading. It was a Godsend, really, a welcome distraction from missing Dar, and it helped pass the time during the long, endless days.

Celeste had never considered herself book smart, so what someone like Maggie or even Gwen, she suspected, might pick up quickly, Celeste struggled to learn. Then, one day, Celeste noticed a marked change in the house—everyone around her was speaking French. She'd giggled at first in the dining hall, and they'd chuckled with her, but did not explain themselves. Sweet really. And brilliant, because they kept up the immersion, and after weeks of frustration, suddenly the tide turned and Celeste began to pick up bits and pieces—hellos, goodnights, where's so and so, have you seen, names for places and objects, and the like.

It was an accomplishment, still in its infancy, yes, but it was a big deal to Celeste, and she sat up a little straighter at the table, knowing that Callum and Maggie and Aunt Cateline were proud of her too. It felt good.

To reinforce her efforts, she began writing letters to Dar in French, which she kept in the letterbox that Callum had made for her wedding gift. One each night before bed, even if just a sentence or two.

Monsieur mon mari,
Tu me manques tous les jours.
Pour toujours à vous,
Votre femme,
Celeste MacTavish

It was a simple message—just telling her husband that she missed him and would belong to him forever—but the practice was helpful. She wasn't even sending the letters (not that she could), telling herself that keeping them with her meant Dar would return alive and whole, that he'd read them when he was back. Superstitious, sure, but when had Celeste *not* been?

The letterbox held only a few pieces of parchment at a time, so Callum made her a tabletop chest to store the letters in. It was just as beautiful and intricate as her box, and was even fitted with the same lock, a match to the keys she and Dar already had.

However, despite the fact that she had settled into a routine, a life of sorts, at Dunhill, as summer turned to fall, Celeste grew anxious. Almost two months had passed without word from Dar, and not only that, but her mother's birthday was approaching, and it would be the first year she didn't visit the cemetery. She hadn't realized how much the ritual meant to her until the day grew closer, and she began to panic, which manifested in Celeste being short and snappish with everyone.

When the day came, October twentieth, two months, one week, and six days after Dar's departure, Celeste was beside herself. She spent the morning in the church, which at least felt somewhat like paying respects, though her parents hadn't been particularly religious.

Maggie came by a few times in between Isla's feedings and naps, knowing what an important day it was, but she never stayed long, and Celeste was grateful for that. She liked that Maggie cared, and was acknowledging the importance of the day, but mostly just wanted to be alone. She was still there in the late afternoon when she heard footsteps again, though these were heavier than Maggie's. She turned at the sound to see Callum approaching.

"I'm sorry," Callum said quietly after lighting a candle and coming to sit by her. "I know what it's like to pass a day like this and not be close to mark it."

"You do? Really?"

He nodded, looking ahead. "I left for Seagrave a few months after Fiona died. I didn't even think about missing her birthday at the time. I just wanted to be away from here and the memories. With Aunt Cateline gone, it was so quiet and lonely in the estate, where once it had been so vibrant and alive. When I realized I wouldn't be able to put a stone on her marker on that day, I was filled with guilt." He swallowed hard. "It's something I do to this day."

"A stone?"

"Aye, like this." Callum took a small stone out of his pocket and handed it to Celeste. "Your mother may not be there, but our family plot is a peaceful place. There's even a bench you can sit upon, and the stone markers may help you feel like you are close. Mayhap closer than sitting in here."

She was interested at once. "Would you take me?" she asked, feeling energized for the first time that day.

They rode to the family plot and Callum left two stones atop his first wife's headstone before squatting down to say hello to his own mother and father.

Celeste smiled at the ritual, glad he'd brought her here. It wasn't the cemetery at home, but she felt a connection just the same. She sat on the ground wiping the dirt from all three of the markers, then, by rote, she took out her little wolf and tapped it across the stones. As she did so, she felt Callum's hand covered hers, turning it so he could see the figurine.

"What's this?" he asked.

"Derek made it for me. There's a mama and papa and a brother wolf, too, but this is the one I always carry with me." She looked up at him then and admitted something she'd never told another soul, not even Maggie. "But this is the only one I have left." A tear rolled down her cheek. "Somehow, over the years, I lost them all, save for her."

Callum stared at her, his eyes filled with understanding,

then they both turned abruptly at the sound of someone approaching.

"Hey, there you are!" It was Maggie, coming up the hill, likely on one of the long afternoon walks she took while Isla napped. "Are you okay?" she asked, her voice filled with concern.

Celeste shared a look with Callum. His eyes said *your secret is safe with me*, and she nodded. "I am," she said, turning to Maggie. As she spoke, she realized that after her time with Callum, she truly was.

LATER THAT EVENING, she was walking from the solarium to her room, a book under her arm. As she made her way toward the stairs, she heard a voice that stopped her in her tracks.

"Celeste," Dar said.

She cried out, turning to see him standing there, looking tall, and proud, and handsome. His arms opened, and she flung herself at him, overcome with gratitude and relief that he was home. Loving the grunt that sounded as they made contact.

"I would have washed you and rubbed your neck and helped you," she said, patting his damp hair that indicated he'd washed up in the stream before coming inside.

Dar grinned. "You still can, I've been dreaming of a hot bath for weeks." Then, he noticed the book in her hand. "Wait, are you speaking French now?"

"*Oui*," she said, leaning farther against his chest, finding it hard to let him go.

"You'll have to tell me all about it." He held her, nesting his chin on top of her head.

"I've missed you so much," she said, squeezing him tight.

"Let me see you, love." He pulled away to cup her face. "I got rather used to you being there all time," he told her, looking at her as if drinking her in, before bending to kiss her.

It was magical being in his arms again after so long, the feeling of his lips on hers, and the rumble deep in his chest. She would have stayed right there for hours more, but Dar pulled back, grinning at her pout.

"Come, I'm starving," he said, taking her by the hand. "Ide's making supper for us."

"Us?" Celeste asked, feeling dazed.

"Lachlan and Gavin. They're putting their things away and will be down shortly."

"Ah, of course," she said, nodding. "How long have you been home?"

"Only a few minutes. They went right up to their rooms, but I wanted to find you first."

Celeste didn't really care about the logistics, she was just thrilled he was back, and clung to his arm all the way to the dining hall, where Callum and Maggie were already seated. Ide set a few platters down and Celeste filled Dar's plate extra high. Gavin and Lachlan joined them soon after, and they spent a long while sharing stories of their travels, which thankfully included no violence, and did include success in finding the parcel of land and securing it.

When everyone finally headed upstairs, Celeste wasn't

surprised to see a hot bath waiting in their room. Dar was well-liked by the staff.

"Come, I want to help you undress," she told him as she guided him toward the tub.

"So do I," he returned, turning her to face him.

After a very passionate soak in the tub, Dar carried her to bed. He laid her on the blankets and shook his head as he looked down at her. "I've truly missed you," he said.

Celeste grinned, thinking of what had happened in the bath only moments before. "I could tell," she teased.

Dar returned her smile, but softly. "Aye," he breathed, "I missed that. But what I meant was that I missed *you*, Celeste."

"Me, too, Dar," she reassured, gesturing for him to join her. "Come to bed and hold me. Please."

He needed no further prompting, and lay beside her, gathering her close as she snuggled against him. A short while later, as she was falling asleep, she remembered the dozens and dozens of letters she'd written him and she smiled, excited to show him her full-to-bursting letterbox and matching chest in the morning.

CHAPTER 34

SCOTLAND, 1431

A week had passed since his return to Dunhill, and in that time, Dar had fully reacquainted himself with his wife. After so long without having Celeste nearby, it was heaven to spend his days around her again.

They lazed away many a morning (and the odd afternoon) in bed with one another, his passion ever stronger after their time apart. But it wasn't just lovemaking that preoccupied them— sometimes they were content to just lie in one another's arms and talk, about anything and everything under the sun— Celeste's dream of the home Dar would one day build her, stories about Dar's mother, which would naturally prompt Celeste to tell stories about her parents too.

Often, he'd pull out the letters Celeste had written him while he was away, marveling over how she'd begun writing in French; he'd even tucked one or two into his satchel to keep with him always.

This was the first time since they'd met, Dar realized, that things could simply *be*. There was no worrying about delivering a message or being found out as a man out of time. There was no impending leap back through centuries to tiptoe around delicately. There was no fear that he and Celeste would be separated by those centuries, and no rushing of plans for weddings or property purchasing. Nay, right now, he was simply enjoying his time with Celeste.

He and the men would be returning to England shortly, but now that they knew what they were heading into, there was an ease around it that had not existed previously. After such a long absence, Lachlan had left for Pembrooke to check on his affairs, and Gavin had taken his leave, too, eager to see his wife and family before he had to depart again early next month.

Aidan had offered to stay behind at Abersoch to prepare for the actual construction, which would begin in the spring. Dar had forgotten that Aidan had fostered with Lachlan at Pembrooke, and had learned much from him about building, among other things, while there. Although Dar remembered being envious of his friend at the time, now he was grateful. Though, with Aidan getting things set up at Abersoch, Dar felt he couldn't stretch his stay at Dunhill any longer than absolutely necessary. As soon as Lachlan and his men returned, they would be on their way.

In the meantime, however, Dar was helping Callum inventory Dunhill's food stores and supplies for the winter months ahead. Just the other day, Greylen and Gwen had returned from Seagrave so Gwen could check on baby Isla, who'd been miserable with a cough and a low fever. Of course, as was often the case, by the time Gwen had arrived to offer her professional expertise, Isla was back to happily crooning, smiling, and playing with her toes.

Taking advantage of the impromptu visit, he, Callum, and Greylen were off to a few neighboring towns in search of laborers, hoping they'd be able to hire a few skilled ones for Abersoch. They'd considered taking the women along, but Maggie and Gwen had claimed Celeste for a day of apple picking, which was fine with Dar—he'd worry less.

"Be mindful, love," Dar said, kissing the tip of Celeste's nose as she stood to see him off, a handled basket over her arm. Och, he'd missed her so much while he was away, he still couldn't stop touching her. "I'll see you this evening," he promised, before tugging her cloak closer together, worried she might catch a chill, and already thinking about sharing a bed later.

Her pretty eyes went wide, and she grinned from ear to ear. "Thank you, my lord," she said dramatically as she curtsied.

He chuckled, giving her bottom a playful swat as she turned away.

"Be careful, my lord," she cautioned livelily, looking back at him. "I might start to like that."

He'd have laughed, if not for the shock at what had just come out of her mouth.

"What?" Celeste asked, grinning coyly. "I was just flirting with you, jeez. Now who's the prude? Don't make me feel bad."

He wasn't sure he could speak presently, not while thinking of her perfectly rounded bottom upturned over his knee. He felt his cheeks flush, which only made Celeste laugh.

"Oh, I was only teasing you," she said.

He cleared his throat, finally finding his voice. "Noted. Stay out of trouble."

She shrugged, looking mischievous. "Maybe," she demurred, and if he wasn't mistaken her look said otherwise.

Maggie called her name then, and Celeste said nothing more, only laughed, running to catch up with her and Gwen, leaving Dar dumbfounded. He shook his head, then headed over to Grey and Callum, who were waiting by the horses.

"Tell me of Abersoch," Grey requested, having been out of the loop since Dar's return. "I was gone when Gavin passed through on his way home and we've not spoken since."

If not for Grey and Gwen's visit to Dunhill, they wouldn't have had the chance to speak in person at all. Dar was glad to have his counsel now, and began filling him in on what had transpired and what they'd accomplished thus far, beginning with the ten-day journey to Abersoch. They'd been moving as quickly as possible, but it was a monumental undertaking and one he wasn't sure he would have been able to accomplish without Gavin, whose name carried weight in the region.

"The rock wall's astounding," Dar said, shaking his head at the natural wonder they'd seen once they'd arrived. "We rowed out far enough to see what Alex—the Montgomery in the future—was talking about. If you know what you're looking for, it's clear as day."

The maps that Alex had shared with him had helped them find what they hoped was the correct parcel of land, but until they saw the portal at the edge of the property with their own eyes—or at least what they all believed identified it, the two swirling lines that crawled up the entire surface from beneath the sea line to the top of the cliffs—they couldn't be sure. When they'd found what they'd sought, they'd all been astonished, passing long minutes just staring at it, speechless. It was the evidence they needed.

Luckily, when they went in search of the proprietor, he'd been all too happy to sell when he saw what they were offering. Apparently, he'd been barely getting by on rents, and, if the speed at which he'd completed the transaction were anything to go by, he hadn't believed his luck at the offer. That step secured, Dar hoped to lay the groundwork by the end of the year and start construction in the spring.

"When will you return?" Grey asked.

"A week, mayhap two at the latest. I just haven't told, Celeste yet." He wasn't looking forward to another long separation and knew that though she seemed to be faring well at Dunhill, being in the fifteenth century was not her preferred option.

Grey nodded. "Whatever help you need from us, you know you have it."

"Thank you, my friend."

Unsure how long this endeavor would take him, Dar knew that at the least he'd have to stay until they set the stone that would bear their names. In the meantime, Celeste was his main concern. Her safety and welfare, and most importantly—her happiness.

Dar had never been one to wish away time, but in this case, he wished for the changing seasons as never before.

CHAPTER 35

SCOTLAND, 1431

Celeste skipped to catch up with Maggie and Gwen as they trekked to the apple orchard at the outskirts of the property. She wasn't sure how they did it, but they looked like they belonged here, *here* in this time, happy and carefree.

Maggie with her dark curls blowing in the wind and a big smile on her face, and Gwen standing there looking like a queen. It was at times like these that she wished she'd brought her phone, not only to capture a snapshot such as this, but for something to look at, and photos to remind her that the twenty-first century exists and she was there.

Even so, there were countless images, pictures in her mind, that Celeste knew she'd carry with her when she returned to her own time, and this was one. The two of them wrapped in stunning cloaks, standing side by side at the base of the meadow. It was a memory she would keep with her always.

Celeste was so excited that Gwen and Greylen had returned.

Today, they'd skipped their usual morning yoga session for a long walk and what Maggie hoped would produce a haul of apples before the first frost. It was a good thing Celeste was in shape, because what Gwen considered a brisk walk was basically power walking on steroids.

While she'd been told that Dunhill stretched for miles, with beautiful rolling hills, craggy mountains, and lush waterways, Celeste had never ventured so far from the castle. Instead, she'd been given a stern warning from Dar *and* Callum that a league —three miles—was the limit if she was on her own. She'd never bothered to question it because it was enough to give her plenty of freedom while still remaining in view of the keep.

Now as they veered south, the rolling hills and small streams gave way to rougher terrain, prompting a warning shout from Andrew, one of Callum's men who was following them, to watch their footing.

"There," Maggie said, pointing to a copse of trees somehow wedged between some lush greenery and a ravine, "my favorite spot. But be careful, the ground's uneven here," she warned, as if it wasn't visible with the naked eye.

Curious, Celeste made her way through the trees to the edge of the ravine, and peered over. It was more of a gentle slope than a mountainside, but still, there were a few rough divides and what looked to be some deep gaps. Land, she decided, best left unnavigated.

Returning to her friends and taking turns on the ladder that was left in a small lean-to to pluck the higher-up apples, Celeste thought about how nice it was to have Dar home again. He had loved all her letters. When he went to unlock the letter box and chest, Celeste had been pleasantly surprised to see he wore the key around his neck, just like she did. "I can't imagine why that surprises you," he'd said. "You both *are* and *have* the key to my heart."

They'd sat on their bed then, her leaning against his chest as he'd read each one aloud, grinning and filling her with praise as he showered her with kisses and hugs. In fact, they'd been so occupied with each other since he'd returned, talking about their future, and their families, that she'd barely had time to sink into one of her "I miss the twenty-first century" moods. At least, not too deeply or too often.

Thinking about the time she and Derek had gone apple picking—and ended up with more apples than they could eat, living off of pies and strudels for a month—Celeste took out her wolf, and traipsed it across a branch, setting it down when she noticed a particularly ripe-looking apple.

When everyone's baskets were full, Maggie set a brisk pace in guiding them home, worried about Isla's next feeding. Good thing, too—when they returned, Aunt Cateline was waiting on the steps with a fussy baby in her arms.

While Maggie saw to the baby, Celeste and Gwen took the apples to Ide, and then went to clean up the sweat and dirt they'd accumulated on their morning trek. After lunch, they all decided a nap was in order, and though she wasn't normally a napper, Celeste laid down, surprised when she realized that she was falling asleep.

When she woke, it was with a start. Deep in her slumber, she'd remembered her wolf, and more alarmingly, how she could picture taking it out of her pocket and setting it on the branch—but that she wasn't sure she'd ever retrieved it. In a panic, Celeste leapt onto the pile of clothes she'd left on the ground before her nap and started pawing through them. Her wolf wasn't in her dress pocket, or the one she'd worn to the apple orchard, and it wasn't in her cloak pocket either. She searched her room, looking under the bed before she moved onto the courtyard, kitchens, and back up to her rooms, though she knew by then that it was fruitless.

Sitting on the end of her bed, almost in tears, she pictured the last place she knew she had it. The orchard. It had to be there. And Celeste had to go get it, or she'd have lost her last remaining family treasure.

She briefly considered asking the girls to go with her, but then vetoed that idea. What if they told her not to go? Or suggested she wait until morning? She couldn't do that. Not for something this important. Celeste figured if she ran, or better yet, rode, she might be able to get there and back with enough time for a hot bath before dinner. And with no one the wiser.

Celeste hadn't planned on running into Andrew again in the stables, or for that matter having to give a reason why she was saddling her mare. But then again, she'd never gone riding in the late afternoon. Already knowing an explanation would be necessary and dreading it for the same reason she'd decided *not* to include the girls, she told him the truth, that she needed to go back to the orchard, that she had left the figurine, something of great value to her, behind.

From the compassionate look in his eye, she thought he was going to give her the green light, but then Andrew peered outside, shook his head, and said, "I'll take you first thing in the morning."

Trying to hide her disappointment and growing panic, Celeste plastered a fake smile on her face, thanked him, and slowly walked back to the keep, knowing he was watching. When she reached the path that branched off from the main one and led to the gardens, Celeste paused, feigning an interest in some heather that grew there. After a moment, she looked behind to see whether Andrew had turned and headed back inside. He had.

Not knowing how much time she had until he came back out, Celeste darted right and skirted around the courtyard, using the back of the outbuildings for cover as she made her way to the meadow. It was unfortunate that she wouldn't be riding, but she'd made the trek on foot once today, and was confident she could do it again.

Colder now as the late-afternoon sun fell, she pulled her cloak tighter against the windy chill. It wasn't long, though, before she warmed up from switching between walking and jogging as she kept a close eye on the ground. The last thing she needed was to trip and sprain an ankle. She grinned when the orchard came into view and she reached it with just enough light left to grab the ladder from the lean-to and shimmy it against the tree she'd last visited with her wolf.

Celeste held her breath as she climbed the rungs, giddy when she spied her little treasure on the tree branch just above her, sitting by his lonesome, exactly where she'd left him. So excited to have found it, she braced one hand on the trunk, while reaching up with the other, her fingers closing around her figurine just as Celeste realized the ladder was teetering beneath her, thrown off balance by her lunge toward the wolf. She tried to steady herself by reaching for a closer branch with her free hand, but it was too late.

Celeste tumbled backward, the ladder coming down with her. She landed flat on her back, which stunned her, knocking the wind out of her lungs, and in the moment that she couldn't move or breathe, she could only watch as her wolf flew from her hand.

The instant she caught her breath, Celeste scrambled to find it, knowing time was short as daylight quickly waned. In a panic now, she searched the area, her heart soaring when she spotted it on one of the nearby rocks. Filled with relief, she dashed toward the figurine, grabbing at it for the second time that evening.

She had only a second of elation before she realized she'd run straight toward the ravine's drop-off and would be unable to slow her momentum in time. Shoving the wolf deep in her pocket, Celeste scrambled for something, anything, to hold on to as the seconds seemed to slow. She gripped the boulder the wolf had been sitting on, but it was damp, and she could not find purchase in time. Knowing what was about to happen a moment before it did, Celeste let out a shriek as she fell through the air to the ravine below.

CHAPTER 36

SCOTLAND, 1431

After visiting two towns, the second in which they discovered another skilled mason who was eager for work, Dar was happy to be back at Dunhill with time to spare. He, Grey, and Callum entered through the kitchens to let Ide know they would be seated at the dinner table tonight, then they all headed straight to their rooms.

"Celeste," he called upon entering their chambers. "Love?"

When she didn't answer, he put aside his disappointment, figuring she was with Maggie or Gwen somewhere in the keep. After changing his clothes, he wrote her a quick note:

Mon amour,
Je t'aime.
Votre mari,
Darach MacTavish

Simply telling her that he loved her, his wife. He withdrew his key and secured the note in their letterbox, a marked spring in his step at the thought of surprising her with his early return.

After looking in the dining hall, the solarium, and the great room, but finding only Aunt Cateline, Dar dug deep for a spot of patience, pouring a brandy to help. It wasn't until Callum and Maggie, then Grey and Gwen appeared, that a feeling of unease took hold.

"Celeste isn't with you?" he asked to all, as if he couldn't see that with his own eyes.

"Nay," Maggie confirmed, shaking her head, along with Gwen.

Sensing his alarm at Celeste's absence, they all went in different directions, calling out her name. When it was clear she was not inside, they dispersed out into the courtyard.

Andrew was just coming up the path, and noting their alarm, asked, "What is it?"

Grateful for the man's concern, Dar urged, "Have you seen, Celeste?"

Andrew nodded, and for a moment, Dar allowed himself relief.

"Aye," Andrew said, "a few hours ago. She wanted to take a horse to ride back to the orchard. I told her with dusk upon us it would be best if we went in the morning."

Relief gone. The orchard was miles away. Dar tried to rein in the panic in his voice and asked, "Did she tell you why?"

"She said she misplaced something, a figurine of some kind," Andrew said, then a look of realization crossed his face. "I thought surely she would wait."

Aye, anyone else would have, but not his wife, who treasured that wolf above all else. It was the only thing she carried with her always.

"Right," Dar said as he started grabbing supplies—torches and ropes and whatever else might be useful—and securing them to his saddle, Grey and Callum following suit.

"We'll find her," Dar pledged when they were ready, more to himself than anyone else.

With Andrew in the lead, they headed toward the ravine, hoping she'd merely lost her way. She'd been gone now perhaps three hours if she'd left before dusk. By horseback it took little time to reach the spot, even at the slow pace they took to carefully scour the land as they went. They took turns calling her name, waiting a moment each time for a response. When they reached the orchard, Dar spotted her tracks and the old ladder laying on the ground beside one of the trees close to the edge.

The sight of the ladder ignited a new flush of panic in Dar, and he called her name loudly, his voice echoing down the ravine. They waited but heard nothing in return...until a weak, broken whistle sounded from afar. Could it be? His eyes shot to Callum, who, by his look, had also heard the sound, and he gave a call in return. Dar held his breath, listening. Sure enough, it sounded again.

"We hear you, Celeste!" *Thank You, God!*

Lighting their torches, they searched the ravine, noting among them how slippery the rocks were. Between the dark and the chill, 'twas a dangerous combination.

"Again, love!" Dar called out, trying to keep the fear from his voice. All he needed was a sound from her so he could make a path downward.

Celeste managed another whistle, even weaker this time, and Dar started off in the direction of the sound, holding his torch high. After a few paces, he caught a glimpse of her down below, lit faintly by his torch.

"Here! She's here!" he bellowed, calling the others toward him and silently praying for her to be okay.

Picking his way carefully toward Celeste as quickly as he could, Dar held his torch aloft to get a better look at the gorge she'd fallen into. What he saw was not welcomed. She was sprawled out over a rock at an odd angle, and though she could surely see him by now, she wasn't moving.

Dar quickened his pace toward her, as Grey and Callum caught up to him, spooling out the rope they'd brought with them. Dar nodded to his brethren, lowering himself into the gorge, then knelt beside Celeste, putting his ear to her chest. At the sound of her heart's steady rhythm and the cadence of her lungs taking air in and out, he allowed himself a calming breath. His worst fear had not been realized.

Bringing his face up toward hers, Dar saw that tears spilled from her eyes. Holding back tears of his own, he brushed the hair from her face, whispering, "Shhh, it's okay, love," and praying he was correct. "Let me look at you, aye?"

She nodded, wincing and releasing a high-pitched sound as she did so. Clearly even this small gesture put her in great pain.

Considering her awkward angle, Dar feared a broken back. Remembering what Gwen had told him once about what she called "basic first aid," he asked if she could move her fingers and flex her feet. At first, Celeste seemed to struggle, her brain trying to tell her body what to do, and in this long moment, Dar held his breath, eyes glued to her feet and hands. Then, miraculously, he saw the slightest movement in her fingers, a small flex at her ankles. He nodded, but noted she made no other movement.

Careful not to cause her further pain, Dar ran his hands over her legs and arms, feeling for any signs of injury, bruising, swelling, or a break. As he did, he saw that Callum had brought down the ladder from the orchard, and was now digging for purchase in hopes of securing it against rock wall and vegetation. Cautiously, Dar determined that other than some minor scratches, her limbs appeared sound.

Having successfully secured the ladder, Callum knelt behind her, steadying her head as Dar ran his hand behind her shoulder and back. When his fingers encountered a sticky substance he suspected was blood, Celeste winced and gave a sharp intake of breath.

"Hurts," she whispered, though so faintly, Dar could not be positive he'd even heard it.

He grimaced, looking at Callum. "She's bleeding."

From there they worked slowly, trying to determine the location and severity of her injuries. Not willing to move her too much, at the risk of causing more damage, or to expose her to the cold by cutting through her cloak or her dress, they went off of feel and Celeste's responses.

It seemed that her shoulder and ribs had taken the brunt of her fall, though the question of how badly she was truly injured would have to wait until they were back inside, by a fire with

Gwen's expertise. Deciding the best course of action was to bind her as tightly as possible, both to inhibit further movement of her bones, and perhaps to offer her some relief, he lifted her gingerly and placed her back against his chest as Callum wound cloth around her.

By the time they were finished, Grey had found a way back to higher ground, which meant Celeste wouldn't have to be hoisted out of the ravine. That was a boon he was grateful for.

Dar did his best not to jostle her as he carried her in his arms, and in the end, it wasn't too far back to where they'd left their horses. Celeste gave a few yelps, but otherwise seemed to handle the short trek. He considered walking her all the way back to the keep, but knew getting her home quickly was more important than the discomfort she would endure from a slow ride on horseback. So, he laid Celeste carefully in Callum's arms, and climbed atop his steed, where Callum and Grey gingerly lifted her up into his lap.

Dar was never so grateful to have Gwen in residence. She was a wonder in a crisis and had already prepared for whatever Celeste might need.

Celeste tried to explain to Gwen what had happened, but it was clear she could barely speak.

"It's okay, you don't have to talk right now," Gwen told her, shooting Dar a reassuring look. "This is normal," she said to him, which worked to soothe his nerves only a wee bit.

After getting his wife cleaned up, Gwen doused her wounds with vinegar and stitched up a gash atop her shoulder blade—the source of the blood, Dar surmised. Although not too long or deep, Gwen said it wasn't worth the worry of leaving it to chance. She also confirmed that Celeste had suffered a broken rib. To Dar, this seemed catastrophic, but Gwen assured him that although painful, it would heal with time.

When he asked about the binding he and Callum had done, Gwen said that it had been a good short-term solution, but was not a practice she would advise. Aghast that he might have done something to hurt Celeste, Gwen assured him again that for the short time they'd bound her ribs, they'd most likely helped her pain, especially for the ride back.

Now, standing by the bed where Celeste lay, he rubbed her forehead, then held another dram of whatever it was Gwen gave her for pain to her lips, tipping it as she swallowed.

"Better?" he whispered, still emotional from the danger she'd been in, and overcome with relief that she was safe and home, a bit worse for wear, aye, but she was whole.

As Gwen left, she brushed his shoulder. "She'll talk in the morning, I'm sure. Considering her injuries—not to mention whatever shock she's likely still in—it's no wonder she's quiet. I'll be back every few hours to check on her, just in case anything changes."

Dar nodded and said a prayer that they might be out of the woods, then kissed the top of Celeste's head.

Realizing only then how exhausted he was, Dar washed and changed, keeping a close eye on his wife the entire time, then pulled a chair up to the bedside, where he dozed off and on throughout the night.

CHAPTER 37

SCOTLAND, 1431

When Celeste awoke, Dar was asleep in a chair next to the bed, his head bent at what looked like an uncomfortable angle. It took her a minute to remember what had happened, why her body ached so much.

When it all came back to her—the missing wolf, her run-in with Andrew, the fall off the ladder, and then the tumble into the ravine—she realized how lucky she was to be alive now. She dared not wonder if, after all of that, the wolf had indeed been lost again; this time, likely, for good. There was a chance it was still buried somewhere in the pocket of the skirt she'd been wearing, but given how hard and fast she'd tumbled, Celeste wouldn't bet on it.

She reached out toward Dar, but he was too far, and she could tell that stretching would be a bad idea. Swallowing, she breathed his name, but nothing came out. She must have lost her voice. It was with that thought that she remembered how she'd called for help for what seemed like hours, even though taking a breath, especially a deep one, had been excruciating.

Scooching herself off the rock she'd landed on had been out of the question, let alone climbing back up out of the ravine. *Stupid*, she told herself now. She tried his name again. "Dar." It was barely a whisper, but his eyes shot open, and he leaned forward, drinking her in. She'd never seen him cry before. A misty-eyed look, yes, perhaps a couple times, but this morning, it was full-on tears. Seemingly unable to talk—though for a different reason than Celeste's—his forehead came to rest on her bedside, and his shoulders shook. She swept her fingers through his hair, offering him the only comfort she could right now.

A rap at the door sounded and Dar sat up, kissed her palm, then wiped his face.

"I love you," he said, as Callum entered the room.

Callum looked as bad as Dar, but offered a comforting smile and a "morning." He squeezed Dar's shoulder as he came up behind him and when he reached her, he placed his hand on her head, nodding as if to say, *you're alright*.

"Morning," he said again, and Celeste noticed he had a pouch in his hand. "I hope you were able to rest."

Without fanfare, Callum opened the pouch he'd brought in, dumped its contents into his hand, and placed three small figurines on her nightstand. When he moved away, allowing Celeste to see what had been in the pouch, emotion overtook her.

It was a wolf family, all carved from the same kind of wood as *her* wolf. In fact, her wolf was there, too—looking a little more worn than the three Callum had carved, but no worse for the wear, considering. She glanced first at Dar, who nodded, smiling, and pointed to the dress she'd been wearing, now draped over the back of a chair. He must have searched it for the wolf, and put it there for her to see. She looked to Callum next, but was so overcome with emotion that she covered her eyes with her hand, trying not to sob, one, from embarrassment, and, two, from pain.

Callum smiled, saying, "The family is again complete," before he turned to leave.

Throughout the day, she had a stream of visitors, and slowly, Celeste began to feel better about the whole thing. Not physically, not yet, but she was allowing herself some grace. No one brought up how lucky she was, or how irresponsible—not even Greylen, who she knew was the sternest and a stickler for following the rules. Everyone just showered her with love and attention and offered things they thought might comfort her. Aside from feeling bad for the worry she'd caused, Celeste let herself bask in the feeling of familial love. It was a gift.

But a few days passed quickly, and then Grey and Gwen were gone, returned to Seagrave once Gwen was certain that Celeste was on her way to a full recovery. She had said good-bye, feeling sad about it before they'd even made it out the door. She knew she'd miss their energy and Gwen's flair.

With the long and uncomfortable days that followed, all spent in bed, Celeste thought more often of home. It had always been there, in the back of her mind, and yet she'd refrained from telling Dar just how often she thought of it. More than once, she'd wanted to discuss it with him, if for nothing else than to share the burden, but she'd always talked herself out of it.

He'd promised they'd go back, and she believed he was true to his word. She'd been able to manage her feelings of intense longing for home so far with finding a routine, and then having Dar back at Dunhill again, but convalescing with only fifteenth-century methods to rely on was bringing back all of her feelings of longing for home.

When she awoke from her latest nap about a week after Gwen's departure, her thoughts turned first to her daily rumination of *what I wouldn't give for*—a hot shower, a real mattress, a Diet Coke (something she always craved when she wasn't feeling well), a movie to pass the time. She was just about to start trying to recount the entirety of *Sleepless in Seattle* in her head when she spied the letterbox on the nightstand, her key on its chain next to it. She smiled, at once finding it difficult to be morose, and walked her fingers to the key, feeling giddier by the second. Dar came into their room just as she retrieved his note, so she patted the bed.

"Come, sit with me."

He looked at her skeptically, knowing it was difficult enough to find a comfortable position on her own, let alone with the two of them on the overly soft mattress.

"Please," she said. "Let's try again."

A few grimaces later, she was pressed against his side, his arm around her, not completely comfortable, but blissfully content. She'd missed that.

She read his words aloud, fumbling the accent a bit, but getting the pronunciation of the French down:

Mon amour,
Je chéris votre bien-être par-dessus tout.
Votre éternel,
Darach MacTavish

She read it once more to herself, to make sure she'd parsed the meaning, and then smiled. He'd told her he treasured her welfare above all else, and she melted at his words. Then, she told him he'd better grab her a stack of parchment and an ink pot and quill.

Another week later, Lachlan and Gavin rode into the court-yard, a sign the men would be leaving soon for England.

By then, Celeste was out of bed and moving around as best she could, using walls for balance and taking frequent rests. Lachlan had been horrified when he saw her walking in such a sedate, stiff manner.

"Oh, piseag, what happened?" he'd asked, the gentle concern on his face at odds with the strong warrior presence he carried about him. It was endearing, really. And, strangely, he didn't reprimand her either. Celeste had thought for certain that if Grey hadn't given her a what-for, surely Lachlan would have done so. But, maybe, they thought she'd suffered enough. Which she had. Seriously, she was grateful for whatever Gwen had plied her with, but she sure did miss ibuprofen, ace bandages, and ice packs.

Dar told her that evening that he and the men would be leaving in the morning, though he promised to be back by the end of the following month, December. It was much earlier than the original plan, thanks to his worry for Celeste's injuries, but still, a long time to be separated—again. And another reminder of holidays she would have celebrated back home, or at least commemorated with a trip to the cemetery.

All at once, all the things she missed started to cycle through Celeste's mind, and she began to wonder again if she'd made the right choice in coming here. She couldn't deny that she loved the family she had here, the friends, and, of course, Dar, but it wasn't *home*. Not in the literal sense, nor in what it provided for her—stability in the face of uncertainty—which she was losing again with Dar's imminent departure.

Noticing that she was a bit melancholy throughout dinner, he'd asked what he could do to help her. It was on the tip of her tongue to tell him she wanted to go home, but as she looked at him, this man who had crossed centuries to fulfill a pledge, and who had, in the process, promised his undying and eternal love to her, she just didn't have the heart.

"Just make love to me tonight, Dar. I need to be close to you." Aside from the times they read letters to each other, they'd barely even cuddled since her accident because of his worry of hurting her, but honestly, she really needed human touch right now. His touch. She knew he'd be gentle.

He let out a deep breath, looking resigned.

"Really?" Celeste pressed, raising her eyebrows. "Well, that makes me feel better."

He chuckled, and at the sound, her heart swelled in a good way, pushing her woes and worries aside. It was just what they needed, and after a careful, but no less intimate night of passion and talking and careful cuddling, it felt like maybe she could find her footing again.

She thought once more about telling him of her moments of doubt, thinking that maybe it would make them better and even stronger than before. But then Dar pulled her closer, whispered his love for her, and assured her that everything would be okay, and Celeste knew it would break him if she told him her thoughts now—especially just before he was setting off for more than a month. Instead, she sunk into his embrace and forced her thoughts away, crossing her fingers in hopes that she would be able to do this, for him.

CHAPTER 38

SCOTLAND, 1431

As the weeks passed, Celeste's desire to leave the fifteenth century and return to her own time only increased, becoming more and more unbearable by the day. Dar arrived back at Dunhill in mid-December, in advance of when he'd said he would, and it helped, but soon he would leave again. And in a way, *she* was the reason why things would take longer. It's not like he needed to come home to visit Callum and Maggie. He was coming back for her.

And, even though she loved being with him and having him near, it was almost easier to keep up appearances and maintain a brave face when he *wasn't* there. Whenever they were alone together, all she wanted to do was tell him. It was getting more difficult to keep her feelings to herself, but she told herself she had to—that to reveal just how unhappy she was would be whining, would make her everything she didn't want to be; namely, childish and selfish.

After all, he'd uprooted his life to deliver Maggie's message —even the Abersoch project was to help someone else. He sacrificed so much of himself for others, it seemed silly that she was having trouble doing this one small thing. It didn't help, either, that in all the time she'd been here, joking and reminiscing aside, never once had Maggie and Gwen spoken of a desire to go back.

On Dar's second day back, Celeste found herself standing in the great room and staring at the fireplace, feeling like her whole world was crumbling, and trying, for the millionth time, to talk herself into being happy here.

"What is it?"

Celeste startled, and whirled around. Dar had come up behind her, and she'd been too lost in thought to notice.

"I can tell something is troubling you," he said, putting a hand on her shoulder.

Whether he'd caught her in a weak moment, or Celeste made some kind of unconscious decision, before she could stop herself, she said, "I...I don't want to be here. I miss home, Dar," feeling guilty the moment the words escape her.

Tears welled in her eyes. She hated that she'd put voice to those feelings, but it was the truth, and that truth was crushing her from the inside out.

Dar said nothing at first, but his eyes were filled with compassion, and he brought her into the comfort of his arms, holding her while she cried. So many things crossed her mind as they stood there, but in this moment what she felt most was loved and secure...and safe in the confines of his love for her.

He didn't hurry her or push her away too soon, just waited until she was calm enough to step back on her own.

"I'm sorry," she said, wiping her eyes while noting he'd shed a few tears of his own.

"Don't be." He shook his head. "You're right, you don't belong here, not truly. I'll take you back."

Stunned, Celeste took a step back. "You can do that? You *would* do that?"

He looked at her, his eyes filled again with love and understanding. "Celeste. Your happiness and welfare are more important to me than anything else."

If anything, she'd expected a list of reasons of why things would be okay, a long and thoughtful discussion of the merits of the path they'd chosen. Something about patience and how he needed to fulfill his duties. Not an instant offer to take her home.

Celeste wiped away a last tear. "What's wrong with me? Your happiness should be my priority too."

He shook his head. "It's hard to give to others when you're unhappy yourself. I'm grounded in a way I've never been before. I have my wife, whom I adore and would give my life for, my father, and purpose, too, Celeste. *That's* what gives me the power to endure. And it's true, I do feel at home here—it's easier for me to spend my days in a world I've always known. While you, you've been uprooted from the one place you'd found security, and those who you found comfort in. Let me remind you of the woman I met only months ago, quiet but filled with strength. She fought for me, and for us, and she came into my arms courageously, on an errand that few would. So forgive me if I don't fall on your sword of woe."

For a moment, Celeste just stared. "That was amazing," she breathed.

Dar pressed a finger to her lips. "In all seriousness, let me take you home and then I'll come back to finish what I started."

Still in shock, Celeste just nodded, overwhelmed by how much he understood her. She'd never expected him to be so willing to take her back. "You'd let me go," she said, and pouted around his finger, fully realizing the contradiction in what she was saying—*she* was the one who'd asked for this.

"I will *never* let you go, Celeste. From now through eternity, you are mine. Don't ever forget that."

"Never," she repeated.

"Why don't we tell Maggie and Callum, then we'll go," he said surely, quietly.

She nodded again, her heart swelling with possibility and excitement. Part of her felt like she was abandoning him, all of them—and the thought of leaving Maggie again, this time probably forever, made her feel as if she were being ripped in two— but her home was where she belonged. She didn't fit here, even if some of her favorite people were here. Home was where she belonged, where she felt most herself. It was where her parents were, and Derek, and all the memories that she cherished. She was rooted *there*, in the future. And she didn't understand how or why, but it was calling her back. She couldn't deny the pull anymore.

. . .

CELESTE WATCHED as Callum went to the wall and retrieved the wolf sword. Maggie, silent tears streaming down her face, stood in the doorway with the baby, a safe distance from the sword, she'd told Celeste, to ensure she would not be whisked away from the life she'd found here.

"I'll see you again, my friend," Callum promised as he extended it to Dar. They'd said their goodbyes already, but now Callum turned to Celeste, and shook his head fondly. "You will be missed," he uttered tightly.

Celeste nodded, overcome with emotion again. He'd given her so much these past months, and feeling like she should offer him something in return for the love and kindness he'd shared with her, she reached into her pocket, pulling out the family of miniature wolves. She hesitated only a moment before singling out the baby, the one Derek had carved for her, and setting it atop her palm. "I would like you to have this," she said of her most prized possession.

Callum stared at the little wolf, then back to her, realizing the enormity and significance of her gift. With great aplomb, belied only by the moisture in his eyes, he shook his head, gently closing her fingers around it and pushing it back toward Celeste.

"A generous offer, truly, but let's keep them together, always," he whispered as her tears flowed freely.

With a final nod, Callum kissed her forehead and walked from the room, pausing in the doorway. With his arm wrapping around Maggie, he said, "You are eternally cherished, by us both, little sister."

Her heart cleaved as she stood there. The enormity of her

decision weighed like an anvil around her neck. She knew this was her family, Maggie, Callum, and of course, Dar, but this wasn't her home. She didn't feel the same way Maggie felt, or even Gwen. She loved Dar with every fiber of her being, but she needed to go back. She knew that now, and could no longer try to deny it.

"Are you ready?" Dar asked once Callum and Maggie had taken their leave.

She nodded, and stepped into his arms like she had that day in her basement. It had only been a few months ago, but it felt like centuries. He held her tight, his lips to her forehead, and she closed her eyes and waited.

And waited.

Confused and worried all at once, Celeste looked up at him. "What's wrong?" she asked.

Seeming just as confounded as she felt, Dar looked at the sword and the jewel, ever vibrant, but not shining, not animating as it had before.

Wanting a closer look herself, Celeste reached out and took the sword by the hilt, pulling it closer. Only half a second passed before Celeste jarred—suddenly, she felt the sword buzz, and her eyes widened when she heard its hum. Startled, she tried to let it go, but found that her hand was literally glued to the hilt.

She looked at Dar, who gave her a questioning look in response, clearly also not sure what was happening. Then a thought crossed her mind: what if she was always meant to go back, but he wasn't? Terrified at the possibility, she flung her arms toward the floor, but the sword didn't budge from her hands.

"No, no-no, not yet, not like this," she pleaded, and it was then that Dar realized what was going on.

He leapt into action, trying to pull the sword from her hands.

"No! *Celeste!*" He wrapped his arms around her, trying in vain to go with her; but though she could *see* him enveloping her, she couldn't feel it.

The jewel heated suddenly, and a blinding spray of light emanated from it, blocking Celeste's view of everything around her.

"*Dar!*"

"No! No!" The desperation in his voice cut straight through her and she cried as the room spun and she felt herself being pulled away. *No!NoNoNo!*

"DAAAR!" she cried, but she already knew it was too late. She was gone.

CHAPTER 39

SCOTLAND, 1432

Sitting at the desk in his chambers, Dar dipped his quill in ink, looking out over the courtyard as he thought of what to write. He'd filled the little chest Callum had made already, but decided to leave one more. This one in the letterbox. His heart was heavy; he knew it would have to be his last. So much had happened in the months since Celeste had disappeared, literally slipping right out of his arms and through time.

A knock sounded on his door, interrupting his thoughts. He called, "Enter," fearing it was news of his father.

Lachlan had been his rock these past months. All of that time Dar had wasted hating the man—the irony of it all. Dar himself had done the same thing his father had, he'd fallen in love with someone out of reach.

His father had taken the news of Celeste's departure with a heavy heart, though he hadn't been much surprised at Dar's explanation. Apparently, his father was open to a wee bit of magic. Lachlan had even offered to search out Esmeralda and demand answers, surprising Dar yet again since it was news to him that his father even knew the mystic.

"How did you manage?" Dar had asked him in the early days, feeling like a large part of himself was gone.

Lachlan had sighed and patted him on the back. "You get up and you carry on, son. You do your best every single day, forever. If you're grateful for what you had, I promise you'll find some grace."

"I'm sorry, father."

Understanding his offspring's meaning, Lachlan had shaken his head, eyes misting. "I am, too, son. Why don't we make ourselves useful?"

And so they had. He'd arrived back at Abersoch with Lachlan just as winter took hold. At the time, they had but thirty men and had built temporary shelter, then set out to begin construction of the castle. The undertaking was immense, but a Godsend too.

For six-and-a-half months, they labored day and night, and their efforts had paid off. With the break in the weather, footings had been dug and filled, cellars excavated, and by spring, stakes and ropes outlined where they'd lay the castle walls. And, on the first of June, he, Gavin, and his father had laid the stone that bore their names.

It was bittersweet, though, for, by then Lachlan could no longer hide his condition, something he'd kept secret for months.

Gwen couldn't be certain what it was, only that it affected

his heart. Dar was devastated at the thought of another loss, but he was grateful for the time they'd had together.

As Gwen came into the room, he jotted a quick note, not what he'd first intended, but it was obvious by the look on Gwen's face that time was of the essence. And it was better to leave this, he thought, than nothing at all—even if no one would ever see it.

CHAPTER 40

"The past is merely the past, unless it's your future."

Celeste's head dropped to the table with a *thwack*. She'd gone to the crone the moment she'd returned home—like, literally, she was still wearing her fifteenth-century clothing—but the old bat was proving no help.

Here she was, panicked, in shock, terrified she'd ruined everything and would never see Dar again, and the one person who could help her refused to give her a direct answer. Didn't she understand how crucial this was? Somehow, she had taken both the sword and the jewel with her, meaning the man she loved, the man who had given her the most important part of her life back, was without any means to return to her.

With Dar, Celeste had again found the part of her that lived in feelings and emotions and didn't have to pretend. The part that felt safe and whole. It seemed like once that switch had been turned back on, there wasn't an off button. Those feelings and emotions were now raw and exposed, and she couldn't tamp them down or stuff them inside and pretend they didn't exist, not like she used to before Dar. No longer could she distract herself from her emotions, or dismiss them. There were no new-age fixes. It felt like she was in the middle of eclipse season and all of the planets in her chart were tipped at a fatal degree.

So here she was, the side of her face on the tablecloth, living out her latest tragedy while staring at a plate of cucumber and dill tea sandwiches and wishing she were dead.

The crone's frustratingly ambiguous words echoed in her mind again. *The past is merely the past, unless it's your future.* No, duh. The past *wasn't* her future, never *had* been her future. That was something that had never really been in question. But that had been before Dar was stuck in the past. Before she'd gone and messed it all up. Now he was there and she was here, and *that* was the whammy she couldn't wrap her head around. She just wanted a straight answer from the old woman sitting across from her.

So, no, the past was never her future, but seeing what that actually meant in reality still cut like a knife. Why hadn't she talked to him about her unhappiness sooner? Maybe it would have relieved some of the pressure she'd felt, and she could have held on a little longer.

From this side of things, it was hard to imagine that she couldn't have made it the few more months it would have taken to begin constructing Abersoch and setting the stone. A few more months in the fifteenth century wouldn't have killed her. It's not like she'd been dirty or starving or uncomfortable.

There'd been soap to bathe with in a hot tub. And she liked clean eating, right? What better place to indulge in healthy food with no pesticides or preservatives? They'd had meat, they'd had vegetables, they'd had cheese, hell, they'd even had coffee and caramel lattes thanks to Gwen. They'd had books and jacks, and horseback riding, dinner parties, and even friends who came and stayed with them. Friends she really liked. And, even if being separated was always the ultimate endgame (though Celeste still couldn't believe that to be true), she could have stayed longer, had more time with him.

If all of that wasn't an awful enough reminder, the look on Dar's face when he'd realized what was happening was the last thing she saw; and that horror that had crossed his beautiful dark eyes in those last seconds was permanently etched in her mind. *Oh, Dar.*

What was it that made her choose that day and that time to break? And more importantly, what was it that sent her back without him? If they were truly fated to be together, why had the sword torn them apart? *This* was what bothered Celeste the most: the possibility that she and Dar were not meant to be, that there wouldn't be a happily ever after for them.

"There, there, sweet," crowed the mystic, in her infuriatingly placating way, patting her hand and pushing the plate closer. "Have a treat."

Celeste never wanted to eat again and was about to tell her so when her stomach rumbled loudly. She peered at the old woman, wondering if she'd used magic to make that happen, but it was more likely that now that food was near, her body had responded on its own. She honestly couldn't remember the last time she'd eaten, and at the realization that it was probably with Dar, she had to choke back another sob. Like a child, she walked her fingers to the plate and nabbed a triangle, realizing after her first bite she'd have to sit upright to swallow it.

She did so with a sigh, silently chomping away at first one and then two of the crustless delicacies, getting hungrier with each bite. Ten minutes later, when only crumbs remained on the plate that had been plentifully stacked, she leered across the table.

"Did you cast a spell on those or something?"

"Oh, pfft."

As far as Celeste was concerned, that was a resounding yes.

Celeste slow-walked through a month of devastation, deprivation, and depression. She never thought she'd be a triple D, but there it was.

Then, one day, without ceremony, she experienced a rush of dizziness that shook her out of her fugue, at least temporarily. Her jaw started to tingle and she dry heaved all over the foyer floor, kneeling there in a cold sweat. A few moments later, she felt fine, which struck Celeste as odd, and as she walked into the kitchen, her mind churning, she came to an abrupt halt.

Could she be pregnant?

She'd had a period just the other week, but it had been a light one, kind of just spotting, now that she thought about it, though honestly, she hadn't really paid too much attention to it because of the aforementioned triple Ds. But now...now she allowed herself to consider the possibility of a baby for a moment—before rushing to the drugstore for a test to confirm it one way or another.

Was this something she even wanted? she asked herself as she drove to the store. But the second she asked herself the question, she knew the answer: yes, it was. She would love to have Dar's baby, even if she couldn't have Dar. Especially if she couldn't have Dar.

When she'd been at Dunhill with him, they'd talked about having children, about filling that house he was going to build her in the country. They had never used protection, and after that first conversation about children, she'd grown more conscious of tracking her cycle, but each of the few months she could have been pregnant, she wasn't. And that had been fine in the moment, because they'd had their whole lives ahead of them.

Without consciously realizing it, when Celeste had been launched back to the future alone, she'd given up hope of ever being a mother.

So now, retching bile onto the cold stone floor was a welcomed surprise. It was the first sliver of hope Celeste had had since her return.

At the drugstore, she bought four two-pack pregnancy tests and then drove home, immediately peeing on stick after stick when she got there. Of course, it didn't take long to figure out she'd been an idiot to buy so many tests—seriously how many times could you pee in a row? Not eight, she realized after she ran dry at three.

It didn't matter, though, because two minutes later, all three were lit up with " Pregnant."

She was able to get in with her ob-gyn right away—it helped that they couldn't make out a word she was saying on the phone and ended up telling her, "Just come in."

Once she was there, one of the nurses drew blood and told her she'd have to wait a bit to speak with the doctor, but, lucky for her, the ultrasound tech had a cancellation. And, after shimmying onto the table, and saying a silent prayer for the millionth time, she finally heard what she'd been waiting for: a tiny heartbeat. Her and Dar's baby!

Unbidden, she thought: *And so, another griffin rises.*

As she watched that little blob that was their baby, Celeste imagined how happy he would have been. *Oh, Dar, our baby.* She cried again and the technician stepped out of the room to give her a moment.

When her head stopped spinning, she clutched her medallion, the one Lachlan had made for her. She'd put it on the same chain that held her key to the letterbox, and as she grabbed it now, she realized that this whole time she'd been carrying a treasure from Lachlan, a treasure from Callum, and a treasure from Dar.

It wasn't the same as having the men with her, but it helped, just a little.

THE BABY NEWS gave her enough strength to get up and live her life again. Really live it. She had a responsibility now to guard a priceless treasure; just as Dar's responsibility, by dictate of the griffin, had once been to protect her. And by God she would live up to her responsibility, as he had lived up to his.

She hit her stride after that first trimester was over, and a couple months later, decided a trip to Scotland was in order.

New Celeste was decisive. New Celeste didn't question her desires or feelings. Bolstered by the confidence in herself that Dar had given her and the weight of responsibility of the baby growing inside of her, New Celeste felt much surer about things. She wanted to visit Dunhill, if only to drive to the property and talk to Dar and Callum and Maggie from outside its walls.

It helped Celeste to consider that fate had separated them not because they didn't love one another or deserve one another, but because she and Dar had worked out whatever it was their souls needed to in this lifetime. Personal growth, she decided, came first, and she vowed to embrace life head-on. She could live for their baby. And she'd be the best mom ever.

Celeste recalled something the old crone had said before she'd left for the Hamptons last summer—that regardless of what happened, she would know true peace eventually. And, just like always, the woman had been right. Celeste felt true peace now.

Plus, according to griffin lore, she and Dar were mated for life; and, even better than that, according to the vows she'd exchanged with her husband, their souls were united for eternity. Even if they were just words, she believed in them, and that gave her hope. So, if their time together was all they'd have in this lifetime, she knew the next would only be that much better. And the next one and the next. She would live happily with what they'd had this time.

The girls—Amanda, Sam, and Jenny—came to visit a few

times, coordinating with her doctor's appointments. In between they sent baskets filled with goodies, including her saving graces, ginger tea and hard candies. It was with their support that she decided to skip her usual summer in the Hamptons plan and instead face the past, albeit in the present, and visit her husband's homeland.

Alex insisted she take one of the jets, and even made up an excuse about needing to do something or other across the pond. She knew he was just watching out for her, though, picking up the slack Dar had left behind. They'd all been deeply sympathetic about what had happened, and told her often that Dar had been well-liked and would be missed. Besides, they'd said, they owed him.

She was grateful for their support and offerings; not only was it comforting to know that people were looking out for her, but it definitely made traveling that much easier.

She wanted to go to Abersoch first—she was going to do that thing that people do at memorials, trace the letters in the stone onto paper and have it framed. She'd hang it in the foyer next to the étagère that she'd added a few pictures of Dar to, taken during those brief weeks they'd had together in the twenty-first century. It was an area of her house she didn't avoid any longer. She even kept a pretty vase filled with fresh flowers on it. Celeste was no longer that little girl lost, and it showed in everything she did.

When they arrived at the Abersoch estate, Celeste was five months pregnant, and was beginning to feel the stirrings of the baby inside of her. Holding her belly, she stared in awe, thinking of how this castle was here because of Dar. Her husband and father-in-law had built it so future generations would benefit from its magic. She knew it had been added to over the years, updated and restored, but still, what a monumental accomplishment.

After unpacking, she explored the property, marveling at its beauty, the lush great lawn and sweeping vistas to the sea. Amanda had told her that the first time she'd come to Abersoch was actually to perform at a black tie event, and seeing it in person, Celeste could understand why someone would choose this space for something like that.

At first she just meandered, and she did meander, savoring every bit of it, but eventually she found herself standing in front of the old original entrance. It reminded her a little of the portico at Dunhill, but this one had a plaque next to the steps, shiny and very clearly new. It was stamped with big numbers denoting the current year and Celeste moved close enough to read: *To our comrade Darach MacTavish. Our eternal thanks, dear friend.* The words brought a rush of tears to her eyes, but she swiftly brushed them away, dismissing the underlying tidal wave of emotion brewing beneath the surface—there was a proper place and time for that, but it wasn't now. She was trying her best to be stoic.

Moments later, kneeling on pretty paver-like bricks set in an odd pattern, Celeste saw the marker, the one that had shown Dar his destiny, and noted that her life seemed to revolve around these. Markers. It was a statement of fact, not her feeling sorry for herself. She reached out and brushed her fingers over the letters, glad that Dar had taken Lachlan's name and set it in stone. It was fitting. She was grateful they'd had each other in the end.

After a few days of exploring and enjoying the estate, she traveled to Scotland. Alex wanted to go with her but she insisted that this was something she needed to do alone. He won when it came to the use of the jet, however, and so she flew into a private airport, where a rental car awaited her.

It took her some time to figure out the whole driving on the other side of the road thing, but she eventually got a shaky handle on it—enough, at least, to take her the hour or so to Dunhill. Pulling into the long drive that led to the castle, Celeste had to concentrate even harder than usual on driving, so blown away was she by the sight of the building that had been her home for several months; the place where she'd last seen Maggie and Dar, where she'd met so many people who meant so much to her.

Seven hundred years had certainly changed things, but in a way, it looked exactly the same. This was Dunhill, a place she'd called home.

When she got to the end of the paved part of the drive, she rolled down the windows and turned off the car, just sitting there, staring at the castle. Emotion threatened to overtake her, but Celeste held it back, knowing that if she broke down now, she'd never make it inside. *If* she made it inside.

She'd done her research before making the trip, and had discovered that not only was Dunhill still a private residence, it was still in the O'Roarke family—generations had lived on because of Callum and Maggie. She was wondering if she should get out and actually knock on the front door when she was startled by the doors opening. An older couple stepped outside, calling out, "Can we help you?"

Not sure what else to do, Celeste got out of her car and waved to the couple. "I'm so sorry," she called to them, trying to figure out how to explain her presence. "I didn't mean to trespass." She shrugged, a tide of emotion slipping to the surface. She took a few seconds to tamp it down, then said, "My name is Celeste MacTavish, and… I was close once with an O'Roarke, and…well…"

She searched for the right words even if they wouldn't be the exact truth—obviously they couldn't be, not if she didn't want them to think she was nuts, but now that she was here, she knew she had to try.

"She told me so much about this castle, it's almost like I've been here before. And, when I found myself in the area, I had to come and see it for myself. I honestly didn't mean to disturb you, and I'm not sure I would have even gotten out of the car if you hadn't come outside. But…" Celeste paused, very nervous, but knew she had to try. "If it's not too much trouble, I would love to see the inside of your home?"

It was the first time she'd claimed the MacTavish name, at least publicly, since she'd returned to her own time, and it felt good to say it. Sure, technically, legally, it wasn't actually her name, not anymore, but in her heart, it was.

The couple looked at each other and smiled. Celeste let her hopes lift for a moment, praying that they would let her in, and not wave her off like some crazy person who'd driven up to their property and demanded to see inside.

"Well, Celeste MacTavish, my name is Christian O'Roarke,"

said the man, something like excitement glittering in his eyes, "and this is my wife, Michelle. Please come in. I think, if you are the Celeste MacTavish I hope you are, that we have something that might belong to you."

Something that might belong to me? Confused and surprised both that this couple not only seemed to know who she was, but had possibly been waiting for her, Celeste paused only a moment before following them up the steps. Weirder things had happened to her, she supposed.

She took the steps slowly, trying to feel the stone beneath her feet, remembering all the times she'd done so before, both months and centuries ago. She held her breath as she walked through the castle doors, then stopped for a moment, flooded with memories of Dar, Maggie, Callum, and the time she'd spent here with them.

More than seven hundred years of wear had settled on the place, yet it still felt familiar. It didn't smell the same, or look the same, but there was a feel to the air that was comforting, that was right.

The O'Roarke family had obviously taken great pride and care in the upkeep of Dunhill. The castle looked beautiful filled with modern-day art and furnishings. If the old couple thought her behavior odd, they didn't say so, just waited patiently until several minutes had passed.

"Please," Michelle said then, reaching out to lightly touch her arm, a pleasant smile on her face.

Celeste nodded and turned to follow her and Christian to the great room. They stepped inside and said nothing for a moment, just looked at her expectantly. Suddenly feeling put on the spot, Celeste wondered if she was supposed to say something.

"Your home is beautiful," she offered, pretending to admire a piece of art as she ran her hand along the stone wall. It was astounding that she'd been here centuries ago. As she continued around the room, she pictured it the way it had been, with the large wooden table and chairs where they'd eaten on special occasions—her wedding day being one—and the sitting area on the other side where they'd spent many a night.

She continued through the room, glancing back at Christian and Michelle, who were just watching her, big smiles on their faces, seemingly enjoying how she was taking everything in. If only they knew she was not admiring their furnishings, but remembering what once was.

Celeste stared wistfully at the floor in front of the fireplace, where she and Maggie had played jacks, and then looked up and froze. Her breath caught and her hands flew to her mouth. Displayed on the mantle, and looking as new as the day they were made, were Celeste's chest and letterbox.

She really hadn't wanted to cry, at least not until she left, but as she reached out to run her hands over each one of them, tears filled her eyes.

After a minute or two, Christian took a few steps forward, coming to stand beside her. "You know," he said, his voice soft, "family lore says a laird lost the lady of his heart, right here in this very room, and she's the one who has the key to these. Not a laird, nor a lady, of our own blood, but a couple very dear to the O'Roarke clan. It's been said for generations that she would come back for her box and her chest; and while it was a good family story for many a year, according to my father, the lady was foretold to return in my lifetime. I've never known whether to believe him or not, but I've always remembered her name. You see," he said, pointing to the box, "her initials were inlaid in the wood."

Barely believing what she was hearing, Celeste stepped closer to the mantle to find what she already knew was there. Her initials. CEM, Celeste Elizabeth MacTavish. She smiled as she looked from the boxes to the O'Roarkes, still marveling that the treasures Callum had made for her were here, whole and preserved so many years later.

"Yes," she said, when she finally found her voice. Celeste sensed she didn't need to explain. Christian was presenting these to her so readily, that it was clear he knew they were hers, even if he couldn't know how. "These are mine. They were gifts from my brother, things he made for me. One he gave to me on my wedding day, and the other shortly after."

It was a small piece of a much bigger truth; one that warranted much explanation, but the O'Roarkes only had one question.

"Do you have the key?" Christian asked excitedly, staring at her like everything he'd told her—everything he'd been brought up with—rested on her answer.

She nodded again. "I do," she whispered, unable to help herself from being caught up in his glee. She smiled as a few tears fell, then took off her necklace to show them the key, which exactly matched the locks in style.

They weren't full-on gasps, but the intakes of breath Christian and Michelle each took were noticeable. Then, without another word, Christian took down both boxes and placed them on a table in front of the sofa. They stepped aside as she placed the key in the chest's lock and turned it, and when the lid snapped open, he and his wife *did* gasp.

"I have to tell you, lass," Christian said, a catch in his voice, "seeing our family lore come true right before our eyes is an inconceivable marvel." After another long moment, he said, "We'll give you some privacy."

Once she was alone, Celeste slowly lifted the lid, crying as she carefully ran her hands over dozens of letters. She gingerly picked one up, scared at first that it might disintegrate, and opened it slowly, holding it to her chest before wiping her eyes so she could read it.

It had been written the winter she'd left, updating her on their progress with the building of Abersoch and as ever, he'd ended the letter by telling her he loved her and missed her. *Oh, Dar.* She opened a few more, all outlining his days without her.

While it was nice—no, incredible—to see his handwriting, to read his words, words written specifically for her, as she laid the last letter from the chest aside, she wondered if maybe he'd left something more personal. Reaching out to the box, her fingers brushed the wood, remembering all the letters they'd written to each other, notes of love and devotion, and how she would lie in his arms as they read them to each other. When she turned the key and opened it, she found only one letter inside.

My dearest Celeste,
Until we meet again, my love,
Yours eternally,
Dar

She wept. Hard. Those were his final words to her.

She sat on that sofa for nearly an hour, then composed herself and had lunch with the O'Roarkes. They insisted, especially seeing as she was pregnant. They were a lovely couple, animated and filled with questions about the letters and how she came to have the key. It was of course impossible to explain how she was at the center of this family's lore that dated back centuries, but when she shrugged and said, simply, "Maybe a wee bit of magic was involved," Christian's eyes lit up.

"Aye, my father thought so too." Christian carried her letterbox and chest as they saw her to the car, and insisted she come back and visit anytime. He hesitated only a moment before handing the items to her, giving them each an affectionate pat. "These should go with you, of course," he said. "We'll be sad to see them go, but are very proud to have finally fulfilled my family's duty."

When she returned to Abersoch, Alex was there waiting for her with open arms and kind words. She was happy to see a familiar face, but also knew she was ready to go. She'd gotten what she came for—more than she'd came for, actually.

They left for the States the following morning, and after an exhausting day of travel, Celeste was thrilled to be home again. She pressed the door combination and stepped inside, where she immediately blew out a deep breath and kicked off her shoes. Tired and overwhelmed, she leaned against the door for a moment, holding her letterbox and chest close.

A true sense of peace rushed through her, just as the crone had foretold. She had something she'd never imagined she might get—the chest and her letterbox, both filled with words from Dar. She still had her memories, of course, and she had their baby too. Today she could be grateful just for that.

It was on the tip of that thought that she heard a voice, a voice she'd never thought she'd hear again.

"Celeste."

She froze, clutching the boxes tighter, terrified to look up in case she was just imagining things. Gathering her courage, she closed her eyes, and said a prayer, slowly lifting her chin.

And there he was—Dar—standing not ten feet away. "I see you've started filling the house with flowers," he said nonchalantly as his eyes drank her in.

She felt it like a true caress. God, how she'd missed that. "Someone has to make sure our baby is surrounded by sunshine and happiness."

"Our baby?"

She nodded, putting the box and chest down so he could see her expanding belly, still trying to fathom how what was happening in front of her was real. "He's growing by the day," she said, her voice faltering as she started to crumble. "Oh Dar, what took you so long?"

"Och, Celeste, come here, love."

She couldn't get there fast enough. She threw herself against him, sobbing in his strong all-encompassing arms. She'd missed this so much, just being enveloped by him. She'd missed his size, his warmth, his strength. She tried to tell him but by that point she could barely string a syllable together. So, he carried her upstairs, his lips to her forehead, whispering his love for her over and over again. He laid her on the bed, then followed her down, holding her tight. He didn't stop telling her how much he loved her, how he'd missed her, and how sorry he was that she'd felt that she couldn't talk to him.

He told her how devastated he was when she disappeared right before his eyes. That she'd taken his heart and what he'd believed at the time to be the only possibility for uniting them —the sword and the jewel—with her. It was only later that he'd realized he did indeed have a way to her—the portal that had opened for the Montgomerys. It merely included a jump off a cliff.

He told her all about Abersoch, and that with her gone, he'd thrown himself into the one and only task that stood in his way of going back—or forward—to her. How when they finally laid the stone, he'd found out that Lachlan had been suffering from health problems but had hidden them so he could do his best to help Dar return to her.

Then he'd laughed when he told her about Gwen, and how she knew of another portal on the Abersoch property—tide pools beneath the rock wall she'd learned about from her favorite aunt, a mysterious Aunt Millicent. How they didn't just have Maggie to thank for bringing them together with the sword, but Gwen, too, for offering him a way to return that didn't involve a jump off a cliff, a jump he'd had every intention of taking to come back to her, but one that Gwen had worried Lachlan wouldn't survive.

"Wait!" Celeste cried, the gears in her head turning rapidly as she pieced the whole story together. "Lachlan—your dad's here too?"

Dar nodded. "Aye, he needed modern medical attention. He's out of surgery, but still in the hospital. I left him only a few hours ago, when Alex texted me that you had landed."

Apparently, the Montgomerys had been in the loop before she was. No wonder Alex had given her that odd smile when she'd gotten off the plane that afternoon.

For a moment, as she laid there in Dar's arms, feeling blissfully content, she thought her mind was playing tricks on her. "You're real, right? This isn't an illusion or a dream."

"Nay, lass. I'm home. Here in the future, with you, forever."

EPILOGUE

UPSTATE NEW YORK

Dar leaned against the kitchen counter, watching through the window as Celeste exited the barn and made her way back toward their home. Basket in hand, she smiled, almost skipping her way back inside.

"Breakfast in about thirty," she announced, kissing the top of baby Grif's head and depositing her goods by the sink before stopping in front of Dar. He was on the phone with Alex, so he just smiled and winked, then pulled her in close, loving how perfectly she fit against him. He tilted her chin and went in for a quick kiss, mouthing, "I love you."

When she made an exasperated face, he grinned—she wanted him to say it for real, out loud. He liked feisty Celeste. He liked pouty Celeste too. Hell, he just liked Celeste any way she came at him. "I love you," he said, clearly, giving her what she wanted, then to Alex on the phone, "No, not you."

She smiled and rolled her eyes. "Was that so hard?" she asked, then bumped into the island, wincing out an "ow."

He reached out, covering her growing belly with a hand, and whispered, "Be careful, love."

Ignoring him, she pierced his eardrums when she yelled, "Daaad!" Still he chuckled. Grif laughed in his high chair, hands banging on the countertop.

At this point, Dar knew he'd get no work done, and so told Alex he'd call him back later, just as Lachlan hollered back, "Coming, kitten."

The door opened, and his father, arms full, came into the kitchen and placed a few bags on the counter before taking off his baseball cap and kissing Celeste's cheek.

"Groceries procured," he announced, then winked at Celeste. "*Including* your bushel of oranges and requested sticky buns."

"Ooh, thank you. What did the doctor, say? Everything good?" she asked.

"Aye, the hearts as strong as ever. Might need a new pace-maker in a few years, but for now, this ticker, as they call it, is sound."

Dar shared a grateful look with her. Yeah, his da had made it through, not only a trip to the future, but surgery as well. Thank God for Gwen. Without her knowledge and the timing of his separation from Celeste, they wouldn't have been so fortunate. Looking back, his da had been right all along, Divinity was most definitely at play here. With all of them. Gwen and Grey, Callum and Maggie, and the Montgomerys too.

"Did you see the garden this morning?" Celeste asked Lachlan. "The tomatoes and zucchini look amazing."

"Aye, the fruits of our labor—all that hard work is paying off nicely."

The smile on her face was worth everything they'd gone through. His wife was whole again from the inside out. Secure. And, to be honest, he was too. He had a family the likes of which he'd never imagined.

They'd sold Celeste's house and bought a huge parcel of land upstate, with a large house already on it. It needed some work, to be sure, but had good bones, so Dar had hired an outstanding contractor to remodel it to their liking. In fact, it was Nick's brother Lance who owned the company.

He and his da had kept a few projects for themselves, though, like building the new front porch, refurbishing the stables, and constructing an enormous pergola out back next to the pool. He loved the long days of work, the tasks that needed to be done around the property, because they allowed him plenty of time at home with his growing family. In essence, they had a sustainable farm, with plenty of animals, from cows, to goats, chickens, pigs and many in between. Stress on the word *essence*, though, since Celeste had named every one of them and made him and Lachlan promise they wouldn't end up on the dinner table.

"Did you get that message from Brianna O'Roarke?" his father asked, once the groceries had been put away.

Dar nodded. He had, her name and number were jotted on a pad of paper in his office. Apparently, Brianna's grandfather was the person who'd originally sold the sword—which was now safely tucked away in their lower level, in a large safe—to Derek. Unlike the O'Roarkes Celeste had met when she'd visited Dunhill, the younger generation seemed more insistent that their relics stay in the family. Brianna's message had merely said she had "some questions about my family's sword," but Dar could read between the lines—and he just wasn't sure how he was going to answer them.

He looked at Celeste as she broke apart sections of an orange to give to Grif.

"Hey. Come here," he said, still leaning back against the counter.

She smiled and made her way over to him, wrapping her arms around his neck as he bent to kiss her. It wasn't the quick peck he'd intended, but a slow and poignant kiss as he felt her weight against him, their new baby between them.

She knew it, too, and whispered, "I love when that happens."

Aye, so did he.

THE PROPHECY

EXCERPT FROM BOOK I OF THE LAIRDS OF THE CREST SERIES

The dream was always the same.

Gwen pressed deeper into the warm embrace, sighing as strong arms tightened around her. She rubbed her face in the crook of his neck, running her hand over the solid mass of back and shoulders until her fingers tangled in thick, soft hair. Large powerful hands followed her movements, pressing her closer as he cupped the back of her head and gently tilted her face.

She never felt his hesitation before. Tonight she did. She tugged on his hair, a silent demand to be kissed. Then he covered her lips, completely sealing them within his own. A deep sound rumbled through his chest.

This dream was different.

She felt the warmth of his lips and the pressure of his hands, the texture of his hair and the heat of skin. She heard sounds given and returned.

It seemed so real.

His thumb coaxed her chin, and her lips parted as he moved between them. He spent an eternity simply joining their mouths...in every possible way. His tongue, reverent at first, was slow to explore, then became wholly demanding.

She gave in to him completely. In truth, she kissed him back with everything she had. They shared an urgency—taking satisfaction as they'd never been able to before.

She traced her fingers over his face—his broad forehead, straight nose, high cheekbones, his smooth, strong chin—and she pulled him even closer.

My God, it had never felt so good.

She made a sound as he pulled back, a whimper he hushed with slow, passionate kisses over her forehead and cheeks. Then he covered her lips again before tucking her within the crook of his neck. "Sleep, love," he urged in a murmur. "The morn's but an hour away."

Gwen burrowed against him, silent tears wetting her cheeks —oppressive longing crushing her from the inside out.

She'd never heard the sound of his voice.

It would haunt her forever.

NEVER SAY GOODBYE

EXCERPT FROM BOOK 1 OF THE BROTHERS MONTGOMERY SERIES

Amanda had just reached down for Zander when she heard Stan swear behind her and Callie whisper "Mama" as she latched on to her thigh. Stan was telling someone to back off. Obviously on his earbud since he wouldn't be saying that to her. She picked up Zander instinctively and Callie said "Mama" again, this time with more force.

"What, sweetie?" she said distractedly while turning to Stan. Jeez, he looked furious. The other two men guarding them closed in. Really tight. Callie shouted this time, drawing Amanda's full attention, and pointed toward the street. Amanda felt a moment's hesitation before turning. And when she did, she gasped.

She'd seen this picture before. Last night, as a matter of fact. She'd been preparing dinner while Callie sat on the sofa in the kitchen. One second the TV had been muted, then it was blaring. Amanda had startled at the noise then turned. Callie was standing on the coffee table, her whole body shaking with excitement, remote in hand.

Amanda had rewound whatever had caught Callie's attention and listened as the TV news anchor spoke: "From our business desk—exclusive and rare footage of billionaire Alexander Montgomery, president and CEO of Montgomery Enterprises. Mr. Montgomery is seen here, leaving his New York headquarters. His entrance to America happens to coincide with a masterful power grab of JDL Security."

They showed a caravan of black Lincoln Navigators pull up to a prestigious Manhattan address. The cameras of course focused on him. The impressive, handsome man in question stepped from his vehicle. He ignored the press as he and his entourage entered the building. The newscaster continued: "While still in London, Mr. Montgomery amassed a brilliant staff, hand picking, if not plucking, some of the savviest technical, military, and medical minds. He's apparently settled in the States indefinitely.

Stan swore again, jarring Amanda back to the present as the caravan came to a stop. The doors opened in unison and Mr. Montgomery and his men emerged. Callie was right, her papa had come. And jeez, they meant business today. All in black suits. All wearing sunglasses. And she'd bet her life that they were all armed. They were large men and had a way of taking up the most space possible with a stance. Using hand signals to communicate, his men formed a perimeter, shutting down the street as he continued toward her.

Something about the way he looked now—dressed to the nines, storming so powerfully toward her, so totally in command—set her body thrumming right there on the street. Seriously, Amanda Abigail Marceau! How did you forget him?

He was her every girlhood fantasy come to life. All six and a half feet of him. Tall. Broad. Dark. And so wickedly handsome. Straight nose, strong chin, and a mouth, she would swear, that was made to give orders. In fact, she watched him order Stan and his men just now to stand down as he walked right up to her. Like almost touching right up to her. She had to tilt her head back, which wasn't something she was accustomed to doing, not at her height. He stared at her a good few seconds, his eyes softening just a bit, before saying quite forcefully, "It seems there's a security problem."

"Wh…" Amanda had to wet her mouth; it had gone bone dry at his accent. She did after all have a thing for his voice, and apparently after just two days without it, it worked its magic on "on her again. She tried once more, "What security problem?"

"I'm in charge of your security," he shouted as he got right in her face, "and you're my problem!"

ABOUT THE AUTHOR

Kim Sakwa is the author of multiple bestselling romances, including *THE PROPHECY, THE PRICE, NEVER SAY GOOD-BYE,* and *NEVER TOO LATE.* When not writing, you can find her walking the hills of her Michigan subdivision, listening to the soundtracks she creates for her novels. She's a hopeless romantic, hooked on happily ever after.

ALSO BY KIM SAKWA

The Lairds of the Crest Series

The Prophecy

The Price

The Pledge

The Brothers Montgomery Series

Never Say Goodbye

Never Too Late

Never Say Never

ACKNOWLEDGMENTS

I am so thankful for my talented, amazing team at Taggart Press. They are the reasons why my books are beautiful on the inside and out, and work tirelessly to get my books discovered by readers.

Sarah Beaudin
Design and production · C'est Beau Designs

Kim Haulena
Copy-editing and proofreading

Marian Hussey
Audiobook Narrator / Voice Talent

George Long
Cover design · G-Force Design

Bonnie Paulson
Business consulting · Finding Your Indie

Katie Price
Website development and design · Priceless Design Studio

Liz Psaltis
Content creation, advertising, and promotion · EHP Marketing

Mandie Stevens
Social media management, promotion, advertising
management, and conferences · Finding Your Indie

Rachel Stout
Developmental editing · Rachel Stout Editorial Services

Jane Ubell-Meyer
Luxury hotel amenity placement, major media coverage, and
events · Bedside Reading